Lead Me Home

"Cortright's sophomore novel, the second in her Grace Alone series, is a continuing testament to "write what you know and learn the rest." Her avid love of history and family heritage make her story-telling warm and endearing. Maggie and Romy will draw you into their world of the Great Depression in America's heartland, with all the heartaches, hunger, faith, and romance to help you feel at home."

–Lisa Lickel, author of *The Last Detail*

"Journey to the days of the Great Depression with its myriad challenges for survival. Connie Cortright weaves a story of young people challenged to assist their families through difficult times yet still find their own happiness."

–Terri Wangard, author of *Soar Like Eagle*

Grace Alone Series

Book 2

The heartwarming story of *Lead Me Home* continues the GRACE ALONE SERIES, the saga of three sisters facing times of change and challenge in the 1920s, 1930s, and 1940s. Also look for Book 1, *Guide Me Home*, available on Amazon.com.

Lead Me Home

CONNIE CORTRIGHT

Author's Note: This novel is a work of fiction. Names, characters, places, and incidents are either products of the author's imagination or used fictitiously. All characters are fictional, and any similarity to people living or dead is purely coincidental.

Scripture quotations are taken from the King James Version of the Bible.

http://www.conniecortright.com

Copyright © 2017 Connie Cortright / Milk Door Publications

Published by Milk Door Publications

Edited by Lisa Lickel / Lisa Lickel Publishing

Cover design by Lisa Hainline / Lionsgate Book Design.

Printed by CreateSpace, An Amazon.com Company

Available from Amazon.com and other bookstores

ISBN: 978-0-9968441-2-3

DEDICATION

To my four wonderful sons and their wives who have supported and encouraged me for many years while I take on this new "career" in my life. Also, to my mother who has believed in me from the very beginning, twelve years ago.

In loving memory of my father

- WILLARD A. LAABS -

who shared many of his remembrances of the 1930s with me

ACKNOWLEDGMENTS

This book would not have been possible without *Little Heathens-Hard Times and High Spirits on an Iowa Farm During the Great Depression* by Mildred Armstrong Kalish. I read and reread her book to understand what life was like for Romy and his family living on a farm in Iowa. Also thanks to Richard Schnering, President of the Cassville Historical Society, for giving me information regarding the Cassville Ferry during the mid 1930s.

There are so many other people I'd like to thank for helping me get this book published. My critique partners at ACFW Scribes 218 helped me hone my writing skills. Inga Bauer and Sandy Armstrong, my beta readers, gave me their reader's perspective. Many thanks to Lisa Lickel and Belinda Cortright of Cortright Editorial Services, my editors. They helped me to wordsmith my story and turn it into the novel it is today. I send my sincere thanks to my book designer Lisa Hainline, who created my wonderful cover. A special thank you to Janet Ransdell for a fun photo shoot. Most of all, my heartfelt thanks go to my husband for being so supportive during the editing process. I couldn't have accomplished this without all this help.

Above all, to God be the glory for His many blessings.

CHAPTER 1

The steering wheel slipped through his sweaty palms as Romy Iverson careened around the corner. An ice delivery truck, parked too far from the curb, loomed in front of him. Cranking the wheel to avoid slamming into it, he exhaled. Close one. He couldn't crack up Pa's truck while doing an errand for Ma. Putting a foot on the brake, he struggled to concentrate on his driving rather than on the task ahead.

The annoyance inside him threatened to take over. Or maybe it was the embarrassment he knew he was about to face. His mother insisted on thrusting him chin deep into a quagmire. He was twenty-one years old, too old to be put in these awkward situations.

She'd volunteered him to pick up Pastor Hannemann's sister-in-law from the train depot. Here he was, dressed in his old barn clothes. What would Mrs. Hannemann's sister think when she saw him? Or maybe smelled him?

Ma shouldn't have dumped this so suddenly in his lap. She had tried to assure him it was an easy thing to do. Was she kidding? She knew he got nervous around dames. He couldn't manage to talk to one—ever—especially someone he didn't know. He slammed his palm on the steering wheel.

Besides, he didn't want to *pick up* someone from the train station. He wanted to *get on* the train and go somewhere, anywhere. Someday. If only he could get away from the farm to have adventures out in the world. One day he'd settle down. But not yet. The love of the land was in his blood.

If truth be told, he wanted to escape from Harry. His perfect older brother could do no wrong, at least not in Pa's eyes. No matter what Romy did, it was never good enough. What would he have to do to prove himself to Pa? Why couldn't Harry let him live his life the way he wanted?

Sighing, he wound his way around the streets of Dubuque toward downtown. The bluffs, hugging the city center, rose against the blue western sky with stately red brick houses skirting the rim. Curls of smoke rose from nearby chimneys, the odor tickling his nose. The streets grew wider the closer he got to the river, abandoned buildings dotting the road as he passed. According to what he'd read in the paper, they used to be alive with factory workers. Now they were home to hobos.

At least he had an hour and several errands to do before he had to face her. Give him time to talk himself into this. All he had to do was pick her up and get her back to the parsonage. He could do this simple task.

First stop, the feed mill. Pulling up in front, he took a deep breath to calm down. Why did talking to women make him so nervous?

The mill was crowded with the usual Saturday morning busyness. Romy cautiously backed his 1928 Ford truck to the hopper. Pa would detect a new scratch on the seven-year-old vehicle in no time, even though the truck had taken a beating before. Harry would tease him mercilessly, as usual, if he managed to bang up the truck like he did last year.

On the opposite end of the lengthy building, other farmers were parked at the loading dock, packing bags of feed into their trucks. They must have arrived before first light.

"Howdy, Ralph." Romy shivered as the cold March wind crawled down his neck before he got a chance to button his ragged brown coat. No money for a new one these days. He grabbed his shovel and jumped into the back of the truck. "Pa wants this corn ground up."

"Got it. We s'posed to add anything to it?" Ralph lowered the tailgate.

"One hundred pounds of oats. We're out already." Dust invaded Romy's nostrils as he shoveled corn into the hopper.

"Looks like you're in a hurry there. I bet you're goin' to meet a doll." Cackling, Ralph grabbed a shovel and jumped into the back to help. "You're always looking for pretty girls."

"Oh, baloney, Ralph. You don't have to pester me about dames every time you see me."

"Sure I do." Ralph wiped his forehead with his bandana. "Since I'm your Pa's best friend, I have to help him keep you in line when you're in town." Scraping the last of the corn from the truck bed, he slapped Romy on the back. "You'll get over your shyness someday."

Romy shook his head. If only. "I'll be back in an hour to pick up the feed."

He jumped to the ground and headed toward the front of the truck. "Thanks for the help."

After putting the pickup in gear, he pulled out. He'd prayed, asking the Lord to help him over his bashfulness. So far, the prayers hadn't helped much. He couldn't even talk to girls from church without his gut clenching.

Come to think of it, he didn't even know this girl's complete name. Ma called her Margaret, but, of course, she wouldn't be Margaret Hannemann since she was Mrs. Hannemann's sister. He didn't know what she looked like, either. What fun.

Romy headed toward the post office to check on the mail. He pulled out his pocket watch. Half an hour to do some quick shopping before the train was due. He stuffed the timepiece back into the upper pocket of his bib overalls. Still time to think of a way to escape this mess.

***

Maggie Ehlke watched the buildings of Dubuque crawl by her window as the train slowed. The trees weren't a blur any longer. Crossing the expansive river a few minutes back had been the clue that she was reaching the destination. She had never imagined that the Mississippi was that wide.

After the long trip from central Wisconsin, she was more than ready to get out and stretch her cramped legs. She'd buried herself in her favorite Jane Austen novel, but by the end of the long journey, she couldn't even sit still for *Pride and Prejudice* any longer. Time to face her new life.

If only her twitchy stomach would settle down. The last time she had seen her sister's family was before three-year-old Denny was born when they lived in Racine. Now here she was in Iowa, visiting them at Neil's new church. What would their house and church look like? How big would the kids be? A million questions swirled in her mind.

She bit her lower lip. Who would meet her at the train station? It certainly wouldn't be her sister in her condition. Neil would probably come. Maybe he'd bring the children.

She couldn't wait to see how big Lucy and Denny were after all this time. Lucy must be six years old by now. And she'd be meeting Denny for the first time. There had been no money to make a trip earlier. Neil and Emma had sent several pictures. Nearly a year ago.

Would Neil be able to fit her large trunk into his car? Back home in Juneau, Ma had helped her pack all her belongings into the steamer chest so she knew the thing was heavy. Mostly books.

She had to stop worrying so much. She took a deep breath and let it out slowly.

When Emma's letter announced the possible arrival of twins, her parents had decided it was the ideal answer to their prayers.

One less mouth to feed.

Ma declared that since Katie would be graduating from high school in spring, she wouldn't need Maggie's help with Frank any longer. But Maggie had to go somewhere and do something.

Maggie's original plans had gone up in smoke the year Frank had been paralyzed with polio. Ma couldn't manage all the work of being a farmer's wife with a paralyzed nineteen-year-old son to care for day and night. The burden had fallen on Maggie to stay home and assist Ma.

After graduation, Katie would be the one to help Ma shoulder the housework. Her youngest sister would take Maggie's place, so she had to leave. Now there was a place for her to go.

Surely Neil and Emma would have enough food since he was a pastor. They'd need her help when the babies came. Logical.

Maggie could still hear Ma when she dug out the trunk. "Lots of girls are farmed out for room and board to strangers in these hard times. Be thankful you're going to your sister's house."

Was that supposed to make her feel better? Squeezing her eyes shut, she willed the tears away. She wasn't upset that Katie would be taking her place, but Emma's house wasn't her first choice of a destination when leaving the farm.

All she'd ever dreamed of was to go to college. She loved to learn. History. Science. Anything she could. That's why she had been counting on more education. Was this too much to ask?

After all, Emma was fortunate enough to go school to become a teacher. That's when she'd met Neil. That one year of teaching had changed Emma's life forever.

Maggie swallowed past the lump in her throat. In the end, Emma wasn't any smarter than she was. Life wasn't fair.

Of course, Ma and Pa had to do something to make ends meet. Life during this Depression was hard to bear. No money. Period. She'd move away from home to help them out, but nobody seemed to care what she wanted. It didn't end the deep-down ache of being unwanted. Her unshed tears wouldn't wait any longer. One coursed down her cheek.

Her gloved hand reached up to swipe the tear away as she looked out the window.

Gulping in air, she struggled to calm down. She'd have to be satisfied with the books she brought. She had to use her mind one way or another.

Three of her siblings were already married, but it didn't mean that was her major goal in life. She wanted to get an education and become somebody. Some day.

At twenty-two, she was old enough to move out, but moving in with her sister's family to help with the babies would not be a permanent home. Changing diapers wasn't a lifelong dream for her. She'd help Emma out with the babies when needed, but she'd be studying as much as she could during her free time.

This was a temporary fix at best. *Lord, show me which direction You want me to go.* She would trust that He was leading her home.

The passenger train shuddered to a stop, the hissing steam announcing its arrival. After straightening her outdated hat and tattered checked wool coat, she gathered her bags and headed for the platform. Stepping into the cool air, filled with the pungent odor of coal cinders and smoke, she searched for her brother-in-law while workers pushed rattling baggage carts in her path.

People scurrying to get out of the cold wind filled the station platform. Snow banks, piled halfway up the north side of the building, stood as a testimony to the waning winter. As the wood-planked area emptied, Maggie realized neither Neil nor the children were anywhere in sight. Now what should she do?

She tugged off her black cotton gloves to check the watch pinned to her lapel. She glanced at the hole in the right fingertip. The seam was coming open again. She'd repaired it as best she could before leaving home, but they'd been sewn so many times already. If only there was money for a new pair of gloves. Or a coat for that matter. She ran a hand over the cuff of her coat where the threads were bare. No money. She shook her head.

"Ma'am, is this your trunk?" The porter pointed to her old German chest sitting nearby.

"Yes, sir." Maggie looked down at her watch. "I guess my family hasn't arrived yet. I can't imagine where they are." Her teeth clamped down on her lower lip as her stomach quivered like a bowl of gelatin. "Would it be possible to put it inside until they get here?"

"Why, sure." The porter loaded it onto a wheeled cart. "I'll help you. Don't want you to freeze."

***

Romy raced along the last block toward the station. Oh, great. He had gotten so involved with his mother's grocery list he had neglected the time. Now he was late. No more time to get nervous. Since the crowd had already dispersed, he pulled into a parking spot close to the platform.

Jumping out of the truck, he spotted a young woman juggling two smaller bags. A porter trudged behind her, struggling with a large black trunk. No one else paid any attention to her.

Was that Margaret? He climbed the three steps to the side platform. What should he say? "Ummm . . . Miss?"

Romy faltered into silence because he still didn't know her last name. He couldn't very well call her by her first name without being introduced. Ma would not approve at all.

She turned toward him, her voice carrying across the short distance in a near whisper. "Are you talking to me?"

He approached her in an I-don't-want-to-disturb-you manner, not looking directly at her. Swallowing, he took a breath to calm his racing heart. "Um . . . Do you know Pastor Hannemann?"

"Why, yes. He's my brother-in-law." Her bags slid out of her fingers and fell onto the wooden planks. "Has something happened to him? I thought he would be here to meet me."

"Uh . . . He's at the hospital . . . for an emergency . . . this morning." At last Romy got the courage to look down into the young woman's brown eyes set in her oval face. Her curly brown hair, smooth creamy skin, and perky upturned nose reminded him of Mrs. Hannemann. She sure was pretty. "I . . . I . . ."

Nothing more came out.

"Is everything okay? Is my sister in the hospital?" Biting her lip, she glanced wide-eyed among the pile of luggage, the porter, and Romy.

"N . . . no," he stuttered. "Somebody else, uh, from church."

Romy tried to swallow. Dry as sawdust.

With furrowed brows, she scanned the emptying platform. Biting her lip, she turned back to him. "My name is Maggie Ehlke."

"Miss Ehlke." He nodded, but his mind drew a blank. At least he knew her name. "Romy, uh, Roman Iverson . . ."

She pulled on her gloves, hiding them behind her back, but not before he noticed a hole in one of the fingers. "Are you taking me to Emma's house?"

He avoided eye contact with her as heat rose up his neck faster than a mouse scurrying to find cover. "Yes, um, to Pastor's house."

Miss Ehlke stepped back. "Thank you for picking me up then. I have a large trunk and these two smaller bags. I hope that won't be a problem. Will you have room for them?"

Oh, man. How was he going to fit the trunk, the groceries, Miss Ehlke and all the feedbags into the truck? "Umm . . . I think it will fit."

This errand for his mother was becoming a real pain in the neck. He pointed to the battered red truck parked nearby. "In the back."

"I'll help you with that, sir." The porter steered the cart toward the truck. "This here is one heavy trunk."

As Miss Ehlke bent to pick up the remaining bags, Romy reached for them, his hand grazing her fingers. Her lilac perfume tickling his nose, he stepped back. Drawing in a breath, he glanced at her face. "Let me . . . help you."

***

Maggie inhaled. The barn smell on Mr. Iverson's clothes assailed her. He obviously lived on a farm. Good thing she was familiar with that odor, but it didn't mean she liked it.

"Thank you." She shook her head. She'd never seen such a timid person in her life. At least his mother had taught him some manners. Walking with him toward the truck, she smiled to put him at ease. Jitters were hard to deal with. She knew firsthand. "How far is it to Emma's house?"

"They . . . about ten minutes." Mr. Iverson opened the truck door and placed the smaller bags on the seat. "Have to fit in here . . . Watch the groceries." He pointed to the box lying on the floor. "Stopping at the feed mill first."

He pushed the bags toward the middle of the seat, forcing Maggie to sit close to the door. That was fine. Leave as much room between them as possible. After Maggie was settled, he shut the door. What a gentleman.

He and the porter jockeyed the hefty trunk into the truck bed and slid it to the side. Maggie couldn't help but wonder what else would have to fit in the back. Mr. Iverson extended his hand in a gesture of thanks to the man before climbing behind the steering wheel.

Maggie sat in an uneasy silence as her new city flew past her window. Not used to being with someone who barely spoke, she racked her brain thinking of a topic to discuss. With six siblings, she'd grown up in a household filled with constant chatter.

She touched her brown hat to make sure it was straight. Was she brave enough to break the silence? "I've never been to Dubuque before. Neil and Emma moved here from Racine several years ago, but no one from our family has come to visit."

There was no response, so she tried again. "Since you're stopping at the feed mill, do you live on a farm?"

"Uh, yup." Nothing more was offered for several long seconds. He glanced in her direction. He pointed out the front window. "We live, uh, north of town."

Maggie rubbed her forehead. Couldn't he say anything else?

"I grew up on a farm, also. In Wisconsin." This topic might be more successful. "It's been so hard on my family during the last three years with the price of corn so low."

She stole a glance at her driver, a somber-faced young man with short brown hair. Her father would describe him as a "bean-pole." He would be more appealing if he weren't clenching his teeth so hard. If only she could say something to calm his nerves.

She swallowed before trying again. "The low price of milk and beef doesn't help either." Still no response. Maybe she should try the direct approach. "How are things here in Iowa?"

"Uh, kinda hard . . ." Mr. Iverson kept his eyes on the road. "Been dry lately. Not much growing."

Silence reigned once again. This was ridiculous.

Maggie closed her eyes. "What do you raise on your farm?"

"Uh, mostly pigs . . ."

This was a conversation?

"So how's that doing?"

"Pa says the feed costs more than the pigs are worth."

Silence.

He pulled up to the feed mill loading dock. "Things aren't good."

After jumping out of the truck, Mr. Iverson and an older gentleman loaded several bulging bags into the back of the truck. This reserved young man could stack the bags on top of each other as if he were throwing pillows.

She clenched her fists until her nails bit into her palms. His confidence handling the heavy feedbags surely didn't transfer to his social skills. Her head snapped up at the sight of him talking and laughing with the miller.

Revealing a deep dimple on each cheek, his toothy smile transformed his face, as if she were observing a different person. That irritated her. She gritted her teeth. Why couldn't he talk to her?

CHAPTER 2

Romy tossed another burlap sack on the growing pile in the truck bed. He would take his frustrations out on the feed today. The more he felt like kicking himself, the faster he heaped the bags.

Why couldn't he think of anything intelligent to say to Miss Ehlke? His mind had frozen as solid as the fishing pond at home. He could have told her about the farm. He even could have told her about Dubuque. Anything to fill the overbearing silence stretching between them.

If only he could be somewhere else right now. Why couldn't he get on a train and travel to new places like Miss Ehlke did? Explore new cities. She sure was lucky.

Ralph tossed the last feedbag onto the truck. They'd piled a couple of them on Miss Ehlke's trunk for lack of space.

"Well, you take care of that pretty gal." Ralph patted him on the back. "We'll have to keep our eyes on you."

"I told you I picked her up at the station for my pastor." Laughing, Romy dismissed the comments with a wave of his hand. "I probably won't see her much, except at church."

Oh, that it were true. Now he had to survive the long trip to Pastor's house.

***

Maggie took a deep breath as they started on the last leg of the trip. The end couldn't come soon enough. The trees along the road looked like marching skeletons with their bare branches reaching toward the sky. While inside the truck the silence was deafening.

Could she get him to talk to her? After all, if he could talk and joke with the mill worker, he should be able to converse with her. "You sure have lots of feed in the back."

"Uh, yup."

Was that any kind of answer? Anyone with good manners knew in polite society you didn't answer a question with one word. Ma had made sure she learned it when she was little. Her four brothers knew if they grunted at their mother, they would get reprimanded.

She'd try again. "You must have a large farm."

"Eighty acres."

She looked out the window at the passing red brick houses. What a blessing for him to have a place to call home. Since his father would always need his help, he'd never have to leave. She sighed. He'd never feel unwanted. He sure was lucky.

It'd be nice if he talked more, though. She didn't want to sit the whole time in silence. "Do you and your father work the farm alone? Do you have other brothers to help you? How large is your family?"

If she asked more than one question, maybe he'd open up.

"Seven . . . Four boys and three girls . . ."

"Oh, my! Your mother must be very busy." Maybe she should ask him the names and ages of the six siblings, but it took too much effort right now. She rubbed her forehead where a dull ache had started.

"Actually she's at Pastor's house, with my five-year-old sister, um, helping Mrs. Hannemann."

Dropping her hand, Maggie glanced toward him. Well, the young man was able to speak in a complete sentence. Could she keep him talking? No, she was too exhausted from the long trip to continue the struggle. She only wanted to see Emma's family. The pain, shooting through her head, had grown past the point of ignoring it. She closed her eyes.

✳✳✳

Romy's brakes squealed when he stopped the truck in front of the parsonage. Somehow he'd lived through her stony silence during the remainder of the ride. He couldn't help it if his mind raced for things to say and came up blank. As he looked up at the yellow clapboard house with the wide white porch, he took a deep breath. Now what? "This is—"

Before he could get another word out, Miss Ehlke bolted upright, opened the door, and jumped out of the front seat. She turned to him and smiled. "Thank you for the ride and the *wonderful* conversation."

Somehow, her words did not mirror the smile on her face. She shut the door and raced up the sidewalk. As her foot touched the porch, the front door flew open, and Mrs. Hannemann met her in a fierce hug.

She wasn't very friendly. She didn't even wait until he could open the truck door for her. She'd probably been uncomfortable in the silence, but she didn't have to be sarcastic with him. He smacked the steering wheel with the heel of his hand. Why didn't his mouth cooperate with his brain? This was the story of his life when it came to females.

At least his dream of traveling would get him away from the dame problem. He could ride the rails to places unknown and never have to make small talk with girls. It sounded more and more appealing all the time. It would take him far from a certain Miss Ehlke who couldn't stand him right now.

He looked down at her bags. Perfect. He'd be the one to get them into the house. Those sisters surely wouldn't be thinking about luggage. He carried the two smaller valises to the porch.

Ma stood in the doorway, wiping her hands on a towel. "How many more are in the truck?"

"Only her huge travel trunk." Romy set the bags down inside the front door.

Ma closed the door after them. "Did you survive the trip from the station?" Her eyes twinkled as she tried to hide the don't-try-to-fool-me smile spreading on her face.

Rubbing the back of his neck, he frowned. "Yeah . . . She didn't have much to say."

"Hmm. I bet you didn't either." She shook her head. "I can never figure out why you are always so shy in the company of girls since you aren't like that at home. You certainly give as good as you get with your sisters." She looked at the watch pinned to her dress bodice. "Maybe I should ask what took you so long."

Running his fingers through his hair, Romy exhaled. "I had to stop at the feed mill after I picked her up." He pointed toward the curb. "I piled the last of the feedbags on top of her trunk since I ran out of room."

"Need me to help you, or can you get it in the house alone? How large it is?"

"The guy at the train station had to help me load it up, but I'll manage." He put his hand on the doorknob.

"If you needed help there, it must be really heavy. I'll come out to give you a hand since Pastor's not home yet."

"No, Ma. I'll figure out something."

"Don't argue with me. I'll come out to see if I can help you."

"Then give me some time to move the feed so I can get to it."

"I'll be out in two minutes, then." She reached for her tan frayed winter coat as Romy closed the door.

Ma was treating him like a kid again. Not what he needed today.

In short order, Romy managed to move the trunk back to the tailgate. He brushed the dust from the feedbags off the top. Now, could they move the thing? It was heavier than any feedbag he'd ever lifted.

When the front door closed, he glanced toward the porch where Ma hustled down the steps. "Let's see if we can get it out of the truck."

Time to get this done and head home.

Romy took one end while she grabbed the handle on the other end. As they slid the trunk from the truck bed, her end thudded on the pavement. Color draining from her cheeks, she gasped and straightened up as if she had been poked by a branding iron.

Romy's heart raced faster than the windmill in a storm. He set down his end and hurried to his mother's side. "Are you all right? What's wrong?"

"I had a bit of a pinch move down my arm, but I'm fine now." She waved her hand to dismiss his concern. Her smile belied the drawn look on her face. "It sure is a beast."

Should he believe her words, or the look on her face? He took a breath and let it out slowly. At the sound of an approaching car, he glanced down the street.

Pastor Hannemann drove up in his black Chevy. "Hello, Mrs. Iverson. Hello, Roman." He walked around to the curb. "Is Maggie here yet?"

"Yes, we were trying to get her trunk into the house." Rubbing her arm, his mother pointed to the source of frustration. "It's very heavy."

"Well, Mrs. Iverson, you go on in." Pastor looked at Romy. "We'll get it into the house, won't we?"

Probably not. Wait until Pastor felt how heavy it was. But of course, he'd never say so out loud. Romy smiled.

The two men struggled with the trunk all the way up the sidewalk. They hoisted its bulk up the seven steps onto the edge of the porch. Both of them puffed from the exertion.

Pastor rubbed his back. "I know we need to have our houses built higher off the ground in case of spring floods, but sometimes it sure is an inconvenience." He moved Romy's end of the trunk two inches back. "Better make sure it's squared up here."

Romy nodded. That's as much as he wanted to do. What a way to end this trip to town.

"I imagine Maggie has packed it with her large collection of books. I think we'll take the books out before we move it another inch."

"Good idea." Exactly what Romy wanted to hear. He had wasted enough time for one morning and wanted to get on the road as soon as possible.

Opening the front door of the house, Pastor motioned for Romy to enter first. "Come on in for a bit."

"We have to head home before long since Pa is waiting for me." Romy removed his hat when he entered the foyer. "I'll wait here for Ma and Janet to come."

He spotted Ma towing his five-year-old sister down the stairs. Lucy and Dennis, Pastor's two children, followed close behind.

Pastor turned to shake Romy's hand. "Thanks so much for getting Maggie from the depot." He looked over his shoulder into the living room at his wife and Maggie. "I felt I had to go to the hospital this morning for Howard and his family."

"That's fine." Romy motioned for his mother and sister to go out the door. "We'll see you all at church."

That trying experience was now behind him.

✳✳✳

Maggie heard the outside door open and glanced over. Mr. Iverson walked in followed closely by Neil. In the midst of her conversation with Emma, she stopped cold.

Why had she been so harsh to him when she got out of his truck? After her long trip, she'd been irritated by the silences stretching between them. It wasn't logical. If only she hadn't gotten a headache. Since she'd probably hurt his feelings, she'd better apologize to him before he could get away. But he shook Neil's hand and headed out the door faster than a scared deer. She would have to deal with him later.

She smiled at the chaos suddenly descending on the house. Lucy and Denny jumped up and down talking a mile a minute, vying for Emma's attention. Neil entered the living room with arms outstretched. "It's so nice to see you."

Maggie welcomed his embrace. "I'm glad to be here." She crouched down to put herself at the height of the children. "My, you two are so big! Lucy, you were about Denny's size when I saw you last."

Standing beside Emma's chair, Lucy looked at Maggie out of the corner of her eye. "Lucy, this is your Aunt Maggie." Emma pushed her in Maggie's direction. "We told you she was coming to help."

Lucy nodded her head as she stepped back. "Oh yeah, she's going to sleep in my old room now since I had to move into Denny's room."

She offered Maggie a smile that didn't quite reach her eyes. Looking down at her feet, she stayed glued to Emma's chair.

Maggie turned her attention to the wiggly three-year-old with sandy brown hair who was an exact miniature of his daddy. What a cutie! Denny looked like he was not going to detach himself from Neil's leg anytime soon.

"Denny, it's so nice to meet you." Maggie smiled at her nephew, trying to break the ice. "You're such a big boy. I've waited so long to see you."

"You'll never believe this by looking at them, but these two have been talking about your coming for a week straight." The joy on Emma's face radiated across the room as she massaged her protruding belly. "I think we're all so relieved to have you here. Now we're ready for our addition to come into the world."

"Wait a minute." Neil approached Emma's chair with Denny still attached to his leg. He bent over to pick up a sliver of paper lying on the floor. "You may be ready at this point, but don't you think Maggie should get settled in first?"

His wife nodded. "You're right."

Maggie settled onto the couch. "Yes, I need some time to get acquainted with the children."

And time to get rid of her headache.

Grinning, Neil rubbed his hand down his wife's hair. He straightened the pillows sitting beside her. "That won't take too long. They're usually not so shy."

Emma shifted in her chair. "I know that, but I'm not sure when these babies will decide to arrive."

"I think they will wait for God's timing." Maggie nodded. She had never imagined Emma would be so large. She'd watched her expand before Lucy was born. If memory served her correctly, Emma was twice the size now. Must be twins for sure.

"Very true." Neil turned to Maggie. "Would you like me to show you around?"

"Sure, I've heard so much about your house. I want to see if it's how I imagined." She relaxed for the first time since she got off the train. The headache started to subside. "Emma, why don't you rest where you are while Neil gives me a tour?"

With the children shadowing him, Neil led the way through the dining room and into the kitchen. The sun's rays poured through the window sending warmth all the way to Maggie's toes. A white round table stood in the center of the red-and-yellow-checkered linoleum floor.

Neil pointed toward the modern-looking cupboards with glass doors. "Em has done wonders in here. She painted the cupboards and window frame white to lighten the room."

"It looks so cheery." Maggie ran her hands over the large white sink under the window. "It's so nice to have a sink with running water in the house." She glanced at Neil. "Until two years ago we still had to carry water up from the pump in the yard. At least now Pa has rigged up piping into the kitchen so we can have water in there."

"One thing nice about city living . . . indoor plumbing. Wait until you see the bathroom upstairs." Neil brushed crumbs scattered on the countertop into his palm.

He pointed to a cylinder standing on four legs in the corner next to the sink. "A while back, we managed to purchase a used washing machine, which has helped Emma out immensely."

Maggie noticed the wringer rollers on the top of the covered cylinder. "I'm sure I'll learn how to use—"

"This is where I help Momma bake cookies," Lucy blurted out while hopping from one foot to the other. She must have gotten over her shy streak.

With wrinkled brow, Neil frowned at Lucy. "Shush, you shouldn't interrupt Aunt Maggie when she's talking."

Denny pulled on Maggie's sweater, adding his two cents' worth. "Yeah, cookies."

Maggie crouched down to look into both children's eyes. She glanced from one to the other. "Sounds like a great idea. Maybe we can bake some oatmeal cookies for your Momma next week. I'll need help from both of you to show me what to do."

"Hoorah!" Lucy jumped up and down clapping her hands. "I gotta go tell Momma right away."

She tore out of the kitchen and ran back through the dining room.

"Cookies!" Denny followed suit and ran after Lucy.

Giving Neil a half-smile, Maggie stood again. "Maybe I should have checked to make sure Emma has oatmeal and flour before I promised the cookies."

"We're doing all right so far. The congregation gives us foodstuff when they don't have cash for the offering plate." Neil straightened a chair next to the table.

"Anyway, as I was saying . . ." She pointed toward the machine in the corner. "I'm sure I'll learn how to use the washing machine very soon with all the clothes the baby will need."

Neil smiled and nodded. "You're right."

He turned back toward the living room where the noise level had suddenly increased with the cookie announcement. "I'm glad I have a few minutes alone with you. I wanted to talk to you about Roman."

CHAPTER 3

A sudden coldness struck Maggie's core. Had Mr. Iverson told her brother-in-law how rude she had been to him? She'd tried to apologize, but he'd left too quickly. Already in trouble, and so soon after arriving. Gnawing on her lip, she dropped her gaze to the floor. "What about him?"

"Em wasn't happy when I told her I had an emergency visit to make at the hospital." Folding his arms across his chest, Neil leaned against the cupboard. "I wanted to tell you I'm so sorry I couldn't pick you up from the train station."

Maggie exhaled the breath she'd been holding. Not what she'd imagined at all.

"Don't worry about it. I'm glad I didn't stop you from your work." It wasn't necessary for Neil to hear about the ride to his house.

"I'm sure Roman didn't make it easy on you since you had not met him before." Neil smiled with an all-knowing grin. "He can be a bit shy when he meets someone new."

That was an understatement if Maggie ever heard one. Did he read her mind? "Yes, he was rather quiet on the way to your house."

"Don't judge him by your first meeting. He really is a nice guy when you get to know him."

Maggie doubted her brother-in-law, but didn't want to say so. "I'll remember when I see him next."

If only it would not be for a long time. But she still had to apologize to him. "We'd better keep going on the tour so I can get dinner started."

"Okay."

Pushing through a swinging wooden door, Neil led Maggie toward the rising volume of children's voices in the living room.

"The kids are getting so big." Ahead Maggie could see the front door.

"It's been a long time since we've seen you." Neil picked up the two bags left in the foyer and led the way up the steps. "Let's slip upstairs before they get hungry. We put Lucy and Denny in the same room so you could have a room by yourself."

Wonderful news. Maggie trailed him up the stairs. "How thoughtful. I've shared a room my whole life with Katie, so I'm used to sharing, if needed."

"We'll see." Neil made a U-turn when he reached the top of the steps. "Your room will be back here."

He pointed to a small square room with a twin bed in one corner. After following her into the room, he placed her bags on the bed.

The green-leafed wallpaper gave the room the look of spring. The light green quilt on the bed complemented the brown and green oval rug covering part of the wooden floor. A small dresser and old side chair completed the furnishings.

"Oh, this is lovely." Maggie smiled. Much nicer than she was used to. Maybe leaving Wisconsin wouldn't be so bad.

"Most of it is secondhand from church members who wanted to help us out when they heard you were coming." Neil headed toward the next room. "We're pretty well set for the arrival of the babies."

They entered the room where two cribs stood at right angles in a corner. Neil adjusted the doily on top of the large dresser that stood along the third wall adjacent to a window. "Em has worked hard during the last month to get this room to look like this."

"I'm glad the babies will be close to me, so I can help Emma." They headed back the way they'd come.

Maggie followed Neil as they trotted down the stairs. She'd have to earn her keep in her sister's house. She would make sure that they couldn't get along without her. That way she would assure herself a place to live with her sister's family even if it wasn't her first choice. "I better see what to do about dinner before it's too late."

"Good idea. Meanwhile, I'll have Lucy and Denny help me unload the books from your trunk."

"Oh, my! I forgot all about it." Maggie scanned the entryway searching for her belongings.

"It's still on the porch." He pointed toward the door.

"It's heavy . . . All of my books. Just have the kids put them on the floor in my room."

"Okay." Neil peered into the living room and motioned to the children. "I think I have some boards and bricks down in the basement we could use for shelves for your books, if it's all right with you."

"Perfect." Maggie headed toward the living room to seek Emma's help.

***

"I'm glad that's done." Romy let out a long, slow breath as the truck pulled away from the curb. Thankfully, that episode was now behind him.

"Whatever do you mean?" His mother gazed at him over his little sister's head. "I thought Miss Ehlke was very pretty."

"Well, I won't disagree with you there." Romy glanced at her. "You can't imagine what it's like to be in this small truck with someone so cute and not know what to say." He focused on the road again. "I could hardly get a sentence out."

"Oh, dear. Maybe next time will work out better."

"Next time?" Was Ma planning his life again? He'd stay as far away from Miss Ehlke as he could. "She'll run the other way when she sees me coming next time." After a pause he mumbled, "I wouldn't blame her."

"Don't be so hard on yourself. You have to do better when you see her again." She patted his arm. "You just need to come up with topics to talk about beforehand."

Why was his mother always doing this? She kept implying he could change his behavior if he wanted to. He'd get rid of this shyness in a heartbeat if he could.

"Don't forget your pa told you to fill up the gas tank."

"Oh, boy, I forgot in all the rush." He would have been in trouble if he'd gotten home with an empty tank. "Thanks for the reminder."

Romy pulled the truck into the Texaco station, ringing the service bell inside. He rolled down the window when a middle-aged man, with "Joe" printed on his dark green shirt pocket with the red star, sauntered up to the truck. "Howdy, how are you folks today? What can I do fer ya?"

"Fill it up, please." Romy stopped Joe before he walked away. "How much is gas today?"

"Eleven cents a gallon. I'll check yer oil, too." He headed toward the gas cap.

"How long will this take?" Janet leaned against their mother. "We've been gone so long already."

Romy glanced down at his sister. Most Sundays Janet begged to stay and play with Lucy after church. What was different about today?

"I thought you had fun at Lucy's house." Ma patted her leg. "What's the hurry?"

"I figured Blackie must miss me by now."

That was the difference, the puppy. Not a surprise. She had just gotten her new dog from the neighbor a month ago.

"We'll be home soon."

When the tank was full, Joe worked under the hood. After the attendant slammed it shut, he washed the windshield. "I checked the oil, battery, and fan belt. Everything looks okay." He held out his hand. "That will be a dollar ninety-eight." Romy's nose wrinkled as the gasoline fumes surrounding Joe accosted him.

His mother retrieved the money from her purse and handed it to him. "Thanks much." He handed the money to Joe. "We'll see you later." He rolled up the window before starting out. "Let's head home."

The flats of the river valley quickly changed into rolling hills as they headed north out of Dubuque. They passed bare farmland dotted here and there with dirty patches of snow. It wouldn't be long before he and Pa would be busy in the fields planting corn and wheat.

Romy turned right onto the dirt road, a half-mile from home. They drove past the neighborhood farms. "My stomach's telling me it's time to eat soon."

"I'm really hungry, too." Janet looked at their mother. "What are we eating for dinner?"

"I think there's leftover stew from yesterday. I'll have to plan a larger meal tonight since I didn't have any time to cook this morning."

They turned left onto the drive leading up the hill to the house. Glancing around, Romy noted that times had been tough on the farm over the last couple years. The house, as well as the barn, needed a fresh coat of paint, and the hog barn roof sagged. Even the henhouse and corncrib were missing a few boards. There just wasn't enough cash to purchase supplies to do the upkeep. Pa tried to do his best, but he couldn't work miracles in this economy.

As soon as he stopped the truck, Janet crawled over her mother and tumbled out the door. She tore across the yard toward the barn.

Ma's voice brought her to a screeching halt. "Young lady, you get back here!"

Janet did an about face and headed back.

"You make sure you're bundled up if you're headed out by Blackie." Ma pulled the ends of her headscarf tight and turned up the collar of her coat.

"Yes, Ma. I'll be warm when I get to the barn." After Ma nodded, Janet took off in the direction of the barn again.

Ma was good at fussing. She turned back to the truck to retrieve the box of groceries. "Tell your pa and brothers dinner will be ready in half an hour." She looked at her watch. "I know it'll be later than usual, but I need to get the stew heated up first."

"Okay." Romy put the truck into gear. "I'll give them the message."

***

Romy took his coat off as he came in the back door. His stomach growled at the mouth-watering smells coming from the kitchen. Ma always came up with enough food to feed him and six hungry siblings even in these hard times. "It sure smells great."

Sally and Mary scurried around the large table trying to put the finishing touches on it.

"I had to add some extra potatoes and carrots from the basement to make it enough for everyone." His mother stood over her Monarch range, stirring the steaming stew in a large black pot. "Where are the rest?" She glanced at the table. "Sally, can you cut the loaf of bread? It's in the bread box."

Sally pulled the knife out of the drawer and headed for the box. Romy shook his head. How did Ma trust an eleven-year-old girl with a knife when she fussed over him on occasion?

"They'll be here in a minute." Romy proceeded to pump water into the kitchen sink to wash his hands. The water trickled over his hands before disappearing down the drain.

"I know you and your brothers have been using the cistern water during the winter to wash your hands after being in the barn, but now that spring is coming, I'm thinking it's time to start washing at the outside pump again." Ma tasted the stew. "We don't need any more water running out of the drain pipe into the backyard than necessary."

He dried his hands on a towel. "You're right. I could have washed at the pump. I'll take a towel out there after dinner so we remember to wash up there."

How long would it be before they could have indoor plumbing like city folk did? Maybe Pa would find money to buy the pipes this summer.

"I hope Janet knows enough to come in with Pa." Ma looked over her shoulder at Romy, and then glanced at the table again. "Mary, the butter and milk are in the icebox."

"Pa was gathering her up to have her head in with him when I drove away." Romy hung the towel back on the hook. Ma needed to trust Pa more.

"Ma, I can't find the butter." Mary bent low to look on the shelves of the icebox. "I've looked everywhere."

"You know the butter is always on the lowest shelf." Romy stooped to help her locate the butter. "See, it's right behind the milk jug." He looked at nine-year-old Mary. "Cold air falls, so the coldest spot in the icebox is under the ice holder, right here. You'll always find the milk and butter there."

"I forgot. Thanks." Mary carried the container to the table.

"I think I'll have to go get another block of ice for you after dinner." He opened the ice compartment to find only a small chunk left. "At least our ice house is full now."

All conversation stopped as the rest of the family burst in from outside. The bedlam erupting made it hard to hear anything. Ted, Harry, and Jim were arguing about something. Pa carried Janet piggyback style as they entered the kitchen.

"Were you warm enough out there, little one?" Ma stirred the big pot on the stove again.

Janet's cheeks glowed from the fresh air. "Oh, Blackie was so happy to see me again." Janet slid down her pa's back and came to land on her feet next to Ma. "We had fun playing in the barn."

"You better wash your hands really well then." Ma carried the stew pot to the table. "Everyone, hurry before it gets cold."

"Did you have a good visit with Pastor's wife this mornin'?" Pa headed toward the table. "You were gone a long time."

She started scooping stew into the nine bowls as Romy and his siblings took their seats. "It took so long because your son had to get Mrs. Hannemann's sister from the train station."

"Oh, ho!" Harry jabbed Romy with his elbow. "That's why you wanted to go along to town with Ma. So did you have a lovely conversation with her?"

Pa guffawed before covering his mouth with his hand. Ma's hand stilled above the stew pot as she scowled at him.

Great, here we go. Romy clenched his teeth. "You can stop now."

Laughing, Harry ignored him. "I suppose you're ready to propose to her. Did you have a good time?"

Shaking his head, Romy reached for the bowl his ma handed to him. "It was awful, if you ask me."

"You mean she wasn't pretty?" Ted grabbed the bread plate. "I thought she might look like Mrs. Hannemann."

"Not what I meant at all. She was very nice-looking, but she was hard to talk to." Enough about Miss Ehlke.

"I bet I'd have had a great time talking to her." Harry poked Romy again with his elbow. "You're just too shy, Romy. You need to become a man."

This was not news to him. He didn't know what to do about it. There was the problem.

"Okay. Enough of the chatter." Pa folded his hands. "Let's pray. The eyes of all look to You, O Lord, . . ."

When the prayer was finished, silence reigned in the room except for an occasional clink of a spoon on a bowl as everyone dug into the stew.

"Maybe you could introduce her to me." Harry continued the last train of thought.

"Oh, come on, Harry. You have a girlfriend already."

"I'd treat her better than you did when you struck out with Lilah during high school. I still can't believe you took her ice fishing the first time you went out with her. She almost had frostbite when she got home. It's no wonder she talked about you all around school. No other dame would even speak to you after that fiasco."

Romy didn't need to be reminded about that incident. The memory was seared on his brain. Forever.

Harry continued, "I think you should introduce her to me. I'll take good care of her."

"What about Cissy? You don't need to meet another dame." Romy tasted his stew. His brother always had all the luck with females.

"Well, it never hurts to meet more dolls." Harry's smile took on a devilish tenor as he winked at his mother.

Pa glanced up from his stew. "Son, you better stick with Cissy. She's a real pretty gal."

"Harry, stop pestering your brother. I wish you were shyer around girls." His mother took a bite of bread. "You and Romy need to balance each other out."

"Oh, Ma, Harry's fine as he is. No complaints about him." Pa sipped on his coffee.

Romy swallowed a chunk of potato. Pa always stuck up for Harry no matter what the conversation was about. Why didn't Pa think the same thing about him?

"How did it go at the feed mill, Romy?" Pa knew how to change the subject when things got too sticky.

"It was busy, as usual, on a Saturday morning. But Ralph had time to help me get the corn into the hopper." He'd not mention the teasing Ralph had done.

"Did he say anythin' 'bout Elmer's farm when you were there?" Of course, Pa would ask a question about their nearest neighbor.

There had been many meals of late discussing the problems the Zimmermans were having. Mr. Zimmerman had borrowed money years ago to build a pig barn, but now raising hogs wasn't bringing in as much cash as before. Since Mr. Zimmerman couldn't make his payments, Pa worried they would lose their farm.

This morning, Romy had never thought about them when he was at the feed mill.

"No, he didn't." Romy couldn't admit what they had talked about. "Did you hear if Mr. Zimmerman was able to make the payment?"

"Elmer stopped by on his way from town this mornin'." Pa shook his head and took another bite of stew. "He said he tried to pay his bill at the co-op with a calf, but they wouldn't take it." He buttered a slice of bread. "I have a feelin' Elmer will end up auctionin' off his farm just to pay the annual mortgage and interest payment. It's gettin' scary with the Depression and now the dry weather."

Was Pa talking about the Zimmerman place, or their own farm? Romy had never questioned the financial stability of their family. "Pa, are we headed for the same trouble?"

"Well, I didn't borrow money to expand like Elmer did, but you can never tell what's goin' to happen in the future." Pa folded his hands and rested his forearms on the table.

Ma put her hand on Pa's arm. "God will somehow get us through this, Albert. He has always been good to us in the past, and I'm sure He'll continue to be." She looked at him with eyes full of love.

"Yeah, Hilda, it's the only way we'll survive." Pa covered her hand with his.

If Romy followed his dream and left home, he might never find the kind of love his father had for his mother. Would it be worth it?

CHAPTER 4

Maggie watched the children troop up and down the stairs carrying her books at their father's direction. Smiling, she approached Emma's chair. "I guess we better figure out what to feed those hard workers."

"You're right. They're working up an appetite for sure." Emma struggled to get out of the cushy chair. "Mrs. Iverson put a hot dish in the oven, so we only need to get out the rest."

"That sounds great. You need to tell me where things are. I'll take care of it." Maggie led the way through the dining room into the kitchen while her sister waddled behind her. She smiled as she pulled out one of the chairs by the small round table. "Em, sit down and rest yourself."

Emma collapsed into the chair. "I think I'll take you up on that. I feel tired all the time lately." She rubbed her hands on her protruding belly, hidden under her voluminous apron. "I'll be glad when these two come out."

"Would you like a cup of coffee?"

"Sounds good. All we have is instant. The kettle is over there."

After filling the teakettle with water, Maggie put it on the stove. "You have a good reason to be tired all the time. How come you're so sure there are two?" She sat in the chair opposite her sister. "Can you really tell?"

"Not for sure. This is the third time I've been in the family way, and it's much different." Emma again massaged her roundness. "I've never been like this before, and it feels like two babies are kicking. When a friend from church offered to loan us a second crib, I jumped at the chance."

"Now that I see you, I think you may be right." Maggie smoothed her hand along the table before glancing up at Emma. "I can tell you Ma was thrilled to hear the news."

"I figured as much since you're here. Of course, we'll have to wait until they're born, but I'm positive I'm having twins."

"We'll find out soon." Maggie stood up and looked around the kitchen. "Okay. Besides the hot dish, what are we eating?" She noticed a breadbox sitting on the cupboard close to the back door. "Is there bread in there?"

"Yes, but I think we're on the last loaf, so we're close to baking time again." Emma pointed to the icebox. "There's some jam I made last summer in a jar on the middle shelf."

"I'll look." Maggie set the bread on the table. "By the way, where's the bread knife?"

"Over in the drawer by the sink. Oh . . . and when you're looking in the icebox, you should find a brick of cheese. The kids like cheese."

Maggie busied herself getting the food ready. "I guess I never took time to give you the greetings from Ma and Pa." She looked up from cutting the bread. "They miss you and the kids so much, but can't afford to come visit."

"How is everyone back in Wisconsin?" Emma leaned back in her chair, looking like she was settling in for a long conversation. "How's Frank doing? Give me all the details."

"The family is healthy right now. As you know, Frank has stabilized and improved a little. He's getting around in his wheelchair with ease, but that's not much help to Pa outside. He's more underfoot in the house for Ma, but she still has all the extra work of his therapy." Maggie paused before slicing another piece. "I'm sure you're most interested in Vivi and Danny."

Emma grinned. "Who'd have thought my best friend and my brother would have gotten together on my wedding day."

Maggie sighed. "Now they have Pierre, who is absolutely adorable. I can't believe he's almost a year old."

"Is he walking already?" Emma shifted in her chair.

"Not quite, but he crawls all over their house." Maggie's vision blurred with unshed tears. It was hard leaving her nephew. Good thing there were munchkins in this house to keep her busy.

"I wish I could see the house that Danny built for Vivi on the corner of Pa's land."

"Vivi's done a nice job on decorating it. It's so convenient for Danny to help Pa with all the work." Slicing through the cheese, Maggie's hand froze. "Pa slowed down more over the winter."

Emma sat up straighter. "Is he sick?"

"No, I think the economy and dry weather are taking their toll." The teakettle whistled a merry tune, catching Maggie's attention. "Where's the coffee?"

"It's in the pantry."

Searching through the glass cabinet doors, Maggie saw the cups stacked on the second shelf in front of her. She found the Bantam Instant Coffee. "Maybe I'll sit and enjoy this a minute before dinner."

Emma placed her hand on Maggie's arm. "Thank you. And thanks so much for coming to help us. You're always ready to lend a hand."

Maggie spooned coffee into the mugs before stirring the contents and handing one to Emma. "You're welcome. With Katie almost out of school, Ma said she didn't need me around any longer. Ma and Pa were glad I had a place to go. Things are so hard for them with the bad economy. I'm concerned about them even with me out of the house."

"I'm sure they will be fine with God watching over them." Emma took a sip of coffee. "How was your train trip?"

"Long. Nothing much exciting to do sitting on a train besides reading."

"I was pretty upset with Neil when he said he couldn't go to the station to get you. You must have been worried not knowing what was happening when we didn't show up."

Maggie didn't want to trouble Emma in her condition so she downplayed her disappointment. "It did take a while to figure out who I was riding with."

"Do you mean Roman was late?"

Maggie looked down at the dark liquid swirling in her cup. "Not really . . ."

"What happened?" Emma set her cup down. "You're being mysterious."

"It took me some time to find out he was driving me to your house." Maggie hoped she was vague enough not to alarm her sister.

"Oh, I know Roman . . . He probably couldn't get a sentence out to explain the situation to you, right?"

Maggie glanced over the rim of her cup. "That's a good way to put it."

"He's very shy, especially when talking to women. I've seen him talk and laugh with the men at church, but when I walk up, he turns all red and can't say a word—and I'm the pastor's wife." Emma gave Maggie a you-know-what-I-mean smile.

"Then you understand what I went through. It was so awkward." Maggie's teeth sank into her lower lip.

"I think he overcomes his shyness to some extent when he gets to know someone better."

"That's exactly what Neil said." Maggie looked at the clock and jumped out of her chair. "I didn't realize how late it is. Which plates do you want me to use?"

"Our everyday dishes are in there." Emma pointed to the cabinet in the corner. She put her hand on her abdomen. "Oh, wow, these contractions are pretty hard some days."

Maggie immediately went to Emma's side. "Are you all right? Is it your time? Maybe we should call Neil."

"Stop worrying so much. I've been getting these occasionally for a month or so."

Maggie smiled. She shouldn't jump to conclusions like that. Ma had a point when she called her a worrier. She walked over to the icebox. "Maybe they'll come sooner than you think. Do the children drink milk for dinner?"

"No, n . . . not today." Emma glanced down as her hands twisted in her lap. "We're short of milk this week because the Ericksons didn't bring us their usual two quarts." Her cheeks tinged with pink color. "When members don't have money for their church offerings, they sometimes give us food instead. The Ericksons help us out with milk each week."

"I think our pastor has to accept gifts, also." Maggie nodded. "What would you like the kids to drink then?"

"Just water." Emma looked around the kitchen. "Looks like you're pretty well set for dinner. Do you want to call them to come eat?"

***

As Maggie dried the last plate an hour later, Emma and Denny walked through the swinging door from the hallway. Glancing toward the door, Maggie smiled. "Are you feeling better? Have you had any more contractions?"

"No, but it felt good to lie down for a bit while Denny napped." She sat down in a chair by the table.

"Did you have a nice nap, Denny?" Climbing into Emma's lap, Denny nodded.

Emma enclosed her son in a hug before glancing up. "Thanks so much for doing the dishes."

"I hope I put them back in the right place." Maggie hung her towel over the bar on the wall.

Emma gazed out the window. "Since it's Saturday, I need to walk over to church to prepare the altar for tomorrow."

"You're still doing the chancel at church?" Maggie shook her head. "Why would you have to do that when you're so close to your time?"

"I enjoy doing it since I can't go to church now." Emma placed her hands on her lower back. "I'm too far along to be seen in public anymore, so I help out with the altar on Saturdays."

"I never thought of that." Maggie patted Emma's hand. "Did you want me to watch the kids while you're at church?"

"Yeah, maybe you could take them for a walk in the sunshine." Emma helped Denny off her lap. "They can wear their warm coats, but I think the wind has calmed down."

"Great idea." Maggie grinned. What a perfect excuse to get a quick look at their place of worship. "We can walk with you, and then I'll go around the block for a while." They headed toward the front of the house. "How far is it to your church?"

"It's only down the block and around the corner. St. Peter's used to own much more land when the parsonage was built, but they had to sell part of it several years ago to make ends meet." Emma grabbed her coat off the rack. "Now they just own our house and the church."

Maggie started up the stairs. "I'll go get Lucy, so we can leave."

Five minutes later, the four headed out the door and down the steps. "Where are we going?" Grasping Emma's hand, Lucy glanced at her mother. "Are we going to see Papa?"

"I have to go set up the altar, but your Aunt Maggie is going to take you for a walk." Stroking Lucy's hair, Emma gave her a tender smile.

"If you have some time, I'd love to see the church." Maggie walked hand in hand with Denny.

"In that case, we'll get to see Papa for a minute." Emma tipped her head toward Lucy. "I'm sure he's getting everything ready for the service tomorrow."

As soon as they sauntered around the corner, Maggie saw the steepled structure located east of the parking lot. Painted white with four stained-glass windows, it reminded her of the church back home, although much larger. A white cross topped a tall, square bell tower at the west entrance.

After Denny trudged up the ten steps, Emma opened the church door and led the way into a small vestibule. Maggie turned to the left and entered the sanctuary where she spotted Neil straightening the hymnals in each pew. The balcony hovered above the back third of the church while a red carpet led the way down the center aisle to the chancel.

A wooden cross hung above the stone altar against the far wall, a statue of Jesus suspended from its arms. Maggie's eyes misted over with unshed tears at the beauty of it.

"Hello." With arms outstretched, Neil ambled forward to greet them. "Welcome to St. Peter Lutheran Church."

"It's beautiful." Stepping back, Maggie was struck by the splendor of the church windows. The sun created a kaleidoscope of colors playing across the pews, polished with age.

The peaceful scene didn't last long.

"Hi, Papa." Lucy jumped up and down, her eyes sparkling with excitement. "We're going for a walk with Aunt Maggie."

"Auntie." Denny ran to his father's side. This boy never wanted to be left out of a conversation.

Neil scooped Denny into his arms. "That sounds like great fun." He turned to Maggie. "Where are you headed?"

She shrugged. "I have no idea." She smiled and patted Lucy's head. "I'll just have to follow my guide while she shows me around."

Lucy bounced from one foot to the other, beaming at her. Neil set Denny back on his feet.

Emma turned to head toward the altar. "Don't walk too far. This won't take long to finish."

"We'll be back soon, I'm guessing." Maggie grasped Denny's hand, and turned toward Lucy. "Let's go on our adventure."

"Make sure you be good for Aunt Maggie." Neil turned back toward the skewed books.

"Okay, Papa." Lucy hopped down the steps to the sidewalk. She grabbed Maggie's hand and pulled her away from the building. "Let's go this way."

"Slow down, Lucy." Maggie slowed her pace, forcing Lucy to go slower. So much energy in such a small body. "Denny can't walk fast with his short legs."

"Go slow," demanded Denny, mimicking Maggie.

Lucy tugged at Maggie's hand. "I want to show you where all our friends live."

"Lucy, we can see where they live, but we'll have to get there slower, that's all." Maggie set the pace slow enough for both children.

She glanced around as they walked toward the end of the block. The houses all appeared neat and tidy, even if the paint around the windows was chipping and the porches were sagging. Once again, the effect of the terrible economy showed its ugly head. Would things ever get better?

At the end of the block, they turned the corner. "This gray house is where Mary lives." Lucy babbled on during her grand tour. "She goes to Sunday School with me." She peered up at Maggie. "I like her a lot 'cuz she has a Patsy Ann doll. She's so pretty."

"Does Mary let you play with her doll?" Maggie glanced back at her nephew. If only she could ride herd on Denny and keep him moving down the street. He found interest in every ant crawling on the sidewalk. Kind of like trying to herd cats.

"Oh, yes!" Lucy's eyes widened. "That's why I go to her house all the time."

She continued telling Maggie stories about the Patsy Ann doll as they walked along. Suddenly she pointed to an approaching woman wearing a red coat. "There's Cissy, our babysitter!"

The young woman appeared to be about the same age as Maggie. Her flowing blond hair bounced on her shoulders as she walked. When the woman spotted them, her face lit up with a smile. With animated gestures, she waved at the children.

Maggie's dry mouth made it hard to swallow. She looked right and left trying to decide how to proceed. Since the lady was a complete stranger to her, what should she say to the woman in red? Maggie's teeth clamped down on her lower lip. How does one introduce oneself when the children obviously can't make the introductions? She had no time to come up with a solution.

"Hi, there, Lucy and Denny. How are you? I haven't seen you for a long time. I see you're out for a walk on this fine afternoon in the sunshine." Not even a breath later. "My name is Cecilia Bernhardt, but most people call me Cissy. It's nice to meet you."

How did she manage to chew her wad of gum and talk at the same time?

"You must be Mrs. Hannemann's sister. I go to their church. I heard you were coming so she would have help when the twins arrive. I saw the new bedroom that you'll be sleeping in upstairs. She'll definitely need lots of help after those babies are born with these two kiddos in the house. Ya know what I mean?"

How did she do that? She talked faster than the auctioneer back home. She paused long enough to ruffle Lucy and Denny's hair.

Maggie jumped in while she had a chance. "Hello, my name is Maggie Ehlke, and I'm glad to meet you."

"When are you coming to babysit us again?" Lucy jumped from one foot to the other in her excitement. "Will you bring us another coloring book when you come?"

"Lucy, I don't know if I'll babysit anymore since your Aunt Maggie now lives with you. I'm glad you liked the coloring book, though. We had such fun coloring at your house." Cissy squatted down to the girl's height. "But, of course, I'll still visit you sometime, and I can even bring a coloring book like last time if you'd like." She looked at Maggie and kept talking. "I usually try to bring them something small when I babysit so we have a project to do while I'm with them. It's nice to keep them occupied and happy."

Maggie took a breath for Cissy. She must be out of air by now.

"That helps the time go faster, and we don't run out of fun things to do. Ya know what I mean? It's amazing what kinds of coloring books I can find at the dime store for only a couple pennies. I'm always glad to bring something to the kids." Cissy never paused.

Denny pulled on Cissy's red coat. "Go on walk." They couldn't forget about him.

"That sounds like a swell idea since it's sunny and feels somewhat warmer this afternoon. The wind has been so cold lately. I guess that's not surprising for March, but it feels nice today." Cissy put her arm around Denny's shoulder. "Are you taking your aunt for a walk around the block? It's nice for her to see your neighborhood." She pointed across the road. "My house is just down the street. It's the gray house with the black roof." Standing up, she addressed Maggie. "I'd often come during the summer to take the children on a walk or to the park to give Mrs. Hannemann a break, but now I won't have to do that since you'll be right there in the house. Ya know what I mean?"

Cissy finally took a breath.

"I'm sure it was a big help to Emma." Maggie put her hand on Lucy's shoulder to try to get her to stand still. "You can always come play with the children, even after the babies arrive."

"That would be nifty . . . but before Mrs. Hannemann's time comes, we should do something to welcome you to Dubuque and show you around." Cissy shifted her purse from one arm to the other. "Have you seen much of Dubuque yet? 'Course, there's not too much to see these days what with the Depression and all."

"No, I just arrived this morning. The only thing I saw was the train station." The trip to the feed mill didn't count since it wasn't a tourist spot.

"Oh, I just had a keen idea." Cissy clasped her hands together. "The singles group from St. Peter is invited to a box social next Saturday night at another church on the southern edge of town. I'm sure we can take you with us. I'll check with my boyfriend Harry to see what he thinks. It would be a wonderful way for you to meet my friends at church. Ya know what I mean?"

"As long as nothing happens this week." There was no way Maggie would be able to go with Cissy if the babies came. She would be tied down helping Emma. "I'd love to go along with you if it works out for you and Harry."

Was she being honest? She'd be meeting all the young people at the other church, too. What should she wear? What would she take in her box? She didn't want to feel like a fifth wheel with Cissy and Harry, either. Here she was, worrying again.

"Perfect! I'll talk to Harry at church in the morning and get it all squared away." Cissy waved. "I need to get going now, but I'll talk to you tomorrow."

"Bye!" Lucy and Denny shouted in unison as Cissy walked away.

Maggie's ears burned just from listening to her. Too many words.

Denny tugged on Maggie's arm, pointing at the retreating red coat. "Go with her."

Shaking her head, Maggie grasped the children's hands. "We better hurry and finish this walk."

Lucy sighed. "I miss Cissy." But in seconds, she continued her rambling introduction of the neighborhood for her aunt.

Maggie wasn't listening anymore. What had she gotten herself into?

CHAPTER 5

A piercing shriek woke Maggie with a start on Sunday morning as the sun peeked through her window. From the other end of the hallway, a contagious belly laugh soon followed. She had a pretty good idea of the source of the commotion. Denny must be getting into trouble already.

Laughing, she stretched her arms over her head. She wasn't used to waking up with screaming monkeys in the house. Pulling on her floral print shirtwaist dress, she closed the buttons in no time. She'd better see if Emma needed help.

After scurrying around for an hour finding Denny's shoes and getting Lucy's hair braided, Maggie looked for a place to collapse. She needed a nap. Instead, she found herself walking the children toward church since Emma was in her confinement. She'd better get used to this in short order. The coming babies would probably produce four times as much chaos every day. Would she be up to the task?

When they turned the corner, Maggie saw people pulling into the church parking lot. She hurried across the open space with the children.

Before Maggie could stop her, Lucy raced ahead of them and ran up the church steps. She gazed up at her father. "Papa..." She wrapped her arms around Neil's legs as he stood at the door greeting members. "Aunt Maggie is going to church with us."

"Good morning, peanut." Neil gave her a brief hug. "I'm glad you made it on time."

Denny hurried up the last two steps to catch up with his sister. Like a magnet, he attached himself to his father's legs.

Neil pried them loose. "I need to get ready for worship, so you two sit quietly with Aunt Maggie during the service."

He pointed Lucy in the direction of the pews while Maggie clasped Denny's hand. Giving Maggie a good-luck smile, he walked up the side aisle toward the sacristy.

Maggie sat mesmerized, listening to the beautiful organ music filling the church. The stained-glass windows depicting scenes from Jesus' life added to the aura of peace pervading the sanctuary. Maggie let the tranquility flow over her. Tension melted off her shoulders. When Neil came out in his pastoral robe, she focused her attention on him.

Looking a few rows ahead of her, she noticed a family filling the pew until it looked ready to burst. The parents were bookends with seven children between them. Four broad-shouldered young men weighted down one end of the bench while the opposite end held three diminishing girls, each one smaller than the sister next to her. She smiled at the picture they made, all praising God together.

When she glanced again, she noticed the second son looked familiar. Her fingers touched her parted lips when she recognized Roman. He had been so introverted during yesterday's encounter that she had dismissed him from her mind. As hummingbirds bombarded her stomach, she closed her eyes. Would she have to talk to him today?

How should she react to him? She took a calming breath. If she had the chance, she would apologize for the way she acted when they reached Emma's house.

At the same instant, Lucy identified her friend sitting in the overflowing pew. She pointed to his family. "There's Janet."

Maggie shushed Lucy so they would not disturb anyone in the surrounding silence. "We have to be quiet now. We can talk to Janet later."

If only she could concentrate on the service. Maggie caught herself gnawing on her lower lip.

During the offering music, Maggie spotted Cissy on the other side of the sanctuary. Her shoulder-length blond hair was a dead giveaway.

Maggie's thoughts strayed to their conversation yesterday. Why had she agreed to attend the box social with Cissy and her boyfriend? Maybe the babies would come this week. Then she wouldn't have to spend an awkward evening with the couple. *Forgive me, Lord, for not concentrating on Your worship this morning.*

As the last song ended, Neil walked into the center aisle to welcome the congregation and invite them to the basement for refreshments honoring the fiftieth anniversary of two lifelong members.

So much for a quick exit.

***

While the closing music played, Romy sauntered toward the back of church with the rest of his family. He spotted Miss Ehlke in a pew as she tried to get Denny's arms into the sleeves of his little coat. Romy held his breath. Maybe she wouldn't notice him. During the service he'd felt eyes on him. Now he identified who it was. He wanted to avoid any contact with her after yesterday's disaster.

As he passed her pew, Miss Ehlke glanced up. Their eyes collided briefly before both looked away. In the space of one second, her eyes broadcast the message that she wanted to avoid him, also. Why would any woman want anything to do with the likes of him?

His mother interrupted his thoughts. "Let's go downstairs and get some of the refreshments. I need to congratulate the Hendersons."

"That sounds like a terrific idea." At least Romy could retreat from the situation with Miss Ehlke. He headed downstairs with his family to join in the celebration. He followed the line of people as they made their way toward the refreshment table. "That looks great. I don't know the last time I had punch and cake."

While Romy waited his turn, he spotted Harry standing across the room talking to Cissy. His brother had all the luck with the pretty girls. He could talk up a storm anytime, anywhere. A shot of jealousy ran through Romy's veins. It wasn't fair. Romy could only sputter when women were around.

Maybe Harry could give him some tips about talking to Miss Ehlke so she wouldn't dislike him so much. But of course that would never happen. Harry would only taunt him more if he could even get up the courage to ask his older brother for a few pointers.

Deep down, Romy would like nothing better than to get to know her. Once again, his timidity was preventing his innermost wish to come to fruition.

As he took a bite of his cake, Harry and Cissy headed in his direction. "Hey, Romy, we have a question for you." Harry grabbed a plate of cake as he passed the table. "Are you busy Saturday evening?"

"That depends . . ."

"What does it depend on?" Cissy stood with her hands on her hips. "I think you're trying to get out of giving us a straight answer. You always try to wiggle out of doing anything fun with us whenever we ask. We don't ask you very often, so I don't think it's right that you won't help us once in a while."

"That's because you two usually have an ulterior motive for asking me to do anything with you."

"That's not true this time." Cissy pouted even as she chomped her gum. "We really do need your help with this."

"And besides, little brother, it will be loads of fun."

"Yeah? You better spell it out then. What's your plan this time?" Romy didn't have any trouble talking to Cissy, so why did his mouth feel like a dried up creek bed in summer when other girls were around?

"As you know, next Saturday night, the youth group is invited to St. John's up on the bluff for a box social. They're always so nifty." Cissy chewed her gum faster to keep pace with her words. "I've invited a new acquaintance to go with us on Saturday. I wanted to show her around town a bit. I know she'd like to see the huge houses down on the bluff since they're so beautiful. I'm sure she's never seen such swanky red brick houses before. Ya know what I mean? Harry now tells me your pa won't let him borrow the car so we can take her with us to St. John's."

Romy stared at her. How can she talk so much without saying anything?

Harry put his hand on Cissy's shoulder. "Romy, you know how Pa is. He'll want me to take the truck if it's only three people."

Romy nodded. "You're probably right there. Pa won't let you drive the car unless most of the family goes along." Pa was so protective about the car.

"See, that's our problem, Romy." Cissy tucked her hair behind her ear. "If you go with us, there will be four people and no way could we fit in the truck then. Ya know? I really want to take her along since she hasn't seen Dubuque yet. I thought it would be a nifty idea to take her on Saturday, so she could see the bluffs and meet our friends at St. John's at the same time. She's really a doll, so everyone will have fun getting to know her. We really need you to do this with us. What do you think, Romy?"

Romy threw his hands up to halt the avalanche of words. After his head stopped spinning, he had to give them an answer. "I'm sure Pa will have me out in the fields on Saturday, and I'll be dead tired."

"I'll help out with your work, so you can be done early and have time to get ready."

His brother was offering to help him?

"Well, I'll hold you to that one." He couldn't quite believe his ears. Maybe it was worth going if Harry would help him with the work. "If you help me, I'll help you by going along to the box social. I haven't been to one in a long time."

"Attaboy!" Cissy gave Romy a quick hug.

Harry winked. "I'll even let you do the driving, so I can cuddle with my sweetie in the back seat."

Cissy grasped Harry's hand. "Pick us up at six on Saturday at my house. We'll be ready."

She turned around and pulled Harry after her. Had a tornado just swept over him? Romy watched them walk away. What had he agreed to? Why had he said yes to those schemers?

Now he would have to meet yet another girl. He hadn't even asked Harry for suggestions to help him talk to Miss Ehlke. If this new girl were as chatty as Cissy, maybe it wouldn't be so bad, but if she weren't, the night would be a disaster.

***

Maggie looked up when she heard the sacristy door close.

Neil emerged in his black suit and approached the children. "I'm sorry I took so long."

"That's fine." She grasped Denny's hand to stop him from launching himself at his father. "I was telling Denny and Lucy the stories about the church windows."

"Look, Papa, Jesus is talking to the little children." Lucy pointed toward the large colorful picture of Jesus blessing the children.

"Jesus." Denny poked his father and pointed to the windows.

"Yes. We need to go downstairs for a bite of cake, but then we have to go home to check on Mama."

Maggie held her hands out to her niece and nephew. "Let's help Papa get some cake to take home to Mama." She'd have to be sociable downstairs, though she preferred to go home right then and there. She didn't look forward to meeting all the people of Neil's church. She paused in the middle of the aisle. Was she as shy as Roman? Her teeth gnawed her lip.

"The basement is this way." Her brother-in-law led the way.

The lower level, scattered with tables and chairs among the large support columns, resembled a war zone. With everyone talking at the same time, Maggie had a hard time hearing Neil. Before she could ask him what he had said, several cackling women converged on him and drew him into their conversation.

She saw a crowd of people gathered around an older couple in one corner of the cavernous room. Roman's family stood among the large crowd. Roman spoke comfortably with the older people in the group. He didn't seem to be tongue-tied with them.

At the far end of the room near the kitchen area, she saw tables filled with plates of cake and punch. She steered Denny and Lucy toward them. "Let's go get something to eat."

"Janet." Lucy spotted her friend standing with Roman's mother. She wrenched her hand away from Maggie and tore across the room.

Maggie looked down at her nephew. "That leaves the two of us to get some cake." She finally reached the table holding the delicacies. She helped Denny with a plate for himself and grabbed two more to carry back to the table.

"There you are." Cissy bounded up to Maggie with a tall, slender, young man in tow. His narrow face topped with sandy hair reminded Maggie of someone, but at the moment she didn't know whom. "I've been looking all over for you." Cissy continued without a break. "This is Harry, my boyfriend."

"I'm glad to meet you." Maggie looked from one hand to the other before looking at Harry. "I'm sorry. I'm trying to get some cake for Lucy."

"I can see your hands are full." Harry reached out to take a plate from Maggie. "Can I help you with those?"

She handed over the plate. What a polite young man he was. "Thank you very much."

Maggie looked down. Denny's plate tipped precariously to the side ready to dump the chocolate cake.

Cissy noticed the impending disaster and grabbed the dessert. "Wow! That was close there, Denny. We don't want your yummy-looking cake to end up on the floor instead of in your tummy."

Cissy led the way to a table with Denny shadowing her. She turned to look over her shoulder. "Maggie, we need to talk to you about Saturday night."

"Let's get the cake and punch all set for the kids before we chat." Maggie set her plate on the table and turned to retrieve glasses of punch. Harry bent over to help Denny into his chair.

"Oh, this will just take a second, so I'll follow you." Cissy kept pace with Maggie while her jaw kept pace on her chewing gum. "Harry's parents are ready to leave soon, and Harry wants to walk me home first. I'm perfectly capable of walking the block to my house, but he likes to see me home. Ya know what I mean? Then he has to hurry back here before his parents leave."

Maggie grabbed two cups of punch and handed them to Cissy before taking one for herself. "If you only have a second, what did you want to tell me?"

"We have it all worked out for Saturday night." Cissy strolled in the direction of the table. "You should be at my house at six. We'll have to plan during the week how we're going to decorate our boxes of food for the box social. Ya know what I mean?" She set the punch on the table and leaned close to Maggie. "Oh, since Harry and his brother are driving, we'll have to figure out a way to hide the boxes so they don't see them. I know Harry will want to peek at mine so he can bid on it, but we'll have to make sure yours is a surprise. Ya know what I mean?"

Cissy kept talking as she grasped Harry's hand. They walked toward the steps, but Cissy continued. "We'll have to do some planning during the week, but as I said, I only have a second to talk before Harry has to leave, so I better scram. I'll come over to your house sometime tomorrow evening to figure out the boxes." They disappeared around the corner as Cissy said, "I'll see you tomorrow."

Maggie took a deep breath. It was exhausting just listening to Cissy. What had she gotten herself into? How much time would she take up this week planning a box supper for the social instead of getting to know the children better and preparing for the arrival of the babies?

What's more important, she would have to spend time with another unfamiliar man after meeting Roman yesterday. She didn't know if she wanted to spend an entire evening with Cissy, Harry, and Harry's brother.

If he were as nice as Harry, maybe it wouldn't be so bad, but if he were shy like Roman, the night would be a disaster.

CHAPTER 6

Glancing at her watch, Maggie laid aside her book. No time now to finish the chapter. Even though she'd read *Pride and Prejudice* many times, she still loved reading about Mr. Darcy.

She slipped her arms into her coat before picking up the box from the table. What she wouldn't do to get out of going tonight. Not that she didn't want to meet a nice young man her age.

After all, she had to find someone special if she was going to get married like her siblings. Marriage might be the only option for her these days. Now that she was away from home, she had to think about herself more often.

If only she could find someone like Harry, she'd be thrilled. She'd never met such a nice young man, as her mother would no doubt say. Tonight might be her night to meet her own Mr. Darcy. She sighed.

"What's in the bee-oo-ti-ful box?" Lucy studied the blue-and-white gingham-covered box before peering up at Maggie. "Can I open it?"

"No, no. I'm taking it with me to the box social. You stay home and take good care of your momma for me. Okay?" Maggie kissed her niece on the forehead and picked up the box. "I don't know when I'll be home."

Emma smiled and waved. "Have a good time. I think this will probably be the final time you'll get out for a while." She rubbed her hands over her midsection. "I don't think I'll last much longer, so these babies better come soon."

Maggie set the box back down. "Are you sure it's okay for me to go? I don't want to leave if I'll be needed later. I can call Cissy and tell her I can't make it."

"No, don't worry about it. Go ahead and have fun. Neil is here tonight to help with the kids." She put her arm around Lucy, who was leaning against the chair. "You're not here to be my slave or nanny, Maggie. We want you to fit in, enjoy yourself with people your age."

"I'm not sure I know how to fit in any longer. It's just that I've been so busy at home helping Ma with Frank for so long that my social skills are rusty. I'd rather avoid tonight's adventure completely if I could." Maggie sagged into a nearby chair.

"I'm sure it's been hard stuck on the farm all these years. Maybe this is your chance to stretch your wings and meet some young people again."

"It would be easier for me to avoid crowds altogether, but probably not the best thing in the long run. I'll be fine once I meet Cissy's friend. After meeting Roman last week, I'm a bit nervous. Could there be any more men out there like him?" Maggie pulled herself out of the chair and lifted the box into her arm.

"Like I said, Roman's a nice boy after you get to know him. Anyway, have a good time."

"Don't wait up for me." Waving good-bye to her niece, Maggie closed the door behind her.

She struggled with the oversized boot box on the way to Cissy's. The container felt heavy, but that wasn't surprising with the fried chicken, rolls, potato salad, lemonade, and apple pie in it. Someone with an immense appetite better buy this thing.

Maggie had spent the last two days baking and cooking for the social. It wasn't her idea to make so much food. Emma wouldn't take no for an answer. "Of course, we have to put it all in, Maggie. I know just what to pack for these events."

Then came the box. She had searched high and low to find the perfect one. "I stayed awake last night trying to figure out how to decorate it."

"Maggie, you worry too much."

Just because Emma was her older sister didn't mean she could tell her what to do. "I was just thinking about it. I wasn't worrying."

For hours Maggie had fussed over it, trying to get it perfect. Was it worth all the trouble?

She took a deep breath. Time to relax after her hectic week. At least she had accomplished some of her goals in the last few days. It had been fun getting to know the children better during the cookie-baking session. And then there were the walks to the park and subsequent baths. She smiled, thinking of the chaos those two could create. Denny now launched himself at her, sparing his worn-out mother.

The arrival of the twins could come very soon if Emma's intuition was correct. *Lord, please bring the babies safely into this world on Your timetable, not ours.* They had to remember to be patient.

If only she hadn't agreed to do this silly box social event tonight. She should be writing a letter to Ma and Pa instead of meeting Harry's brother.

She put her hand on her stomach. Were grasshoppers invading? She nibbled on her lower lip. Maybe her sister was right. She worried too much. The evening would be over before she knew it.

When Maggie approached Cissy's house, the door flew open. Cissy emerged holding a box covered in rose floral material with two roses fastened to the top.

"How do you like the way it turned out? Isn't it spiffy?" Cissy wore a long-sleeved dress, fitted snugly at the waist before flaring out to midcalf length, made of the exact same material. "My mother found some leftover material from this dress. We decided to use it for my box." The grin on her face declared her joy. "This way Harry can't miss it."

"You're right on that account. We'd better get back inside before you freeze." Maggie glanced down at her skirt. Was she underdressed with her white blouse, navy pleated skirt, and matching navy sweater jacket? At least she didn't match her box.

"I have the perfect way to hide these until we reach the church." Cissy turned toward the hallway table. "We're going to place them inside these laundry bags for the drive over."

She wrapped hers in the off-white broadcloth bag and pulled the string tight.

"That's a great idea." Maggie placed her gingham-covered container on the same table.

"Yours should fit in here." Cissy picked up the other bag and opened it so Maggie could slide hers in. "I thought this way the guys couldn't see our boxes. We don't want them to ruin the secret before the auction starts. Ya know what I mean?"

They heard the squeal of brakes as a car approached. Cissy dashed to the window and drew the sheer drapes aside to peek out. Rushing to the front door, she glanced over her shoulder. "They're here."

No more time to get nervous now.

"Are you gals ready?" Harry was the first up the steps and captured Cissy in a hug, twirling her in a circle. He stepped aside, allowing the first view of his brother from the doorway.

Her hand flying to her mouth, Maggie gasped as her stomach crashed like a wave surging into a rock wall.

Holding his hat in his hand, Roman stood on the porch, dressed in a worn gray suit, a clean white shirt and striped tie.

Maggie struggled to hide her emotions. "You!"

That wasn't a very intelligent thing to say. She spun around and bolted into the house.

Cissy followed her down the hallway. "What was that all about? What's eating you?"

Maggie's heart kicked against her ribs. She had seen Harry in the church basement after the service, but he was with Cissy then, and Roman was nowhere around. "I had no idea Harry's brother was Roman."

How could she face him after her initial reaction?

Cissy's mouth gaped open at the revelation. "You didn't know Romy would be driving us tonight?" She touched Maggie's arm. "I guess I just assumed you knew they were brothers. Harry told me on Sunday that Romy had gotten you from the train station. I thought that in the ten minutes it took to get from the station to Pastor's house, you would have known all about his family, and about Harry and me. It doesn't take me long at all to find out about details like that. I sure didn't mean to keep you in the dark all week. I can find out lots of things about people in ten minutes. Ya know what I mean?"

Maggie didn't doubt it a bit at the rate she talked. With narrowed eyes, she stared at Cissy and spoke in a harsh whisper, emphasizing each word. "Roman isn't anything like you. He hardly talked to me during that very long ten . . . minute . . . ride." She glanced toward the door where Harry and Roman were talking. If only the floor could swallow her up. "I can't go with him tonight. He's impossible to talk to."

Cissy clucked her tongue. "Oh, Maggie, Romy's not really a wet blanket. He's a sweet guy when you get to know him. He's awfully shy around girls he doesn't know well. Ya know what I mean?"

That was for sure. Maggie nodded. However, she had no intention of getting to know him. "But—"

Holding her hand up, Cissy looked over Maggie's shoulder. "Harry's headed our way." Her eyes connected with Maggie as she whispered, "You have to give Romy a chance. It's too late to back out anyway."

Scorching heat engulfed Maggie's neck and ears as she struggled to breathe. Had she ever been so embarrassed before? How could she think of going now?

Harry smiled as he reached the girls. "Are you two ready to go?"

Harry was ignoring her rudeness. What a saint.

As Cissy slipped her arms into her coat and grabbed her black gloves, she answered in a cheery voice. "Ab-so-lute-ly." She pointed to the bags lying on the hall table. "We can't forget the food."

Maggie had no choice but to swallow her pride and face Roman. His brown eyes glared at her. She couldn't blame him for feeling angry at her horrid reaction. How would she survive the rest of the night? "I'm sorry. I'll try that again . . . Hello, Roman."

Her teeth came down on her lower lip.

***

Romy let out his breath. If only there was a hole for him to crawl into. He had watched Miss Ehlke turn deathly pale when she recognized him earlier. She mirrored his shock at finding out the identity of her blind date.

Why had she turned and run away faster than a cockroach in a sudden flash of light? If he had to guess, he'd say she wasn't too thrilled to see him standing on the porch. He didn't blame her.

Looking down, he twirled his hat in his hands. How would he get through this? And here he stood, without a word to say, as usual. "Um . . . it's just Romy."

"Then I'm Maggie, I guess."

Romy placed his hat on his head. "This way . . . we won't need, uh, any introductions."

"Right you are." Harry slapped Romy on the back. Glancing at Cissy, he pulled his watch out of his pocket. "We don't want to be late for the auction."

Cissy picked up one of the laundry bags and handed it to Romy. "Be careful with these. They contain lots of good things to eat."

The old bag obviously had a box enclosed inside, and it was heavier than he thought it would be. The aromas tickled his nose, but he couldn't identify anything specific.

Cissy twisted toward the table and reached for the remaining package, handing it to Harry. "It's not fair to give them a sniff test either."

She turned and sashayed out the door, leaving everyone else to follow. "We'll have to put them in the trunk so you don't get too hungry smelling these goodies. Ya know what I mean?"

She was sure right about the smells coming out of the box. Romy's stomach growled. He'd have to keep his eye on it when they arrived at the church. No clue what it looked like, however.

Harry hurried to open the door of the back seat for Cissy. Romy followed his example and opened the front car door for Maggie. After she settled in the seat, he unlocked the trunk to deposit the two wrapped boxes. His stomach roiling, he walked toward the driver's door. What would tonight bring?

"Which way are we going to St. John's?" Cissy's jaw smacking her gum as loud as a popgun, she leaned forward in her seat. "Since we're trying to show Maggie our beautiful city, we should go through downtown and use the Fourth Street elevator. The church is only two blocks from the upper station."

"That's so far out of the way." Romy met her eyes in the rearview mirror while he drove toward town. Somehow she always had ideas that were so complicated.

"I'm not so sure, little brother. I think it would be closer to go directly up Main Street and end up at Fenelon Place to catch the train than to go around and up the bluff in the car." Of course, Harry would agree with his girlfriend.

"We want to give Maggie the tourist's version of the city, so I think we should let her travel on the tram, also." Cissy eased back against her seat. "That way she can see the ritzy old mansions, the swell stores in the downtown area, and get to ride on the elevator."

"Wait a minute." Maggie held up her hands, palms out. "What are you all talking about? The train? The Fourth Street elevator? The Fenel . . . Whatever you said. Can someone explain?"

"Well, I'll be happy to tell you all about the Fenelon Place elevator." Cissy jumped in with both feet, as usual. "In the late 1800s, a rich banker who lived on top of the bluff wanted to make a shortcut going up and down the cliff. He built a cog train connecting the lower city with his house on the high ridge."

Cissy chewed her gum as fast as she talked. "He built two tram cars linked by cable running up and down the bluff. The cars balance each other out, so they always meet in the middle." Demonstrating the actions, her hands flew as fast as the words escaping her mouth. "It's really a tourist attraction more than transportation for people who live here now, but I love riding it once in a while. I think we need to do this, so Maggie can say she really experienced Dubuque firsthand. Ya know what I mean?"

No one could outtalk her.

Romy glanced in his rearview mirror and saw Harry put his hand on Cissy's shoulder. "Thanks for the history lesson." Romy heard the sarcasm in his voice. "I think you've convinced us to use the elevator."

Maggie peered over her shoulder. "That sounds like fun. I've never even heard of the tram before."

Since he was outvoted, Romy proceeded down Main Street before turning right on Ninth Avenue. "We'll take the elevator, but I'm not driving all the way down Main. I think it's more interesting to drive past the mansions anyway."

Cissy continued to entertain everyone with her one-sided conversation as they drove down Bluff Street.

Romy kept his eyes on the road, trying not to notice Maggie. She wasn't wearing a fancy outfit like Cissy, but there was something so refreshing about her appearance. Dressed simply in her skirt and sweater, Maggie appealed to him more than some of the flapper-type women he'd seen in movies.

Maggie swiveled her head from side to side, glimpsing the passing scenery. Was she more interested in seeing the enormous red stone mansions lining the avenue than hearing the string of thoughts pouring out of Cissy's mouth? She barely added anything to the conversation. But then again, Cissy never let anyone add much to a conversation. Or was Maggie still upset with him?

When they turned right on Fourth Street, Romy glanced over to see Maggie's reaction. She was gazing out the front window with her mouth open.

Her brown eyes looked like saucers when she spotted the two tiny train cars traveling on the bluff, one on its way to the top and its twin on the way to the base of the hill. The parallel railroad tracks spanned the entire height of the precipice, widening only in the middle where the two cars had to pass each other on their repeated journey.

Romy smiled as he pulled the car into a parking space.

Maggie turned in her seat. "I've never seen anything like it. It looks like a tiny train, but I can see why you call it an elevator."

"I think it's the shortest and steepest railroad in the world. At least that's what people here try to tell everyone. Ya know what I mean?" Cissy sounded like she enjoyed being the local tourist guide for Dubuque.

"Come on, Cissy." Harry opened his car door. "This is supposed to be a night of fun, not a history lesson."

"Oh, I plan on having fun." Cissy emerged from the car as Harry opened Maggie's door. "I love taking the train up the cliff."

Romy retrieved both packages from the trunk. "You can carry one of these boxes, Harry."

Romy faced Maggie. "Do you need a hand?"

Her timid smile at least gave him some hope. "I'm fine. Anyway, your hands are full."

Her initial reaction at the house had worried him. Maybe she had gotten over the shock of seeing him. What would the rest of the night bring?

"The train's almost here. Let's go." Harry and Cissy led the way down the short street to the station house at the bottom of the hill.

Romy and Maggie followed their lead in complete silence.

The tiny building, only large enough to hold the waiting train, didn't even have a door to block out the wind. Should it even be called a station house? The four waited outside as they saw the descending train approach the hut.

"I'm glad we decided to go this way." Maggie put her hand on Cissy's arm.

"I know. Isn't this nifty?" When the passengers disembarked from the car, Cissy entered first. The tiny car was built at such a steep angle that each person had to sit on a steplike seat opposite one other person. Harry and Cissy walked up several steps to sit in the highest seats. Romy let Maggie proceed in front of him, climbing to the seat a foot below Cissy. Romy followed after her and sat across from Maggie, below Harry.

"Cissy, you sure were right about it being tiny." Maggie's eyes glowed. She seemed to be as excited as a kid enjoying her first lollipop as she glanced around.

Romy juggled the large food box from one leg to the other as he got situated on his narrow bench. His knees rested against hers in the cramped space. If only he could make himself smaller. After the last four passengers entered the tram, he couldn't move an inch and resolved to enjoy the ride no matter what.

The cog train jerked as it left the station on its short journey to the top of the bluff. The car rose at a snail's pace and, in due course, cleared the treetops. Cissy pointed east. "Oh, look at the view of the Mississippi River. We can see across the valley to Wisconsin and Illinois."

Romy twisted his neck to catch sight of the view out of the dirt-covered windows. When he glanced at Maggie, her face was red enough to light up a Christmas tree. What was wrong now?

She gnawed on her lower lip and stared out the window, ignoring him completely. Was she uncomfortable because of their knees? Romy sat, fidgeting in his seat, but what could he do about it? There was no way he could maneuver to avoid contact with her.

The five-minute ride up the bluff ticked by second by second. Romy was convinced it would never end. The rhythmic slap, slap of the cable rope strained to tow the tram up the cliff. How long would this take? Clenching his jaw, he looked anywhere but in her direction. At long last, the car shuddered to a stop in the upper station house.

"Come on, Maggie. Let's go see the beautiful view." Cissy grabbed Maggie's hand and tugged her out of the seat. Harry and Cissy exited from the top of the car. Romy was surprised how fast Maggie managed to escape the car to get away from him. This was going to be a long night, indeed.

***

Maggie stared up at the ceiling hours after she crawled into bed. Sleep eluded her no matter what she tried to do. She replayed the entire evening from the horrid beginning at Cissy's house to the end when Romy walked her back to the parsonage. Not a night to remember. She still felt the heat inching up her legs as her knees were pressed against Romy's in the crowded tram on the way up to the church. The excessive warmth must have shown in her burning cheeks. At least on the ride down the bluff the car wasn't full, so they didn't have to repeat that embarrassing episode.

The low point of the evening had happened during the auction. The boxes of all the ladies had been displayed on the table for the men to choose. When the auction had started, each decorated package went to the highest male bidder, who then shared dinner with the woman. Maggie had started shaking from head to toe when the auctioneer had picked up her box. "Who wants to put in a bid on this lovely creation?"

Before the first bid had been called out, Maggie had heard someone from the back say in a hushed voice, "Boy, somebody better have a huge appetite for that one." Not her fault. Emma had insisted on putting so much food in her box. It must have been her nesting instincts kicking in before the babies came. The entire room had burst out laughing as she had turned to spot the speaker.

Romy had sat in the far corner with a grin on his face. She thought she had recognized his voice. Covering her face with her hands, she had wished she could melt into the chair. How could he do that to her?

It was surprising anyone had bid on her box at all. Needless to say, the stranger who had won the box got it at a rock-bottom price. He had managed to finish every crumb Emma had packed without leaving much for Maggie.

She buried her head under her pillow. If only she could forget the whole night.

CHAPTER 7

In the dim predawn light, Romy lay on his back staring at the ceiling. Why couldn't he sleep anymore? Pounding his pillow sure didn't help. For almost two months. Every morning. It was hard enough working in the fields from dawn to dusk without insomnia. Why? Was it because of the box social fiasco?

He replayed the moment he opened his big mouth and made the ill-timed comment. He'd only meant to whisper it to his brother and his good friend Cal, but somehow his voice had carried across the silent assembly. After the entire room broke out in laughter, he saw Maggie's beet-red face. If only his usually silent brain hadn't worked so well that night.

Why didn't he wait to find out whose box it was? Then he could have purchased it and sat with her all evening. Preferable to having this turmoil in his gut. The words could not be taken back after they had escaped his lips, but now he didn't know how to fix the problem.

Harry couldn't pass up the chance to mention the comment later. "Hey, little brother, did you manage to apologize to Maggie after putting your foot in your mouth?"

"I tried, but . . ."

Harry had not even let him finish his sentence. "You did a great job of making a huge mess of things by speaking up for once in your life. You had a perfect chance to fix it when you walked her home tonight."

Harry wouldn't miss an opportunity to rub Romy the wrong way, ever.

"I tried to figure out what to say, but my tongue was as dried up as a wheat field after harvest. Total silence all the way to her house. I'll talk to her after church tomorrow."

He had his whole speech memorized so he wouldn't trip over his words. When he had gotten to church, he heard Mrs. Hannemann was in the hospital and the babies had been born. His small problem wasn't as important as having twins. He never even tried to talk to Maggie that day.

Here it was the middle of May. Way too late to apologize now. He wasn't a person who enjoyed hurting other people's feelings, so his misplaced comment weighed heavily on his conscience.

Gone were the days of lying awake planning his traveling adventures. Would he go east and see New York first? Maybe heading toward the western mountains would be smarter. Not anymore. Now the guilt of his ill-timed words invaded his sleepless thoughts.

"Romy, it's time for chores." His father bellowed up the stairs as he did every morning.

Romy sprang from his bed and tore around the room throwing on his clothes. "I'll be down in a minute." Why did he lie in bed so long? He'd be catching up all day again.

He passed Harry's bed as he left their room to head downstairs. Still snoring, as usual. Because he was the eldest, he was allowed to sleep in. Or maybe it was because he was Pa's favorite son. Romy ground his teeth.

Mr. Sleepyhead didn't have to work the fields anymore. Six weeks ago, Harry had gotten a job at the WPA project at Eagle Point Park building the pavilions and gardens. The government paid the salaries of the workers to build facilities on the highest bluffs of the park along the Mississippi River overlooking Wisconsin and Illinois. At least somebody cared enough to find jobs for people.

Pa and Ma had known they couldn't keep the farm running and food on the table for the family without help. These hard times invaded every house in the county. More cash needed to come in. They had decided to send one of the boys out to find a job.

"If you need someone to go work in town, I'll be happy to

go." Romy had jumped at the chance. It wasn't the open road, but away from the farm anyway.

But Pa had overruled any thought of the town job for him. "The love of the land is stronger in your heart. A farmer needs to feel that love. Harry will be going to work the town job, since he's oldest."

Romy had restrained his urge to pound something. Why not him? It was true. He loved the land, but he wanted a way out. Just for a year or so. Then he'd be back.

Now Harry headed to work every morning to lay limestone according to the architect's designs. He came home every night exhausted from moving the heavy stones. At least he got to see Cissy most days at noon when she delivered his dinner.

Romy headed down the steps. He should be happy when Harry brought a check home each week. Why wasn't he? *Lord, forgive my jealous feelings about my brother's new job. Thank You for this money to help with the farm.* At least Harry was out of the house all day, not irritating Romy anymore.

He walked into the kitchen. The sun was barely peeking in the east window. Ma was stooping over to get the cast-iron skillet out of the lower cupboard. As she straightened up, she winced and rubbed her arm. "Good morning, Romy."

"G'morning, Ma. Your arm still hurting like it was weeks ago? Maybe you should get it looked at." Ma scared him sometimes. She always worked too hard.

"Oh, bother. It's just a pinch now and then." She lifted the lid of the stove to stir the banked coals and threw in more wood to get the morning fire going. "I'll be fine. You'd better get out in the barn so you're not late for breakfast." Ma handed him the milk can. "Can you fill this before breakfast? We're out of milk."

"Yeah, I'm on my way." Romy glanced over his shoulder as he opened the back door. "We'll be done in time for breakfast."

An hour later, Romy followed his father into the kitchen carrying the container of milk filled from the big cans cooling in the water tank. The sun streamed through the kitchen window, allowing tiny specks to dance in the rays. His stomach growled in response to the appetizing aroma of bacon and eggs sizzling on the stovetop.

He placed the milk can on the counter. "This is from last night's milking so it's nice and cold."

"Thanks much." His mother continued stirring the eggs,

wrapping her hand in the corner of her apron as protection against the heat of the iron skillet. She set down the pan and shook her hand. "Ow! That's hot. Romy, can you call the rest of the kids down to eat?"

Sally placed the last plate on the table. "I'm not through with the silverware yet." Even at eleven years old, she was Ma's best helper. "I need one minute to finish."

"Sally, don't forget the salt." Ma glanced at the table again. "Romy, can you pour the milk into the white jug?"

"Sure, Ma." The cool liquid bubbled up into a creamy froth as the pitcher filled to the brim.

It looked like everything was all set. Romy headed for the steps. "Time to eat!"

Before he got the words out of his mouth, he heard thundering feet scurrying down the steps. He sidled toward the kitchen before the herd stampeded him. Ted and Jim rushed past him, skidding to a halt before they upended the table. Mary and Janet followed behind while Harry ambled down the steps.

"Girls, you'd better hurry and eat so you're not late for school." Ma brought dishes of steaming food to the table. "Harry, can you drop them off on your way to town this morning since I'm a bit late with the food?"

"No problem, Ma." Harry looked at his silver pocket watch. "I'll leave in fifteen minutes then."

Romy shoveled another forkful of fluffy scrambled eggs into his mouth. Harry probably would be late again. He always was.

"Ted and Jim, are you going to school today, or does Pa need you in the fields?" Ma finished serving the food and sank into her chair. The washed-out look on her weary face spoke louder than words.

Pa glanced up from his plate of bacon and eggs. "Since it rained a bit last night, I'm going to let the horses rest today and work around the barn." He sopped his bread in the bacon grease on the almost empty platter and tucked the soggy morsel into his mouth. "I'm planning on cleaning out the corn planter and getting ready to plant tomorrow, so the boys can go to school today."

"Aw, do we have to?" Jim's face deflated with a frown. The momentary silence as they waited for the answer was broken by the clinking of silverware on the glass plates.

"School is almost out for the summer, so you need to learn as much as you can this month." Ma picked up her white coffee mug for a sip. "Albert, if you're working on the machines today, maybe I could get Romy to help me with the garden. I know we planted the peas last month, but we need to get the rest of the seeds in the ground."

"Yeah, good idea." Cocking his leg over the opposite one, Pa balanced his coffee mug on his raised knee. "The rain softened the garden plot a tad, so the rest can be tilled today."

"Sounds like a plan." Romy scraped the rest of the eggs off his plate. "I'll go till the garden while you clean up the kitchen."

He'd hurry so she wouldn't have to work too hard.

He left the chaos of the kitchen as his younger siblings rushed around, trying to finish packing their lunches and find the correct stack of books.

The chirp of the spring birds in the tree branches was sure nice after the clamoring of all the kids. He headed for the barn to gather the plow and hoes. Sometimes it was hard to get excited about doing field work all day, but he surely didn't want to return to his school days.

Hearing the back door slam shut some time later, he glanced up. His mother sauntered across the barely green grass. He'd worked up a sweat plowing the garden soil. Always a hard job in spring. The warm springtime sun beat down on his back as he broke the clods of dirt.

She approached the garden plot. "You'll have it all done before I can help you."

That was his plan.

She bent over to retrieve a hoe. "Let me give you a hand with the hoeing."

"I don't want you working so hard, Ma." Romy stopped. He needed a breather. "The little rain we had didn't help much to soften the dirt."

"You can't do all this yourself." Ma proceeded to split the large clumps. "The garden always looks so big in spring before it's planted."

They worked side by side for a time making great progress. Sweat poured down his forehead into his eyes. He stopped to wipe his brow.

"Say, I saw Sandy and Jay talking to you in church last Sunday. Are you making progress with talking to girls?" Ma leaned on her hoe.

"Not really. Sandy was telling me they're planning a party at the beach soon and wanted to know if I'd come. Actually, Jay was doing the talking."

"Well, have you had a chance to talk to pastor's sister-in-law again? Those babies are so cute that she's carrying to church with Mrs. Hannemann." Ma bent over her hoe and chopped at the soil.

Romy concentrated on working faster to keep Ma from digging too much. "That's the trouble. She's always surrounded by old ladies admiring the babies. I can't get near her to get a word out. I've been trying every week."

"You just keep trying, son. Miss Ehlke seems to be real nice girl. I pray that you get to know her better soon." Ma pulled her tool back and forth to smooth out the clods.

That was his prayer, too, so he could apologize to her. "I promise that I'll try to talk to her soon."

They worked in silence for a time, but Ma had to take rests from the backbreaking labor often. Romy leaned on the hoe. "Ma, is it time to rest for a bit?"

"No, I'm fine." His mother stopped a minute to catch her breath. "I'd rather get it finished before dinner time."

She continued to hack at the soil.

The peaceful morning seeped into his pores as he wielded his hoe. The scritch, scratch of the tools in the dirt kept up a steady rhythm in the tranquil landscape.

They'd been working a while when Romy heard his mother gasp. "Romy!"

A chill ran down his spine. His hoe stopped dead in midair. He swiveled his head in her direction.

"It hurts so much." She dropped her tool and clutched at her chest.

He rushed to her side. He couldn't panic. "What's wrong, Ma?"

Her flushed face grimaced as she struggled to take a breath. She stumbled toward the garden fence. "I feel so dizzy."

He had to stay calm for her. "Let me help you sit down before you fall." He helped her onto her knees so she could sit on the grass inside the fence.

"It hurts." As beads of sweat coursed toward her eyebrows, she drew her knees up tight. Her eyes, the size of saucers, were filled with fear. The color drained from her cheeks as she rubbed her shoulder and arms. "I feel nauseated. I need to lie down."

Romy's heart raced as if he'd run a marathon. He could see the pain written clearly on her face. What could he do to help her? *God, what's happening to her?* Should he raise her legs? Should he rub her arms? Should he carry her to the house? Maybe she needed a glass of water. He was making no sense. Helplessness crashed down on his head.

"Pa! Pa!" His shout broke the quiet of the countryside. Turning his attention back to her, he asked, "Where does it hurt?"

No response came.

He helped her lie back on the grass. He raised his voice again. "Pa, where are you?"

His level of panic rose faster than the cow tank in a downpour. He rubbed his hand over his eyes.

"I . . . fee l so tired . . . can't breathe." Her eyes fluttering, his mother gasped for a breath. He jiggled her to keep her eyes open. She grabbed his arm. "I have . . . sharp pain . . . my shoulder."

His stomach rolled, threatening to explode, as he massaged her shoulder. How could he stop the pain? He lifted her head off the ground and tried to cradle her in his arms. "Ma, tell me what to do to help you."

"Don't worry, son, I'm not afraid." She grasped his hand, her eyes drooping shut.

A sudden coldness filled him to his very core. Afraid of what? "Ma, what do you mean?"

His pulse pounded in his head. With trembling hands, he stroked her cheek to keep her awake. What was she talking about? It sounded as if she thought she might die. She can't do that. *God, don't let that happen to her. We need her here with us.*

She tilted her head slightly. "Look . . . an angel waiting to lead me home."

Her words almost a whisper, her eyes eased shut again.

He squeezed her hand. "Don't leave me, Ma."

Tears streamed down his cheeks. This can't be happening. What are we going to do?

She inhaled with a long, slow breath, struggling to get out her words. "Tell Pa . . . I love him." Her breath escaped her lungs, and she went limp.

Romy clasped her to him, rocking back and forth. He sobbed

with her head against his chest. Time stopped. Glancing up through tear-streaked vision, he saw his pa running toward them from the barn.

***

Maggie hurried up the stairs toward the nursery to retrieve a crying baby before the other twin stirred. She rushed into the room and snatched Tina from her crib before glancing at Timmy. "Don't wake your sleepy brother. I can't believe how he's been sleeping through your squalls for eight weeks. Let's let him sleep a bit longer."

Now if only the twins would sleep more at night. She could dream, anyway. At least, Emma was feeling much better now and could help in the kitchen again.

As she dashed down the steps, Maggie soothed Tina. The baby was probably hungry, but now was not a good time. Outside, Emma hung up the last load of diapers on the clothesline. The older children ran in circles around their mother. They would be coming in for dinner soon.

Maggie patted Tina's back while looking around the kitchen. The potatoes and carrots needed to get into the boiling water so they'd be done by noon. Good thing she had peeled them already. When she had pulled them out of the root cellar this morning, she'd found the spuds were spongy with age. Maybe they wouldn't take very long to cook that way. Emma told her the gifts of food from the members were getting scarcer all the time, but the Lord would provide for them somehow.

She glanced at the baby in her arms. "Tina, we need to make a big enough batch of stew to last several days, so we better hurry."

Tucking Tina snugly in her arm, Maggie moved between the sink and stove, dropping the vegetables into the stew pot. It was amazing how many things she could do with a baby in her arms. It hadn't taken too long to learn all the tricks in the book. Two months ago, she wouldn't have dreamed she'd be able to accomplish all she did in one day.

After the stew was simmering, Maggie opened the back door. A cool gust of air hit her face. She couldn't take the baby outside without a hat today. "Emma, Tina is awake and fussing. Do you need help hanging up the rest of the diapers?"

"No, I'm on the last one. I'll be right in."

"We'll manage for a couple minutes." Maggie smiled at the baby she held in her arm and received a responding smile. Tina and Timmy were both getting so cute. They were at the perfect age.

Maggie remembered back to the day the babies were born. In fact, it had been the same night as the disastrous box social. She had only gotten a few hours' sleep before Neil woke her. Emma's babies were coming, so they had to leave for the hospital.

After hugging Emma, Maggie had watched as Neil whisked her sister out the door. Her job was to remain home with the older children while Neil stayed in the hospital for the delivery.

The doctor had persuaded Neil and Emma to go to the hospital for the birth. It was more common to have a baby at home, but with possible twins coming, he had been adamant. At least it had kept everyone safe.

The next morning, Neil had arrived home to announce the news of the birth of a baby boy and girl. Maggie had persuaded Neil to take her and the children to the hospital later in the day to visit the mother and babies. When she had seen Timmy and Tina for the first time, she couldn't believe how tiny they were. Denny and Lucy were scared to touch them. Several days later, when Emma had come home from the hospital, Maggie had been overwhelmed with the tasks before her.

Now she wouldn't change places with anyone. She loved being the adoring aunt in the house. Giving Tina a kiss on the cheek, she checked on the stew.

Hearing the phone ring in Neil's office, she wondered what was happening. Usually phone calls meant he had to rush out the door. She hoped it wasn't a serious problem taking him away from his noon meal.

She set bowls and spoons on the table as Neil opened his office door. Emma sat by the table feeding Tina when he burst into the kitchen.

"The phone call was from Roman Iverson." Wiping his brow with his hand, Neil glanced from Emma to Maggie and back again. "Something terrible has happened. Mrs. Iverson died of a heart attack while working in her garden this morning."

"Oh, no!" Emma's hand flew to her mouth. "That's terrible. Hilda was the glue holding the family together. Raising seven children while Albert ran the farm must have been an enormous responsibility. I imagine it took its toll on her. And she told me she was going to have her fiftieth birthday this summer."

"So young." Neil leaned his head on his hands as his elbows rested on the table. "Roman was sobbing as he tried to tell me the news. How will Albert get along without her?"

Maggie couldn't catch her breath. She plopped into the nearest chair. Even though she hadn't talked to Romy or Harry since the box social, she had seen the family in church every Sunday. True, Romy was not her favorite person in the world, but she would never wish anything like this on him. Why did God allow this to happen to such a devoted family?

"I'll have to eat and get out to the farm. I'll assure them Hilda is in heaven, but what about the hole that's left here on earth?" Neil looked at the stew pot on the stove. "Maggie, is dinner ready?"

"Soon." Nibbling on her lower lip, she placed the spoons by the bowls. "I'll check the potatoes."

She saw in her mind's eye the three girls standing like stair steps beside their mother in church last Sunday. Who would mother those young girls now? Then she thought of the half-grown brothers next to their father. Who would feed those hungry young men? What would happen to Romy's family?

CHAPTER 8

Sighing, Maggie wiped the last plate and set it in the cupboard. The dishes were finally finished for the day, and the kids were in bed. Life wasn't boring with four children in the house. At last she could read more of her book. She picked it up off the counter and opened to the new chapter.

Emma burst through the swinging door. The peaceful evening evaporated at her entrance. "I finished talking to Neil a minute ago. We'll have to head to church for Mrs. Iverson's funeral by one o'clock tomorrow afternoon."

Just like that? No discussion about it? Maggie's reaction was swift. "Why should I even go? I don't know the Iversons at all. Besides, funerals make me so uncomfortable." She sounded whiny in her own ears, so why wouldn't Emma think the same thing? "Well, I know Harry a little, since he's Cissy's boyfriend."

Maggie didn't want to mention Romy. She hadn't spoken to him for weeks. The incident at the box social still loomed in her mind, but now it seemed utterly insignificant compared to the crisis in his life. How could she have made the one sentence he managed to get out of his mouth come between them for so long? How foolish. She should have talked to him long ago. Would she have the courage to do that now? What must he think of her?

But Emma wouldn't understand any of this. *Lord, forgive me and help me get through tomorrow.*

"You'll have to go with me anyway." Emma straightened a chair. "Lucy is a good friend of Janet's, so she will be going. Think of the poor girl if she has no friends there. And, of course, I'll be going since Hilda was always helping us one way or another. There is no way I can manage all the children by myself, so, naturally, you'll go with me." The discussion ended abruptly.

***

"What am I supposed to wear?" An hour before the funeral, Maggie looked at the hooks on the wall holding her sparse collection of clothes. Should she wear her black skirt and blue blouse, or her blue blouse and black skirt? Smiling, she pushed her arms into the sleeves.

Attending a funeral was not her choice. She'd rather skip the whole thing. And yet, her heart weighed her down. What was going through Romy's mind? She couldn't even fathom the depths of despair had her own mother passed away. How would Romy's family survive? *Lord, please help the Iversons make it through this day.*

Maggie sucked in her breath as she buttoned her skirt.

Would the three little girls have to run the house? Impossible. At this point, no one was probably even thinking past this horrible day.

Neil had reported Mr. Iverson felt at peace knowing his wife was with the angels in heaven. The family had this assurance, but the devastation to their lives was immeasurable. *Romy and his family will need Your help, Lord, as they learn to live without their mother.*

A cry erupted from the next room. She smoothed her hand over her skirt and hurried to pick up the complaining baby. Timmy this time. Maggie rubbed his back to soothe him as she crept out the door. "Hush now, little one. Don't wake your sister."

"Who's awake first?" Emma stepped out of her bedroom, almost colliding with Maggie. "I'll have to hurry to feed them so we're ready for church."

Maggie handed the baby to Emma. "I'll go make sure Denny and Lucy are dressed and then come back to change Tina's diaper." She hurried down the hallway toward the children's room.

Lucy was struggling to help her three-year-old brother get his shoes on. She was bent over, holding her brother's foot in the air. She pounded the sole of his shoe as he sat on the floor, bracing himself with his arms. One hand held the piece of cheese he hadn't finished from dinner. He stole a bite while she took a break.

Maggie shook her head. "Are you two ready in here?"

"Oh, brother." Lucy thumped the shoe again to no avail. "His foot's too big."

Denny broke off a corner of the cheese. "Have some cheese, sissy. Cheese makes everything better."

Maggie struggled to stifle a laugh.

Lucy glared at Denny. She was only six years old, but sometimes acted like a mother hen. "That's silly." Lucy slid onto the floor and let out a sigh. "I'm gonna tell Momma to make him new shoes."

Maggie squatted down to investigate. "Thanks, Lucy That was nice of you to help." She removed the shoe to try again and found the heel was tipped inward. "Look, the back was just tipped in. Easy to fix." With one little push, Denny's shoe was on. "Thanks for lending a hand, Lucy." Maggie put her arm around her niece. "Let's see if Momma is ready."

"One of the babies is crying again." Denny tugged on Maggie's skirt. Frowning, he crossed his arms over his chest. "One of the babies is always crying."

Maggie ran her fingers through his hair. "Tina is hungry for her lunch. Sometimes you feel like crying when you're hungry, too, I bet." Smiling, she pulled him to his feet. "I think Momma might need our help."

Neil was heading up the stairs. He was already dressed in his black suit and tie with a white shirt. "Do you have time to assist Emma? I really should head over to the church."

"Don't worry about us. Lucy was a big help getting Denny ready. I'm headed to get Tina right this minute." She walked toward the babies' room. "We'll be over as soon as we're all set here."

"Thanks, as always. I should look at my sermon again." He shook his head. "This is going to be a hard funeral."

"I can't imagine standing up there and preaching on such a sad day," Maggie said over her shoulder. She picked up Tina and came back into the hallway. "What a shock for them."

"Giving them the comfort of God's Word isn't so hard. It was just so sudden. Albert didn't even get a chance to say goodbye."

***

Maggie and Emma, each holding a baby, stood in the reception line winding down the center aisle of the church toward the Iverson family. So many people were there. Mrs. Iverson must have been well known. The quiet aura of the church was occasionally broken with a heart-wrenching sob.

As Maggie, Emma, and the children moved closer to the front of the church, Denny bounced from one foot to the other. This was no place for a three-year-old to make a scene. Leaning close to Emma, Maggie spoke softly in her ear. "I'll take Denny and Tina outside, so he doesn't have to stand in line any longer."

"Can I go with Aunt Maggie?" Lucy tugged at her mother's hand.

Emma shifted Tommy from one arm to the other before squatting down. "Lucy, Janet is standing up in front with her brothers. I think it would be a good idea to go say hello to her."

"Then Denny has to stay here, too." Lucy's lower lip shot out, showing her displeasure.

Emma nodded. "Yes, honey, we're all staying." She gazed up at Maggie. "Maybe Tina will smile at one of the girls and cheer them up."

"That's true." Sighing, Maggie closed her eyes for a second. There went her excuse to make a quick exit.

She couldn't swallow. If only her mouth didn't feel like it was filled with cotton. Time to face Romy. What would she say after all these weeks? Maybe the children would be a buffer between them. Her stomach mimicked Denny's jumpiness. She put her hand on the boy's shoulder. "Denny, we're almost there. Hold still just a couple more minutes."

They approached the front of the sanctuary where the casket was surrounded by floral arrangements. The pungent aromas filled her nostrils as the kaleidoscope of colors rose before her eyes. Maggie smoothed her clammy hand down her skirt. Her insides rolled as if on the high seas. Would she say the right thing?

Well-wishers surrounded most of the family members. Standing to the side, Janet clutched her father's hand. She looked as if she didn't have a friend—lost in a lonely world filled with adults who didn't notice the five-year-old girl.

In the near-quiet atmosphere, Lucy blurted out, "Janet, when are you going to come to play with my dolls again?"

"We're in church, so we have to use our quiet voice today." Emma touched Lucy's back. She turned to the forlorn girl. "How are you, Janet?"

"My momma died." Janet responded as tears rolled down her cheeks. "I don't know if I can ever play with dolls again."

Maggie's heart ached to hold her and assure her life would be normal again someday.

"Oh, Janet, of course you can come to our house to play with Lucy again." Emma gave her a warm hug and stood up to speak with Mr. Iverson.

"Janet, your mother's sleeping in there. Why don't you wake her up?" Gazing up, Lucy pointed to the wooden box, its lower half covered by a blanket of flowers.

Maggie gasped before she stooped down to explain. "She's not sleeping, honey. Jesus took her home to heaven." Why had Emma insisted Lucy come along?

In the next instant, Romy appeared by Janet's side. He crouched down and hugged Janet in one arm and Lucy in the other. "Your aunt is right, Lucy. Janet's mother won't be waking up anymore because she is in heaven with the angels." He swallowed and blinked away tears. "We'll miss her terribly, but we know she's singing praises to Jesus. Isn't that right, Janet?"

Janet nodded as tears crept toward her chin. Her shoulders shook as she attempted to hold in her sobs. Taking her in his arms, Romy swayed back and forth, comforting her while tears coursed down his own face.

Maggie hugged Lucy. Was this the same man who had nothing to say the last time she saw him? Amazing. Her throat ached with grief at the touching scene unfolding in front of her. Here was a side of Romy she had never seen before.

"I'm very sorry for your loss, Romy." She looked into his brown eyes and saw the depth of his sorrow. Reaching out to touch his arm, she longed to comfort him, but stopped midway. She didn't know him well enough for that.

"Thank . . . you." Speaking in a too-quiet voice, he averted his eyes from Maggie. Was he retreating into his insecure self again?

She stood up and guided Lucy and Denny past the casket. Though her interaction with Romy lasted only a brief moment, it showed he had a warm and caring heart after all. Had she judged him unfairly?

***

Romy rose from his stooped position and continued to go through the motions, receiving the well-wishers. Pa had been so strong since Ma passed away, but the stress of greeting everyone was taking its toll. Pa's shoulders stooped more as the minutes ticked away. The end of the line couldn't come fast enough for Romy.

Romy's mind wandered back to the conversation between Janet and Lucy. He couldn't swallow past the lump in his throat when Janet had said she couldn't go play with Lucy's dolls again. She must think the world, as she knew it, had come to a complete halt.

In a way, it had when Ma died in his arms. But not only for Janet. Somehow, they all would have to go on living even if Ma didn't anymore. If only it didn't feel as if the weight of their sorrow rested on his shoulders.

Romy had dreaded seeing Pastor's family come through the reception line. He didn't know what he would say to Maggie after weeks of not apologizing for his rude remark. When Maggie offered him such kind words of sympathy, his mind had frozen and all that came out was a bare "thank you."

Why could he talk so fluently to Janet and Lucy, but not be able to utter more than two words to Maggie? What was wrong with him? After all, he'd promised Ma that he'd get to know Maggie. He had no choice now.

The bell tolled, indicating it was time for the service to begin. Romy gathered his siblings. "Let's go to the back of the church. We need to be there when the service starts."

He put his arm around his father to guide him to the rear of the sanctuary. He didn't want Pa to witness the closing of the casket. How hard it was to say good-bye to Ma. Romy's throat tightened as he led the way. It would be over soon.

A few minutes later, Romy started the long walk down the center aisle toward the closed casket, at one point, steadying Pa when he stumbled. "Pa, lean on my arm."

Romy righted himself as he took on the extra weight of his suffering parent. Would life always feel this heavy? His own grief-stricken heart stole his breath away. He didn't have the strength to notice how the rest of the children dealt with their sorrow. Good thing Aunt Charlotte and Aunt Dorothy were close by to help the younger sisters.

Harry was the oldest and should be bearing the burden of the day, but since Ma died, he had retreated into himself. Cissy's presence seemed to be the only thing that brought him.

Romy struggled to concentrate on Pastor Hannemann's words during the service. How could they be sitting at a funeral service for their mother? *God, how can this be happening?* He watched over his family, mostly his father, while keeping one ear on Pastor's words at the same time.

Pastor Hannemann read the text from First Corinthians, chapter fifteen. "If in this life only we have hope in Christ, we are of all men most miserable. But now is Christ risen from the dead, and become the firstfruits of them that slept. For since by man came death, by man came also the resurrection of the dead."

Romy's mind wandered until he heard the pastor talk about a Jewish caretaker from a cemetery in town. "He would often watch the committal services of people who were buried there. Once he stopped me after the burial of an elderly member of our congregation and said, 'I wish our people could have what I just witnessed in your people. Your people left this sad place actually smiling. We have no such joy. There is only weeping and despair.'

"I replied, 'But you can have it. God loved the world so much that he sent His Son Jesus here to save us. Whoever believes in Jesus shall have eternal life.' But he only shook his head, 'I wish I could believe.'

"Brothers and sisters, how important, how comforting to have 'it' *now* for ourselves as we walk through life. 'It', of course, is faith in Christ as our Savior from sin. How blessed to be in this faith as we finally face death, as we face the death of Hilda. 'You can have it.' Jesus gives it to us freely. How beautiful and wonderful to lead others to have it, too. To be able to say: 'You will see her again!' You can give real hope, not just a sympathetic tear, nor the mere sentiment of a card, nor fumbling and clumsy words of condolence. You have the hope and confidence of life, eternal life: 'Because I live, you also shall live.'"

Romy's burden lightened with these words. Here was the comfort he and his family could cling to during these dark days.

As he looked at his father and siblings, the anguish plainly written on their faces crumbled when the peace of God's love invaded their hearts. Life would be forever different because Ma was gone, but she was waiting for them in heaven. This truth would be his life preserver when day-to-day tribulations tried to tow him under with the strong current.

CHAPTER 9

Romy trudged along the cow path behind the barn. Sweat poured into his eyes as the hot June sun sizzled on his neck. He should be working in the fields, not rounding up the cows for evening milking. This used to be his sisters' job. Every day last summer, Sally and Mary had gone down the lane to the cow pasture to bring the cows back to the barn.

Now *he* had to hike the half-mile to call the cows home. How could he finish all the field work if he had to waste his time doing this? He shook his fist. *Why, God, why? Why did You take Ma from us?* So many changes in their lives since her death. Romy wiped the stray tears off his cheeks as he plodded on.

No one had escaped the chaos of Ma's passing. Pa had walked around in a trance since the funeral. He couldn't keep his mind on the important tasks he needed to do. This morning he had loaded Ted and Jim on the wagon heading for the south cornfield to pull weeds.

Romy had tried to dissuade him. "Pa, I could hook up Star to the cultivator and go through the rows to clean them up. It wouldn't take me long at all. The corn isn't tall enough yet to get ruined by the machine."

"Nonsense, the horse will cause major damage out there. I'll just take the two boys with me to help get rid of the weeds before they get too big." Other years Pa hadn't worried about it this late in June. He used to say, "We're not wasting our time over a few weeds."

Out of respect for Pa, Romy hadn't argued, but he knew the boys would have been better used cutting the hay.

They didn't have *any* time to waste since they had to quit working in the fields so early each day. Before Ma died, they would work until the sky was filled with muddy darkness. Now they had to finish up when the sun sat well above the horizon because the girls needed help in the house.

Nobody expected the nine- and eleven-year-olds to fill Ma's shoes. The loss showed everyone how large her shoes had really been. Aunt Charlotte had come for a short time to help out after that terrible day, but she had her own family to take care of.

Sally tried her best to cook supper for Pa and the seven siblings. Aunt Dorothy had worked with her to teach her some things, but in the end Sally had to shoulder the cooking responsibilities every day. She worked all day peeling vegetables and getting a roast in the oven, but most nights the family had to choke down her efforts without complaining.

After her first attempt, Jim had made an honest, but exaggerated, comment. "Boy, this meat is tough enough to nail to your shoes." Amid peals of laughter from her brothers, eleven-year-old Sally had run up the stairs with sobs catching in her throat. No one wanted a repeat of that heart-wrenching moment.

Finally, Romy reached the pasture with Blackie running circles around his ankles. He followed the cow path, angling left. The brilliant sun beat down on his head as bees buzzed near the white clover. If he had more time, he could teach Janet's dog to round up the cows and urge them down the lane toward home without any help, but that would take lots of training. For today, Blackie could just assist him with this mindless task.

"C'm-bos, c'm-bos!" he bellowed to the herd. Blackie rounded up the most distant cows, yapping at them until they began to move. The lead cow, with its full udder, waddled down the lane toward the water trough. The remainder of the herd followed nose-to-tail. They seemed as happy to be heading toward the barnyard as Romy was.

When the cows were fed, Romy walked up the hill toward the house. His stomach growling, he was glad to be breaking for supper. What concoction had Mary and Sally come up with tonight? With any luck, they would keep it simple with fried chicken, potatoes and fresh peas. Two nights ago when that was served, he had been able to swallow his meal without milk washing down every bite.

Ma's absence weighed heavily on the whole house. How would they survive until the girls grew up enough to handle the housework? *God, this is too much for us to bear.* He might have to learn how to cook himself so they wouldn't starve to death.

After washing up at the pump outside, he pushed open the porch door. The smell of charred food greeted him at the door. Sniffles and a hiccup bounced off the papered walls. Drying his hands on the towel by the door, he glanced into the kitchen. Mary sat in a chair holding her arm while she blew on her out-stretched hand. A nasty red welt rose off her index finger.

"What happened?" Romy hurried to her side.

Tears streamed down her cheeks as she tried to explain. "I . . . I. . . I touched the oven door when I tried to get the cake out of the oven." She looked down at the upside-down cake pan on the floor. Mary sank beneath a fresh wave of sobs. "I dropped the pan when I burned my finger."

"I tried to tell her to let me take the cake out." Sally wrung her hands, tears filling her eyes. "We both got the cake mixed up . . . and everything . . . to surprise Pa." The words flew out of her mouth. "I just left for a second to go help Janet and told Mary to wait till I came back to get the cake out."

Romy gathered Mary in his arms to try to comfort the nine-year-old. A damp spot expanded on his shirt as it absorbed the tears from her cheeks. He retrieved the lard, which was always found in the pantry, and smeared it around the burned area. That would keep the air off and stop the pain in minutes. "I'm so glad you tried to surprise us with cake for supper, but we don't want you to get hurt while we're outside."

He heard the family arrive when the back door slammed. How would Pa take this bit of news? Mary and Sally weren't old enough to do this, plus watch little Janet. "Pa, Mary had a little accident right before I came in."

Pa's face blanched when he saw Mary holding her finger. The tears, still coursing down her cheeks, made her look like a little lost waif. Romy stopped himself from hugging her again. His father bowed his head and shook it at a snail's pace before squatting down in front of her. "Oh, Mary, are you all right? I'm so sorry you burned your finger."

Nodding, she stared at the ruined cake. "We tried to surprise you."

His shoulders drooping, Pa's chin trembled. "Don't worry 'bout the cake. We can still eat most of it. It's you I'm worried 'bout."

Wiping her hand under her nose, his sister sucked in a breath and let it out bit by bit. "It doesn't hurt as much as it did before. I just miss Ma so much."

Romy glanced from one sibling to another, seeing tears wash down their faces. The weight on his chest took his breath away. The same question raced through his mind. *Why did You take Ma from us, God?* The girls couldn't manage the house without her. How could they live with the pain?

"We all do, so much." His father gave her a hug before looking at the boys. "Let's help the girls get supper on the table, and then I need to talk to all of you."

Conversation was kept to a minimum as the three brothers bumped around the kitchen trying to rescue the forgotten food. Romy drained the potatoes that were overcooked and mushy. Most of them disintegrated as he tipped them into a serving bowl. Jim held the plate as Ted skewered the chicken pieces and lifted the dark, crispy meat out of the frying pan. Sally poured milk into the glasses. Pa cut the loaf of bread into thin slices. Soon everything was ready, but Romy's hunger had disappeared.

Pa sat in his chair. "Has anyone seen Harry yet?"

"He should be here soon, Pa." Romy pulled the pocket watch from his bib overalls and looked at the time. "He got out of work twenty minutes ago."

"Well, let's pray and get started. He'll have to pray by himself." Pa folded his hands and watched to make sure the six siblings followed suit.

Food was passed around the table in silence. What was this "talk" going to be about? Romy was reluctant to break the silence, waiting for his father to start the conversation. His brothers and sisters were probably thinking the same thing since they were just as quiet.

Finally the door swung open, and Harry burst into the kitchen. "What's for supper?" Harry headed toward his empty chair, not seeming to notice the awkward silence.

Pa picked up the bread plate and took a piece before passing it to Harry. "We've been waiting for you, Harry. I need to talk to all of you."

Harry glanced around the table as he filled his plate. At long last, the silence must have penetrated his consciousness. "What's going on?"

"I burned my finger on the oven, and now Pa's mad at me." Mary displayed her greasy finger for Harry to examine.

Pa blinked twice and looked at Mary. He brushed his hand down her long russet hair. "Oh darlin', I'm not mad at you. I feel so bad you hurt yourself when I wasn't even in the house."

He paused to look at the entire family. "This is hard for me to say. What happened today has persuaded me that I can't wait any longer."

Romy put down his fork as his gut clenched. This was going to be an earth-shattering announcement.

"Our life has changed so much since your ma died. We're all sad and miss her very much, but . . ." Pa swallowed before continuing, "I've decided we can't go on like this any longer. The girls need help in the house since they aren't old enough to do all this work alone. I've talked to Pastor 'bout it and decided I need to hire a woman to come and live at our house to help with the housework."

Romy started to breathe again. That would be great. Now they could have good meals once more and clean clothes. He took a bite of his chicken with a renewed appetite.

Everyone voiced a question at the same time. "When will she be coming?" "Who is she?" "Where will she sleep?" "Do we know her?" "Will she be our new Ma?" The last question came from Janet.

"No, she won't be your new Ma." Pa's loud voice boomed, displaying the conviction he had always shown before that terrible day in May. "I would have to marry her for her to be your new Ma, and I will never replace Ma that way."

He wiped a tear off his cheek.

"All the details haven't been worked out yet as to when she'll come, or where she'll sleep." Pa pushed his plate back. "I wasn't sure how to go 'bout finding someone."

"Do you have someone in mind already?" Romy took a drink of milk.

"As I said, I talked to Pastor 'bout this last time I was in town. He had a suggestion of someone that would work out well for us." Pa put his coffee cup down. "It's his sister-in-law, Miss Maggie Ehlke."

Romy choked on his milk, causing it to explode all over the table.

***

Maggie stood up and rubbed her back. She had been picking peas for the last half hour. Pain shot through her shoulders. Maybe if she stretched for a bit it would subside. She enjoyed working out in the garden on such a sunny day as long as Denny and the twins stayed asleep.

"Where's my momma?" Lucy played nearby in the sandbox. "I want to show her my castle that I built."

"She went over to church to practice organ for the Sunday service." Ah, here was a chance to stretch her back. Maggie bent this way and that as she walked across the lawn. "I'll be glad to come and see what you built."

Her niece pointed to the pile of sand in the corner of the box. "See, it has all these windows in it."

"You did great work there, Lucy."

"Can I come help you in the garden now?" Lucy brushed the sand from her hands.

"No, I'm almost finished anyway." As she searched the vines, Maggie could almost taste the tender sweet peas. It would be good to have the fresh vegetables for supper tonight.

Lately, it seemed the family was eating stew more often–without any meat, most of the time. Maggie had been concerned with the food situation, but she didn't feel comfortable enough to ask Neil about it. Emma would tell her what was happening financially if she felt Maggie needed to know.

During the last couple days, she had a niggling feeling something was wrong. On several occasions, she went into a room where Neil and Emma had been deep in a conversation, but silence had reigned after she entered. Then the dialogue had turned to the weather or other insignificant subjects. They were keeping something from her, but she didn't know how to find out what.

Neil and Emma assured her over and over again they couldn't get along without her. "You'll always have a place in our home, Maggie. Don't worry about that."

The twins were almost three months old now and even slept through most of the night. Emma had fewer tasks for Maggie to do every day, but she found helpful things to do, just the same.

Timmy and Tina were so much fun to play with that she could spend hours getting them to laugh. She would never feel unwanted in this house.

"Aunt Maggie, I think I hear a baby crying." Lucy stood up and brushed dirt off her legs. "Do you want me to go see if the twins are awake?"

"I'm all finished here, so I'll go and check." Maggie picked up her dish of peas and tucked it under her arm. "I'll need help shelling these in a few minutes if you want to lend a hand."

"Sure." Lucy bounced as if she were a Ping-Pong ball. She rubbed her tummy in anticipation. "Yummy peas!"

Minutes later, Maggie and Lucy were in the kitchen popping the bright green pods and pushing out the tiny orbs. Timmy lay on a quilt on the floor, trying to put his thumb in his mouth.

"I can't wait to eat some of these peas." Lucy's smile, with her front tooth missing, was sunshine itself. One of the peas bounced out of the bowl as she worked, and rolled under the table.

Neil pushed through the swinging door and strolled into the kitchen. "Oh, I'm glad to catch you, Maggie."

"I thought you were out on calls this afternoon." Maggie glanced up from her project. "Emma's practicing organ at church during naptime. I'm sure she'll be home soon."

"Well, I was actually looking for you." He pulled out a chair and sat down. "I have something I wanted to talk to you about."

"Is it something about the twins?" Her stomach twisted into a knot. "I so enjoy them, especially when they smile all the time."

"No, nothing about them." Neil looked down at his daughter. "Lucy, do you want to go out and play in the backyard? I'll help Aunt Maggie finish the peas."

"Okay, Papa." She jumped off her chair. "Maybe Denny will wake up soon." She pushed the screen door and ran from the house, letting it slam behind her.

"That little girl sure has lots of energy." The knot in Maggie's stomach grew larger. She racked her brain trying to come up with small talk. If only her stomach would settle down, but the feeling of dread grew inside her.

Neil smiled. "You're right on that one."

The smile faded in the next moment.

"Maggie, you may have guessed things are getting tight

around here." He hurried on before she could reply. "I haven't received any payment from the congregation for the last month. The offerings at church have gotten so low that they pay the electric bill at church and not much else."

"I didn't realize." Maggie's throat constricted. What was coming next? Were they going to send her back to Wisconsin? "What are we going to do to eat?"

"The farmers in the congregation have promised they will still give us milk, meat, and vegetables, as much as possible, but we have to cut back where we can." Neil didn't even make eye contact with her. He stared at his hands as he shelled the last of the peas. "Emma and I have talked about this, but she didn't want to be the one to tell you."

Maggie's insides churned as if she were on the high seas. She hoped her stomach wouldn't erupt. "Tell me what?"

"I've learned a farm family in our congregation needs to hire a young woman to help out. They have several young children that need looking after, plus meals and laundry. He said they have a large garden, also, with canning later in the summer. Since you're used to living on a farm, I assured him you are very capable of handling all these tasks."

Ice invaded Maggie's veins, settling in her midsection. Neil and Emma were sending her away? She had already been sent away from one home because of the bad times. Now it was happening again. This time to a stranger's house.

"Does he live a long way from here?" Maggie blinked hard to stop the room from spinning in circles. "How would I get back and forth every day?"

"There isn't a way to get you back to our house every day. You'd have to live on the farm with them. They would provide room and board as part of the deal." Pausing, Neil glanced up at Maggie. "In fact, he can't pay you cash, only room and board, because he doesn't have extra money either."

Did that mean she would be a servant? How unfair was that? She longed to be more than that. What about what she wanted?

Maggie tried to blink away the tears threatening to spill down her cheeks. How would she endure the separation from Lucy, Denny, and the twins?

Neil steepled his fingers. "Paul says in Romans, 'We know that all things work together for good to them that love God, to them who are the called according to his purpose.'"

She tried to keep her voice from wavering. "I know God tells us that in the Bible, so I have to believe it. I have to trust in Him, but it's hard sometimes. "

She gave him an I'm-trying-not-to-cry smile. How would she manage to live in a house full of strangers? Maybe she should pack up and go home, but her parents weren't in any shape to welcome her, either. In fact, she didn't have any money to get back to Wisconsin.

"I agree with you there, Maggie." Neil placed his hand on her arm. "God has helped us through tough times before and will again if we let him." The sad look in his eyes told Maggie this was hard on him, also. "Emma and I have been praying about this for some time and think this is the best solution for them and you."

Maggie closed her eyes. It might be the best solution for all of them, but no one had asked her what she thought about it. *I love You Lord, but this will be hard for me. Give me strength to do Your will.*

Raising her head, she looked at Neil. "Do I know the family?"

She didn't know if she really wanted to hear the answer. She shifted the dish of peas to a more secure location on her lap.

"Oh, I thought I had mentioned who it was." Neil cleared his throat in the silence. "Of course you know them. It's the Albert Iverson family—Harry's father."

The bowl full of peas clattered on the linoleum floor and tiny green orbs rolled toward every corner of the kitchen.

CHAPTER 10

Romy gently squeezed the cow's teats—right, left, right, left—his fingers working without his brain. The smell of fresh hay didn't even permeate his foggy mind. Neither did the bellowing of the other cattle lined up in their stanchions. As he continued squeezing, the milk landed in the empty bucket. Ping. Ping. Ping. Ping. How could Pa do that?

What will Ma say about all this? Romy shook his head and choked at his thought. Of course, Ma wasn't with them any longer. Sometimes his mind played tricks with him, making him forget the horrific reality. But that's why Pa had made such a puzzling decision. Ma. He worked hard to keep his sudden tears at bay.

"What do you think of Pa's news, Romy?" Jim was down the row milking another cow.

What a *terrible* idea! Pastor's sister-in-law come and live at their house? But of course he couldn't say that to Jim. He attempted to keep his voice steady. "There's no question that the girls can't keep up with the work. The hole in our family is too large, but Miss Ehlke? I have to think of someone else."

"Why not Miss Ehlke?"

"She's so hard to talk to. How would I manage to live in the same house?" He just couldn't get his mind around the situation. "There must be lots of other girls in the area who could help us out. What about Tess who lives over on Pond Road? I used to go to school with her."

"No. That won't work. Her mother had a stroke six months ago. I heard Tess is running the house while she recovers."

Romy had to come up with another solution. "Well, then what about Sandy from church?"

"I heard from Harry and Cissy that Sandy and Jay got engaged last weekend. I'm sure she'll be busy planning the big event."

"What about Cissy then? Harry and Cissy could get married. They could live here, and she could help out the girls."

The milk stopped pinging in Jim's pail. "You want Cissy to live in our house all the time with all her chatter? I think I'd move out then. Besides, you can never tell Harry what to do."

Romy's shoulder's slumped. "Good point."

Romy's mind strained to think of others who could help out the girls. How did his fourteen-year-old brother know all this scuttlebutt about the community? He pressed his head against Bess's flank and continued to squeeze out the milk. The cow chewed her cud, unaware of the turmoil in his soul.

"I wonder what it will be like to have her in our house doing Ma's work." Jim didn't drop the topic as Romy might have hoped.

He hadn't even thought of that aspect of the situation. Maggie would be taking Ma's place in the kitchen and garden. Could they allow her to take over Ma's tasks? He swallowed. They didn't have a choice.

As tears burned his eyes, a fist tightened around his heart. Would she make the loss greater, or would she help fill the hole in their lives? Fatigue seized his shoulders and arms like a vise.

"I'm not sure what to think." Romy forced his hands to continue their gentle pattern. "I know we need help, but it will be hard for anyone to step into the middle of this family and fit in well."

Not to mention the fact that he couldn't think straight around her.

"Well, it will be nice to have a better cook making our meals again." Jim smacked his lips.

"I'll agree with you there." Of course, Jim would think with his stomach. All teenage boys did. Romy hadn't thought of this benefit. He was sure Maggie would be a good cook. "Are you almost done?"

"Yup, I will be in a jiff." Jim stood. "I'll go see if Ted has the separator assembled yet."

"I'll be there as soon as I can." Romy finished up on Bess.

Separating the cream from the milk was a time-consuming task, so he wanted to get started as soon as he could. He hoped Ted had been able to put the De Laval together again after the morning cleaning. Sally used to do this chore every day, but couldn't manage because of all the housework. Maybe having Maggie around would offer some advantage.

Romy entered the milk house. Ted cranked the handle of the separator while Jim poured in a fresh pail of milk. The foamy liquid threatened to overflow the bowl of the machine as the bucket emptied. The cream was collected into the five-gallon can and stored in the water tank to keep it cold until the milk-man came on Thursday. At the creamery, the thick pale yellow fluid would be made into butter, a commodity still in demand despite the Depression. Romy knew having high quality cream was important, because Pa had to get top dollar. The survival of the farm depended on it.

Ted looked up while continuing to crank the handle. "I can't wait until Miss Ehlke gets here. Do you know when Pa is moving her out to the farm?"

"He hasn't said, but at supper he mentioned the weekend." Jim picked up another milk bucket and began to pour. He glanced at Romy. "I wonder where she'll sleep. Do you think Pa will put her in the back bedroom?"

Romy exchanged the skim milk bucket with an empty one. He hadn't thought much about it. "I have no idea."

The back bedroom was off the parlor and not used for much more than storage. In summer it was fine to use, but in the winter months, it would never work. There was no source of heat, so a person would freeze in there. Would Pa really make Maggie sleep in that room? There probably wasn't any other choice, though, since the house was already full of nine people. Eight . . . now with Ma gone.

"If she's going to sleep in there, someone better clean it out and get it ready." Ted turned the handle as fast as he could.

There was a bed, of sorts, in the room, but Romy had no idea what shape it was in. The last time he'd been in there he was storing away the Christmas decorations in January.

"I better check with Pa about it soon, then." He didn't want this to happen at all, but if it was going to occur, he didn't want

Maggie to walk into a disaster from day one. Why did he feel he had to protect her from a bad situation he didn't want in the first place? Maybe, deep down, he wanted a reason to protect her. But that was wishful thinking.

***

Maggie gathered the last of the peas spilled across the kitchen floor. She'd have to wash them several times so they could be used for supper instead of tossing them out. They couldn't afford to waste peas with the shortage of food in the house. While she brushed the remaining green orbs together, she tried to process the revelation Neil had dropped into her lap.

She'd worked so hard when the twins were tiny. They were starting to interact with her more every day. She loved those babies, and Emma was sending her away. Would anyone call that fair?

How would she be able to live in the same house with Romy? Since they'd gotten off to a bad start, things were still uneasy between them. She could be a big help to Romy's younger sisters, but interacting with him might be awkward. Of course, there was no way she could mention this to Neil or Emma since it was so petty. *Lord, help me to know Your will in this situation, and help me to live up to it.*

Neil had gone upstairs to retrieve Tina from her crib when they heard her cry. Maggie was thankful she was alone to try to sort out her thoughts after the earth-shattering announcement. Why hadn't Emma been able to inform Maggie of their problem? Maybe she wouldn't have felt so used and unwanted if her sister had told her the news. *Lord, help me to get over feeling alone and unloved.*

She stood up with the bowl of peas in her hand when Emma came through the swinging door. Maggie swallowed hard and plastered a smile on her face to hide the hurt. "How was practice?"

Emma headed across the kitchen floor, took the bowl from Maggie, and enclosed her in a sisterly hug.

"You can't fool me." Emma stepped back and looked into Maggie's eyes. "I know you heard the awful news. I'm so sorry, Maggie."

"I suppose you have to do what you have to do." Maggie rubbed her forehead.

Emma put her hands on Maggie's shoulders. "Do you think this is easy for me? With less money all the time, I worry about what I'll feed my children."

Maggie hadn't thought about the situation from Emma's viewpoint. She nodded. "I'll go live with the Iversons. Those children need someone to help since their mother is gone. We have to do what God calls us to do."

"I'm sure it will be a relief to them, but we will surely miss you here." Emma swiped at the tears threatening to pour down her cheeks. "I feel like I'm abandoning you."

"Don't worry about me." With her lower lip quivering, Maggie put on a brave front. She waved her hand in dismissal. "I'm a big girl. I can handle the housework."

It was Romy she didn't know how to handle.

Emma shook her gently. "Stop trying to act so heroic. You will be wonderful for the family, but I bet you're feeling like we don't love you any longer. That couldn't be further from the truth."

Maggie shook her head, but the tears that were threatening finally came in a torrent. She leaned her head on Emma's shoulder and cried until her throat ached. She wouldn't be able to help with Tina and Timmy every day and see their smiling faces. She tried to pull herself together. "I know you don't want to do this any more than I want to leave you."

"It's not like we won't see each other again." Emma rubbed Maggie's back. "We'll still see you every Sunday in church. You can stop anytime you're in town, buying groceries and things."

Emma bent to pick up Timmy from the blanket and handed him to her sister. "He will still need to see his Aunt Maggie as much as possible."

Maggie hugged the baby to her chest. She didn't understand it, but this was God's will. Swallowing past the lump in her throat, she resolved to face the move. She would have to figure out how to deal with Romy, but she'd leave that problem in God's hands for now. "When will I have to be ready to move out to their house?"

"Mr. Iverson said they would be ready for you on Sunday after church." Emma picked up the bowl of peas and set them near the sink. "We'll have you packed up and organized by then."

"That will give me tomorrow to make sure all my clothes are clean and ready to go." Handing Timmy back to his mother,

Maggie turned to the sink and started washing the peas. "In the meantime, I better get supper started."

***

Romy sank down on the back porch steps, watching the kaleidoscope of color in the sky as the sun dipped in the west. Pa approached him looking as if he'd aged twenty years in one month, the lines around his eyes becoming more pronounced.

"I was just checking all the animals for the last time tonight." He paused in front of Romy. "Mind if I share your space with you?"

"Not at all, Pa." Romy scooted over. He didn't know what to say to his father at the moment, or if he should bring up some of the questions in his mind. He waited in silence.

"So, what do you think of hirin' someone to help our family?" Pa never did beat around the bush when he wanted to talk about something.

"I think all of us agree we need someone to lend a hand around here." Romy gazed at his father. How much could he say without making Pa sad?

Pa nodded. "It broke my heart to see Sally and Mary's shoulders sag in relief when I made the announcement earlier. Those girls have been under a lot of stress, besides grievin' for their Ma durin' these weeks."

The tears trickled down Pa's cheeks, but his father didn't acknowledge they were there. "I know it will be hard to have a stranger come here and fit into the family, but I think we have no choice in the matter."

"I know, Pa." Romy agreed with the statement, but it was the person that bothered him. There was no way he could voice his uneasiness, because the problem was in his own head, not with anyone else in the family.

His father continued, "I think it will be good for Janet, too." Turning to look at Romy, he rubbed his hands against the knees of his overalls. "She's been lost in the crowd durin' the last month since everyone is so busy tryin' to get by. She needs a woman around here to lean on."

Letting out his breath, Romy concluded Maggie would be moving in. Soon. His head bowed with the certainty. He couldn't deny Janet needed a woman around the house. Nor could he deny Mary and Sally needed help keeping up the house and cooking. "When will Miss Ehlke be coming, Pa?"

"I told Pastor we would bring her here after church on Sunday." He stood and faced Romy. "That means we have tomorrow and Saturday to make plans and get ready for her. And none too soon for me."

Romy peered at Pa. If he would be getting ready for her, the important question had to be asked. "Where are you planning on having her sleep?"

"Since it's gettin' toward summer now, I figured she could sleep in the back bedroom off the parlor. I can't think much more than a day ahead anyway, so we'll have to plan somethin' else when it gets closer to winter." Pa headed up the steps and opened the door. "We can't pay her money, so we better have the room ready when she comes."

"I'll help you tomorrow, Pa."

The door slammed behind him. Romy was alone in the cool evening air.

Bracing his elbows on his knees, Romy leaned his head on his hands. He hadn't realized Maggie would be doing all the work for only room and board.

Things must not be going well at Pastor's house either if they were sending Maggie out here for food and a place to sleep. That was practically slave labor. Romy hadn't thought about this situation from her standpoint.

Now he had more to fill his already aching head.

***

After a restless night, Maggie yawned and rolled over. If only she could stay in bed another hour. Not today. Besides helping Emma, she had to make sure she was set to move out to the Iversons'.

Maggie yawned. How would Emma survive Sunday mornings without her help from now on? Maybe Lucy would be able to step into the gap after Maggie departed. She couldn't be bothered with these thoughts today. She had to survive her transition to the farm herself.

Maggie threw on her navy pleated skirt and white blouse. At least the weather was warmer. She brushed through her brown hair trying to get it under control, but found the unruly curls were more abundant than usual in the humidity. Of course, her tresses would have to be obstinate for her.

"Maggie, can you come here, fast?" Emma sounded desperate. "Tina just exploded in her diaper, and Timmy spat up all over his church clothes."

Maggie hurried into the next room barefoot. She scooped Tina up out of her crib trying to rescue the baby's dress before the diaper leaked through the soaker. She looked at Emma who was sponging off Timmy's shirt. "How are you going to manage both babies by yourself on Sundays?"

"That's a fair question. I think Neil will have to be home longer those mornings until I can get the children ready for church." Emma didn't even look up. She smiled through the chaos. "This will be hard. We have to do what we have to do. Maybe you can sleep over here every Saturday night so I have some help until they're older."

"We'll have to see what works." Maggie finished pinning Tina's clean diaper in place. She hugged her as the baby snuggled close to her shoulder. "I'll surely miss these two little ones. Don't you forget your Aunt Maggie, peanut."

"We'll see you as often as we can." Emma hugged Maggie with one arm. "I'll worry that you're working too hard out there with eight mouths to feed."

"I don't have any other choice." *God help me get through this.* Maggie looked at the clock. "If things are under control here, I better go finish packing my bag, so I'm ready."

Would she be prepared to face the family, including Romy?

"Is your trunk all packed?" Emma laid Timmy down after burping him.

"Yes, I did that yesterday." Maggie laid Tina down in her crib. "I didn't pack all my books until I find out how much room I have out there. Most of the books are still on the shelves Neil put together for me. That way my trunk's not as heavy as it was a couple months ago."

"Okay." Emma headed back to her bedroom. "I'll check on Denny and Lucy. We should be ready to leave for church in fifteen minutes."

Maggie went back to her room to tuck her nightgown and hairbrush into her bag. She heard little feet running toward her.

"Whatcha doin', Aunt Maggie?" Lucy stood in her doorway.

"I'm packing my bag so I'm ready to go. Do you remember that I told you yesterday I'm moving out to live with Janet's family? I'm going to cook their dinner from now on." She watched Lucy's face lose its shiny smile.

"I don't want you to go." Lucy lunged forward hugging Maggie around the waist.

"I don't want to either, but I have to." She knelt down to gather Lucy in her arms. Her throat closed around her words. "I'll miss you lots, but I'll always love you."

"Can I move to Janet's with you, Aunt Maggie?"

"Oh, Lucy, Momma is going to need you here to help her with Tina and Timmy. You'll be her big helper from now on."

"Who will be your helper, then?"

"That's a good question, Lucy. I'll have to wait and see."

Maggie would have to find out the answer later along with the many other unanswered questions. Would she have to share a room with one of the girls? Would she have any free time to read the few books she was bringing with her? Her mind raced with uncertainties.

Looming in the background, one thought always was the same, though. What would it be like to interact with Romy on a daily basis?

CHAPTER 11

"Come on, girls. We don't want to be late for church." Romy helped his sisters out of the back seat of the car. Harry scrambled from the front seat, slamming the car door behind him. Acrid exhaust fumes invaded Romy's nose as his pa and two brothers pulled into the parking space beside them and emerged from the truck. Both vehicles were needed today since Maggie was moving out to the farm.

The plan was to pack her up after the church service. Romy remembered that cold March day when he loaded her trunk into the pickup at the station. Would it be as heavy today?

That had been the first day Romy noticed Ma's pain in her arm. If he had insisted she go to a doctor back then, maybe she would still be with them. Then the family wouldn't need Maggie's help. If only . . . He tried to throw off the weight sitting on his chest and rejoin the present.

"Pa, are we ready?" Romy glanced down the street before heading into church.

Out of the corner of his eye, he saw Pastor's family approach. Mrs. Hannemann carried one of the babies while Maggie followed with Denny and the other baby. With her hat set at a jaunty angle, she sure was pretty. Those brown curls framing her face drew attention to her rosy lips. Why couldn't Romy get the words out to tell her?

"Good morning to all of you." Mrs. Hannemann's sunshine smile greeted the family. "How are things out at the farm?"

"Not so great right now, or we wouldn't need Miss Ehlke to come and live with us." Pa sighed, rubbing his forehead.

Romy shook his head. Pa didn't have to be so blunt even if he was hurting.

The color heightened on Maggie's cheeks as she bit her lip. Romy hoped Pa's comment didn't give her the wrong impression.

Pa peered at her. "Are you all packed and ready to leave after church?"

She looked into his eyes. "Yes, sir, I'm packed. My trunk is ready, but it's still up in my room."

Great. Someone's back would ache carrying that thing down the steps as well as out to the truck.

Pa pointed toward him. "That won't bother Romy. He'll take care of it for you."

Guess it was his back that would be aching. Romy rubbed it in anticipation. He nodded to give Maggie some assurance things would be all right. "Uh . . . it'll work out."

"Yes, we'd better head in for the service before we discuss any more details. We'll talk to you after church." Mrs. Hannemann led the way with Lucy in tow. Maggie followed her into the building.

During the next hour, Romy had a hard time concentrating on worship. Too often, his mind wandered to the situation with Maggie. Were they ready for her to move into the house? With his heart pounding, trepidation flowed through his veins, and yet he looked forward to it. With her bright smile and twinkling eyes, she lit up the room. Why did his anxiety always leave him tongue-tied in front of her? Would he overcome it when he saw her every day?

He and Pa had worked hard yesterday readying the back room. They had carried the bulk of the junk up to the attic. That should have been done ages ago. There were old broken chairs, and even the rocking horse he used to play on, sitting in the room gathering dust. After the items were cleared out, the room was almost spacious.

He had aired out the bedding and beaten the cotton mattress until a dust cloud assaulted his nose. After a sneezing fit, Romy had put it back on the bed frame. "I hope Miss Ehlke's back won't ache because of this sagging beast."

Pa had glanced at the bed. "I'll put a piece of plywood under the mattress to make it firm."

Maybe it wasn't so bad now.

"This three-drawer dresser should be sufficient for her clothes. Her trunk will fill up this space under the window." Romy had rubbed the back of his neck. Would they be able to get the trunk all the way to the back bedroom?

The end result should pass inspection.

The organ music dragged his thoughts back to the church service in time to sing the last hymn. After the postlude, Romy shielded his eyes as they came outside into the penetrating sun. He looked at Pa for instructions. "Should we head over to Pastor's house to start the loading process?"

"You go with Miss Ehlke to the parsonage and get the trunk down to the porch. I'll be over in the truck shortly." Pa headed toward the family to give them directions.

Romy walked toward Maggie, who was surrounded by Pastor's children. She was hugging and kissing them with tears rolling down her cheeks.

"We need . . ." He didn't get any further.

"Maggie, how come you didn't tell me?" Cissy charged toward them, giving Maggie an enveloping hug. "Harry just told me you were moving out to his farm to help out the girls. That's great that you're going to be helping them, but you could have mentioned it to me. We had such good talks when we took the kids to the park lately. I'm going to miss our girl talks and spending time with you. Ya know?"

She stopped to take a breath.

Romy was always amazed at how fast Cissy talked.

"I didn't find out until Friday. I had to pack yesterday, so I didn't have time." Maggie stepped back.

"Well, that was sudden, then. I'm sure they can use your help out there with the meals, gardening, and all the things you're so good at, but I will miss you. Who will I be able to talk to that lives so close to me now?" She looked at Harry. "Of course, I'll still see Harry when he's at lunch from his job, but that's only for a short time most days.

"I know . . . when Harry comes to take me on a date, Romy can bring you along and we'll all spend lots of time together catching up on the latest news. Ya know what I mean?"

Maggie's cheeks turned bright pink at the suggestion. "I'll see you at church every Sunday, Cissy. Now, I have to help Romy with my things."

Maggie waved to Cissy and started in the direction of the parsonage without waiting for a good-bye. Maybe she thought Cissy talked too much, also.

Hurrying to catch up, Romy matched her strides. "She sure likes to talk."

At least, he was able to get out a short sentence without stumbling on his words. He glanced at Maggie to catch her reaction. Her eyes were wide, as if she were surprised.

"I agree with you there. She sometimes drives me crazy . . . talk, talk, talk." Maggie mimicked her words with her hands. "I like her, but only for a short period of time." She turned around and looked back at the church. "Is someone going to drive the truck to the parsonage?"

He nodded. "I told them . . . I'd get your trunk down to the porch."

"I'm leaving most of my books with Neil and Emma for now." Maggie trotted up the steps to the porch. "That way, it won't be so heavy."

"Oh." That would make things much easier. Romy's back would thank her later on.

He followed her upstairs and into her room.

"It's in here." She pointed to the corner.

Romy crossed the room ready to battle the beast once again. Not as enormous as he remembered. He grasped the handles on both ends and lifted it to his chest with no effort. What a difference. "Is there anything . . . in here at all?"

"Only my clothes." Maggie pointed to the full bookshelves. "The extra weight will stay here."

Romy carried it down and waited on the porch with Maggie. So many things he'd like to say before Pa came. He'd like to tell her he was relieved she was coming. He'd like to prepare her for the disaster waiting for her at the house—the piles of dirty laundry, the unwashed dishes, the untended garden, the empty bread box, and the broken-hearted children yearning for a mother who was no more. How could he describe all that to her?

"We're grateful you're coming to help us."

How very inadequate.

✳✳✳

Maggie watched Mr. Iverson pull the truck to a stop in front of the parsonage. At least Romy had managed to verbalize a few sentences when she was with him. Not enough to know what he thought, but it was a start. Maggie turned toward him. "Can I help with something?"

"No, I can get this." Romy once again hoisted the trunk as if it were a bag of groceries and headed down the steep steps. The muscles on his arms bulged beneath his white shirt.

She stifled a gasp. So strong. She followed, carrying the satchel. Breathing deep, Maggie struggled to get her pulse back to normal. Surprised by her response, she buried her reaction.

Following Romy to the back of the truck, she pointed toward her valise. "Do you want me to put the bag back here, too?"

"Yup." Mr. Iverson helped Romy push the trunk to the front of the truck bed and threw the satchel in after it. "Let's get going. Harry is driving the rest of the family home."

Romy opened the passenger door and, without a word, indicated Maggie should sit in the middle. She slid onto the seat, trying to minimize her space between the two men.

Would anyone at the Iverson house be friendly? How would she survive this change? *God, I know this is what You want me to do, so please be with me and grant Your blessing on this family.* "How far is it to the farm?"

"'Bout twenty minutes." Mr. Iverson was a man of few words, just like his son. This would be a long twenty minutes, and half a world away.

As Maggie watched the countryside fly past the windows, she wondered which direction they were going. "Tell me about your farm."

"Typical Iowa farm."

That helped a lot. Since Mr. Iverson didn't offer anything more, Maggie was resigned to sit in complete silence for the rest of the ride.

"The house is good size—three bedrooms downstairs and two up." Romy filled in some blanks. "We cleaned out the back bedroom for you."

Her own room! With so many people in the house, she'd never imagined that luxury. Letting out her breath, she smiled. "Thank you so much. I appreciate that."

Could he read her thanks in her smile? Maybe she would have a place to spend time alone reading when she wasn't working.

"But the house is pretty messy." Romy slanted a glance in

her direction. "With Ma gone, we haven't had time to clean much."

Maggie's eyes widened. Romy was actually talking, even if they were clipped sentences. Maybe in time he'd be more open.

"Oh. I'll do my best."

What other unstated surprises would be waiting for her when they got there?

Would the girls be more talkative than the men? If not, her life would be rather quiet. Harry at least was friendly. Would that change now? The rest of the trip passed in complete silence.

The truck slowed to a crawl as Mr. Iverson made a left turn. Maggie looked up the sloping driveway. A two-story white house stood on top of a small rise with several stately trees towering over it. The driveway curved around toward the back of the house. A short stone retaining wall lined the drive as it wound to the left. Weeds sprouted from the neglected flower-bed on top of the wall. It needed some loving care.

A large screened porch faced her as she studied the house. This would be a great place to do outdoor tasks without being eaten alive by mosquitoes. "What a lovely house."

It needed a good paint job, but what house didn't in these hard times?

"Romy, get her things into her room." Pa stepped out of the truck. "I'll try to find something for dinner."

Maggie lifted her satchel as Romy pulled the trunk toward him.

"Welcome to our farm." Their eyes connecting, his smile said more than his words. The greeting warmed her heart. She followed him into the house, wandering through the kitchen, dining room, and parlor before reaching her new room. Romy set her trunk under the window.

"Hope this works all right for you." He turned to leave. "Someone will show you around after dinner."

With those words, he was gone, and Maggie was left alone.

Was she ready to face the family? She sat on the bed and sighed. She'd better resign herself to this new life. With the way the Depression was going, college was most definitely out. No money. This was God's will for her, for now at least. *Lord, be with me for this new task ahead. Help me to remember that You are leading me home.*

After peeking out the window, she stood and glanced around the room. A bed with a tarnished brass headboard and patchwork quilt greeted her. The hooks behind the door were the only place to hang her dresses.

This would be home for now. She better not complain; many people had lots less than this. She decided to unpack later. Opening the door, she walked back toward the kitchen.

"Will she be my new ma now?" A little girl's voice carried from the kitchen. Maggie assumed she was the person in question.

Harry responded to his sister with the gentleness of a teacher. "We've talked about this before. Miss Ehlke will not be our ma since she isn't married to Pa."

"Janet, you need to listen when I tell you things." Mr. Iverson sounded gruff even to Maggie. "Miss Ehlke is our hired girl."

Maggie drew back, feeling as if she'd been slapped. She didn't consider herself a "hired girl." She wasn't even getting paid for all her work. Although, that's technically what she was since she was here working for the family. Tears filled her eyes.

"Pa, I hope we treat her more like a sister than a 'hired girl.'" Romy defended her. "She's here to help us out, not be something like a maid."

Maggie gasped in amazement. She didn't know Romy could be so outspoken. At least a sister was better than a hired girl. This was a different Romy entirely.

She'd better make her presence known. She stepped into the kitchen. "Can I help with something?"

All eyes turned to her.

"Pa found a couple quarts of canned soup in the cellar. He's heating it up for dinner." Harry managed to cover up the awkward silence. "We'll have some cheese and sausage also, and hope it holds us through to supper. We're out of bread, so you'll need to bake tomorrow."

Maggie expected to be swamped during the first few days getting the household back in order, but she didn't imagine she'd have to bake bread so soon. "I'll be happy to do that tomorrow, but will have to put off the laundry until Tuesday then."

"That's no problem. We've been without clean clothes for more than a month." One of the younger brothers at the table resembled a storm cloud.

"Hush, Jim." Romy's father smacked Jim on the back of his head. "We don't need to tell tales."

Was Maggie seeing a snapshot of this family during the last month? What had she walked into? Where was the Christian love she was used to from Neil's house? She'd have to show patience and love all around. This household needed cooking and cleaning, but more importantly, they all needed the love of Christ—starting with herself.

She tried to alleviate the tense atmosphere in the room. "I'll be able to pull together a larger supper tonight since I have all afternoon."

It would be a challenge—becoming acquainted with a new kitchen and finding enough food for the hungry family all in a few hours.

"First you need to meet everyone." Harry took the opportunity to introduce her to the younger brothers and the three small girls.

So many names to remember at once.

"Miss Ehlke, I'm Janet." The youngest girl grasped Maggie's hand. She squeezed the girl's fingers. At least, this was one name she would remember since she was Lucy's friend.

"Janet, please call me Maggie since I'll be living with you." Maybe this would show she would rather be treated like a sister than a maid.

"Absolutely not." Mr. Iverson snapped, showing his opinion without hesitation. "Miss Maggie is fine, but nothing less."

At least it was better than Miss Ehlke. "Okay."

Without further comment, he pulled out his chair. "Let's sit down and eat."

"Will Miss Maggie sit in Ma's seat?" Sally's hand covered her mouth when the words escaped.

Time stood still as the room froze in place. An instant later, all eyes swiveled to Pa. This subject must not have been discussed before her arrival. Had their mother's chair remained empty during the last month? No doubt about it.

Nodding, Mr. Iverson glanced at his daughter. "Yes, that's fine."

After the table prayer, Maggie ate her soup in silence. She observed the conversation of the family during the meal, watching the give-and-take of the siblings. The teasing between Ted and Jim was surprising. Romy had to defend himself against some of the jabs, also. He had no problems interacting with his siblings. He certainly wasn't as withdrawn as she had at first thought him to be.

The three girls seemed to stick together, especially Sally and Mary. The brunt of the housework must have fallen on their shoulders. Her heart went out to them. She could see herself growing to love them in short order.

"As soon as we're finished here, Romy can show Miss Maggie around outside."

Blinking, Maggie swallowed her last bite of soup. Romy show her around? How would that work? Would he be able to answer any questions she might have? Of course, she couldn't object to Mr. Iverson's order.

"Pa, I don't think that would be a good idea." A ruddy tint spread from Romy's collar toward his face. "I need to go feed the cows and horses since we were at church this morning."

At least Romy agreed with her. The tension poured out of her shoulders.

"Okay. Then Harry can show Miss Maggie our farm." Mr. Iverson turned to the boys. "Ted and Jim can help the girls wash the dishes."

"Wait, Pa, it's so nice outside." Jim looked at Ted before he spoke again. "Maybe we can go down to the fishing pond and catch us some perch for supper."

"Oh." Their father started clearing the table. "I'll help with the dishes, then."

Janet skipped along with Harry and Maggie on the way to the garden. "Our garden is very big." She spread her arms out to demonstrate her words.

"How right you are, Janet." Harry steered Maggie toward the gate.

Her attention was drawn to the fenced-in plot. "It is indeed enormous."

How would she be able to preserve all the tomatoes that were growing in there?

"It's been neglected for the last month, so the weeds are larger than some of the plants. Ma died before she got the garden planted." Staring at his shoes, Harry cleared his throat before continuing. "My aunts came the next week and threw in the seeds. We had no idea how much they planted until the vegetables started sprouting."

He glanced up at Maggie. "I wish I could help you clean this out later in the week, but with my job I'm not sure how much time I'll have. Maybe I can get Jim and Ted to help you a bit."

"Is there something we can find to eat for supper?" Maggie searched the climbing pea vines, the blossoming potatoes, the bushy beans, the leafy lettuce and other numerous vegetables. There should be enough here for many meals later in the summer.

"You and Janet can pick some peas and lettuce. We'll find potatoes for tonight in the basement. That should go well with the fish." Harry grabbed a hoe propped against the fence.

Maggie headed toward the pea plants. "That sounds good." She held her hand out to Janet. "Let's go see what we can find."

After Harry and Maggie had worked for several minutes, Maggie gathered her vegetables before taking them to the house. She put her hand on Harry's arm. "Can I talk to you a minute?"

"Janet, why don't you go find Blackie so Miss Maggie can meet him?" Harry sent his youngest sister running in the direction of the barn before focusing on her. "What's on your mind?"

"What's the deal with Romy? Will you level with me? Sometimes he seems like he doesn't mind talking to me. At other times he avoids me as if I give him the heebie-jeebies."

"Well, he's a shy guy who has never felt comfortable talking to dames in his life." Harry gave Maggie a half-smile. "Actually, he's making great progress. Didn't you hear him stand up to Pa before dinner?" He held up his hands when she tried to interrupt. "At least he defended you, even if he can't talk to you. We'll see who wins the debate—Pa or Romy . . . Will you be more of a 'hired girl' or a 'sister'?"

CHAPTER 12

"What do you mean?" Maggie looked up as she popped a peapod open.

Mary and Sally sat at the table helping her shell the fresh peas for supper. A breeze fluttered the curtains on the window and brought in the earthy scent of farm animals. Plunk, plunk, plunk . . . the peas landed in the empty dish.

Maggie searched Mary's face. "Why would you say your ma didn't love you anymore?"

Mary's lips were drawn into a tight line, her lopsided pig-tails swaying back and forth, as her eyes darted between her sister and Maggie. What was going on inside the head of the young girl? Maggie wanted to help her cope with the recent tragedy, but had to know what the nine-year-old was thinking.

"Romy said Ma's heart was broke when she died." Tears streamed down Mary's cheeks as she snapped the end of a pea. "If her heart was broke, she couldn't love us anymore."

Maggie's hands slipped. She grabbed the dish before it fell to the floor. Mary had lived with this idea for a month? No one had denied it?

"Oh, Mary, that's not true at all." Maggie swallowed past the lump in her throat before continuing. "Of course your mother loved you both." When she glanced at the older sister, tears glistened in her eyes, also. "Romy must have said she had a heart attack, not her heart was broken. That means her heart was sick and stopped working."

Pointing at the younger sister, Sally tilted her head. "I told you so, Mary."

"I'm sure she wanted to tell you herself before she died, but God took her home so suddenly." Putting her arm around the young girl, Maggie wiped a tear from Mary's cheek as a smile emerged.

Mary sat up straighter, her eyes sparkling once more. "Do you really think so?"

"Yeah, really." Maggie hugged them both. "I'm sure she didn't want to leave you, but God wanted her to be with Him in heaven."

"I'm happy you told us. I tried to tell Mary, but she wouldn't listen." With hands on her hips, the older sister put her nose in the air.

"Uh-uh. I listened, Sally. I just didn't believe you."

Sally turned toward Maggie. Her lips curved into a half-smile, not quite reaching her eyes. "Miss Maggie, we're so glad you moved in with us. We have someone to talk to again."

Sally's short brown hair appeared a bit scraggly, patches missing from the waves in the back. Had one of the brothers tried to cut it? This house definitely needed a woman's touch once more.

"What about your pa?" Didn't their father communicate with them anymore?

"He doesn't talk much now, and everybody else is too busy." Sally reached for another handful of peas out of the dish.

These poor girls hadn't had anyone listen to them for a long time. God was showing Maggie beyond a doubt she was needed in this house. Peace replaced the weight that rested on her shoulders. "I'll be here for both of you. Come to me anytime. I want to get to know you better."

Smiling, Maggie popped open a pod, stripping it of the orbs within. The air in the room seemed to be lighter. Could the girls feel the change also?

Giggling, Mary cupped her hands and whispered to Maggie. "I can tell you something 'bout Harry if you want to know him better. He's got a girlfriend named Cissy. She talks a lot."

Maggie tilted her head back and laughed. "Yes, Mary, I know. She's my friend, too. I agree with you about her talking, but she is a very nice person."

Sally poked Maggie's shoulder. Maggie could tell by the

glint in her eyes that she was the next one with news to share. She was glad to see the cloud of sadness disappear from the eleven-year-old's face. Sally glanced at Mary before speaking. "I have a secret too, but it's about Romy. He thinks you're cute."

Could that be true? Maggie's hands froze in midair. "How do you know that, Sally?"

That bit of news seemed impossible.

"He told all of us after he met you in spring."

"Sally, I don't know if you should've told Miss Maggie." Mary shook her head. "Romy doesn't want to talk about girls."

"Oh, you don't have to worry, Sally. I won't say anything to him about telling me the secret." Maggie concentrated on the job in front of her. Were the girls young enough not to notice how stunned she was? Her warm cheeks must be broadcasting her shock to the world.

If Romy thought that about her, he'd show it somehow, wouldn't he?

"That's good." Sally placed the bowl on the table.

"The peas are all shelled. Now, we need to wash the lettuce and potatoes." Maggie looked around the kitchen as she spoke.

She had several questions about her new workspace that needed answers. She saw a bucket of water sitting on the cupboard close to the sink. "Is this the water we use to wash the vegetables?"

Sally and Mary looked at each other and giggled. Mary pointed to the bucket. "No, Miss Maggie. That water is only for drinking or cooking. It's summer. We need to wash them outside by the pump."

"Okay. You girls will have to teach me how to do things around here, then."

Sally headed out the door followed by Mary. "When it's warm, we do everything outdoors that we can. The washing is done by the pump so we don't waste the water in the kitchen for that."

Maggie followed the girls as they headed across the yard. When she carried the pan of potatoes and lettuce across the lawn, Maggie's skirt brushed against her legs in the breeze. They stopped at the base of the windmill, standing in the center of the open space.

"Miss Maggie, when we wash vegetables or get a bucket of water, we have to unhook the water pipe that's filling up the cow tank. Then we hook it to this faucet." Sally demonstrated what she meant by moving a lever that diverted the windmill-pumped water through the faucet.

Mary nodded solemnly, rubbing her backside. "Yeah. One time last year, I forgot to hook up the pipe again and there was no water for the cows when they got home from the field. Boy, did I get in trouble."

Maggie laughed with the girls. She'd have to make sure they continued to find things to laugh about. They used the brush, hanging from a string around the pump, to scrub the dirt off the spuds. Then all three washed the lettuce and checked for any unwanted critters attached to the green leaves.

While they were working, Romy sauntered up from the barn. "I see you're helping Miss Maggie get things ready for supper."

"We're showing her how to wash 'taters at the pump." Mary gave Romy an I'm-so-proud smile.

"Attagirl! What else does Miss Maggie need help with?" Romy looked at Maggie as he spoke, but he talked to the girls. If this was his way of communicating without getting tongue-tied, that'd be fine with Maggie. She'd play along, for a while at least.

"Maybe she needs to know how to get the fire on the stove hot so we can cook all this." Sally put the lettuce back into the pan on top of the potatoes.

"Good idea, Sally. I need to know if your stove is like mine back home. If your brother doesn't mind, that would be helpful." Maggie stood up and brushed her skirt.

"Okay. I'll show Miss Maggie how it works." Romy picked up the pan of vegetables and followed them into the house. "Why don't you set the table, Sally, while Mary and I show her the stove."

He turned to Maggie as he put the pan of vegetables in the sink. "Um . . . Mary, do you know if Miss Maggie knows how to use a Monarch range?"

Was this the only way he could talk to her? "Yes, we had one, but not this large. I know how to start a fire, but just need to know where the supplies are stored."

"Show Miss Maggie where the wood is out on the porch." Stepping into the back porch, Romy showed her the full wood box.

A tub of corncobs sat next to the wood. Maggie pointed to them. "What are these for?"

"Tell Miss Maggie they are fire starters."

Mary looked from Romy to Maggie and back again. She didn't say a word.

This was getting silly. And confusing for Mary. Maggie was ready to stop the charade, for Mary's sake. The ice was broken between them. Romy should answer her directly. "We always used newspaper in Wisconsin."

"There are more corncobs in Iowa than newspaper, so we use those. Mary, show her the can of kerosene-soaked ones behind the stove." Romy pushed Mary toward the stove.

Why couldn't Romy show them to her himself? Maggie stared in his direction.

"See here, Miss Maggie." Mary squeezed into the small space to follow Romy's instructions.

"Can you tell her that we use those in case she needs a quick start to a fire some morning?" Stepping out to the porch, he grabbed some wood before returning to the kitchen. Opening the door to the firebox on the left side of the stove, he threw in the extra wood. "The fire is still going from dinner, so I'll just add some wood."

Maggie could see the stove had four large burners. She imagined all the burners would be used to cook for this family. She opened the shiny white ceramic oven door with the word Monarch written in blue script.

"Ma could bake four pies at a time in here." Mary showed her where they would go.

"Wow, that doesn't surprise me. What water do you use for the reservoir?" Glancing at Romy, she'd see if he'd answer her directly. She could see the water holder on the side of the stove was getting low.

"Tell Miss Maggie we have a cistern in the basement to catch the rainwater for the reservoir."

The muscles in her neck tightened, along with her jaw. Guess he wasn't about to address her when he spoke.

"The water in there is always hot." Mary pointed to the res-ervoir attached to the oven wall. "We use that water to wash the dishes. The buckets of water from the basement are too heavy for me to carry up the steps."

"Of course you can't carry those buckets, sweetie." Romy put his arm around her shoulders. "Ted and Jim are supposed to keep the reservoir full. I'll get them to fill it for you." He pointed to the bucket by the sink. "Can you tell Miss Maggie *that* water is from the windmill? The boys should keep it full, also. That's what we use for drinking, cooking, and making coffee."

The heat climbing under her collar could probably boil the teakettle on the stove. Why was he talking around her, not to her? Maggie struggled to keep her voice even. "Mary, tell Romy that I can ask you what water to use instead of him trying to talk through you."

If only he weren't so condescending to her. She would be better off if Sally and Mary showed her the ropes around the house. Stooping down, she grabbed a pot out of the lower cupboard for the potatoes.

As she turned back to the stove, she slammed into Romy who was standing directly behind her. She lost her balance and was about to stumble backwards when Romy grasped her elbow to steady her. A tingle dashed up her arm. He dropped it as if he had touched a lit match.

"Excuse me." Shuffling toward the sink, she attempted to cover her embarrassment.

Romy headed toward the door but looked over his shoulder. "Mary, tell Miss Maggie we'll be in at five thirty for supper." The door slammed behind him.

What was that all about?

***

An hour later Romy sat with his family enjoying the delicious meal Maggie had prepared for them. How had she managed to get all the preparation finished in time? When he walked in the door, the wonderful aroma of frying fish made his empty stomach groan with hunger. *Thank You, Lord, for bringing Maggie into our house.*

At the same time, the raw taste of resentment still lingered in his throat because of her snippiness. He was attempting to help her out by having his sister be the go-between. Why had such a small thing riled her so? He couldn't help it if he was timid around her. And, he *certainly* couldn't explain the prickle that shot up his arm when he touched her.

"Jim, can you please pass the milk?" Maggie looked at Jim when the milk was only inches from Romy's left hand.

She had been avoiding him ever since he stepped foot in the kitchen. Was that because she was angry with him, or had she felt the current when he bumped into her?

Romy grabbed the milk before Jim could reach it. "Here it is." Romy couldn't resist. "It was closer to me, so you could've asked me for it."

He handed the pitcher to Jim to pass to her.

"Thanks, Jim." Maggie took the milk and filled up her glass. She glanced at Ted, too. "By the way, thanks so much for catching the fish this afternoon."

"Thank you for cooking it." Ted reached for another piece of fish. "It really tastes great. In fact, we haven't had a meal like this for over a month."

Romy choked on his lettuce. He imagined Ted felt like crawling into a hole at the moment. He looked at his sisters and saw them stare at their plates. Silence fell like a boat anchor on the table.

After long seconds ticked by, Maggie cleared her throat. "Thank you. It's not every day you can have fresh fish for supper. I couldn't have done all this without Mary's and Sally's help." She smiled at the girls. They returned the smile.

"I helped, too." Janet looked at her father. "I showed Miss Maggie where we keep the plates and forks. Then I showed her how to set the table."

Pa kept eating, never acknowledging Janet's comment.

"Yes, you were a great help to me." Maggie squeezed Janet's hand.

Romy drank a gulp of milk. Maybe she was perceptive enough to know what the little girl needed.

Janet was the one who needed the stability of another woman's presence the most. She'd fallen through the cracks since Ma died. Romy was torn between the farm work and helping the older girls with the housework. He'd tried his best to be there for his youngest sibling, but there just weren't enough hours in the day.

He studied Janet's hand still cradled beneath Maggie's. Could Maggie help fill the void and heal his little sister's heart? He studied the other girls. Worry lines were no longer etched on Sally's or Mary's brow.

"Janet is always a big helper when she's needed." Romy smiled at Maggie to thank her. She had managed to cover the awkward moment Ted dumped on them. Maybe he'd better work on bridging the gap between her and himself. "Miss Maggie, we really appreciate your help getting supper on the table."

The ice melting from her eyes, Maggie returned his smile. "You're welcome."

Romy swallowed. Maybe it wouldn't be so hard for him to get used to seeing that smile daily.

"I help sometimes out in the barn with Blackie, too." Janet looked around the table. "I can even help in the garden."

"Oh that reminds me . . ." Harry glanced at his father. "Pa, I promised Miss Maggie someone could help with the weeds in the garden since it's been ignored for so long. Will there be any time for that in the next day or two?"

"I'm not sure since we haven't made plans yet." Pa cleared his throat before continuing. "What's goin' on this week?"

Harry whispered to Maggie. "Every Sunday evening we have a family meeting to plan out the week."

"It's time to cut the hay. We've had to put it off for too long already, so it needs to be done soon." Pa pushed his plate back.

"The weather sounds like it should be dry, so we can cut it tomorrow." Romy tried to concentrate on what Pa was saying, but thoughts of Maggie invaded his mind.

She would have to bake bread on Monday. Would she need any assistance in the kitchen, or could they be out in the hay-field working all day? How could he ask that? "Um . . . will you be all right if we're out cutting hay tomorrow, or do you need Ted or Jim to help around the house?"

"I'll be baking bread tomorrow, but I can handle anything in the house with the help of Mary and Sally. We'll be fine without the help of the men." She took a drink of milk.

Pa continued as if no one spoke. "Then it will need to be raked into windrows. That can be done on Tuesday and Wednesday. We should be able to get it in the barn by Friday. On Thursday, Romy will have to go to the feed mill."

It sounded like they would have a very busy week ahead of them. How would Maggie manage everything in the house with the men gone all day? She'd have the girls to help her, but would she need more than that to get used to the routines on the farm?

On Tuesday morning before they headed out to the fields, he'd at least have to show her how to use their ancient washer.

She wouldn't be able to figure out how to operate the beast.

Harry interrupted his thoughts. "By the way, Pa, did you hear we're getting new neighbors?"

His father leveled a look at Harry. "Are you listenin' to rumors?"

"No, Pa. Cissy's father works at the bank. He found out someone bought the Zimmerman farm across the road."

"Is that right? We knew Elmer had to sell out, but I didn't know it was a done deal already." Pa sat up straighter.

"Mr. Bernhardt told me a Mr. Winkler bought Zimmerman's place for a song. I guess Mr. Winkler inherited some money and wanted to get out of the big city. So he spent it on a farm." Harry toyed with his fork.

That brought a chuckle to Pa. "Does he think life on the farm is goin' to be easy in these dry years?"

"I have no idea, but thought you'd want to know what I heard."

Jim piped up. "I wonder how big a family he has."

"Mr. Bernhardt didn't mention the family." Harry glanced at Maggie. "They live just up the road across from us. Now we'll have new neighbors to meet."

"Maybe Romy can go over there and introduce himself since he's so friendly. Then he can tell us about the family." Winking, Jim slapped Romy on the back.

Romy shook his head. "No, not me. Someone else can."

"S'pose that's the neighborly thing to do." Pa pushed his chair back from the table and stood. "I'm goin' to check on the animals and then head to bed early."

Pa'd been doing that ever since Ma passed on. He spent too much time alone, often in the barn.

It seemed he'd forgotten his children, especially Janet. No wonder they weren't coping very well. The man who'd been their rock through all the hard times was crumbling to pieces.

CHAPTER 13

Maggie opened her eyes to a sliver of morning light peeking through a crack in the window shade. A pain in her back shot up to her neck. The bed left something to be desired. She rolled her shoulders to work out the kinks and reached for her yellow print shirtwaist. Slipping it over her head, she planned out her morning.

She had to feed everyone a hearty breakfast and then tackle the problem of baking bread. No one had told her the night before what time the men expected to have their breakfast, but if they were anything like her family at home, they would eat early. She hurried to the kitchen.

The sun shone through the window, dust motes dancing in its rays. What a glorious start to the day. The bucket of well water was full to the brim, as was the reservoir on the stove. Someone had filled them for her already. Probably Romy.

Hurrying to the porch, she grabbed some corncobs and wood to start the fire. Without enough heat, breakfast would be a disaster. She laid the corncobs in the firebox with smaller pieces of wood stacked around them. Finally, she topped it off with the larger wood chunks. Lighting the match from the jar, she watched as the cobs ignited. Within seconds the fire took off. She replaced the lid on the stove.

After some searching, Maggie managed to find all the ingredients for flapjacks. She knew her family in Wisconsin loved the way she made them, so she hoped that would be the case this morning. A good first impression was important. She also found bacon in the pantry and sliced it nice and thin.

"Good morning, Miss Maggie." Mary entered the kitchen rubbing her eyes. "Do you need any help with breakfast after I run out to the privy?"

"Good morning, Mary. Are Sally and Janet still sleeping?"

"Sally will be here in a minute. She's getting dressed. Janet's still asleep. We let her sleep longer since she's so little."

"That's a good idea." Maggie added a bit more milk to the pancake batter to make it easier to stir. "Run along and then you can help me with the flapjacks."

Sally came into the kitchen as Mary ran out the door. "I'll be right back to help you with breakfast."

"Mary just headed out there also, so you don't have to hurry." Maggie got out a black skillet to cook the bacon. "When does your pa usually come in for breakfast?"

"They're almost always finished with chores by seven o'clock." Sally headed toward the door. "I'll fry the bacon for you when I get back."

Maggie only had a short time to finish everything then. Good thing the girls could help. In no time, all three were hard at work putting on the finishing touches for the early morning meal. Sally fried the bacon, the smell permeating the room. Mary set the table and showed Maggie where the syrup was stored. She flipped over the first pancakes just as Harry and Janet came into the kitchen.

Dressed in her nightgown, Janet stood next to her oldest brother. "Where's Pa?"

"He'll be in to eat soon." Maggie took the batch of hotcakes off of the griddle and slid them onto the plate in the warmer.

When Janet saw the golden disks slide onto the plate, her face crumpled. She started wailing like the spring flood. That instant, the porch door opened and the four men walked into the house. The screen door banged shut behind them.

"What happened to her?" Mr. Iverson's accusing eyes glared at Maggie.

Maggie put down the spatula and stooped to Janet's level. "I have no idea. She was fine a second ago." She put her arm around Janet. "What's the matter, sweetie?"

"Ma always made flapjacks for me. I want to see my ma."

Enveloping Janet in her arms, Maggie's heart ached for her.

"Oh, Janet, I didn't realize cooking them for breakfast would make you sad."

Janet pulled away and headed toward Harry. "I don't want to eat any unless Ma makes them. Hers always tasted so good."

Harry embraced her. "All of us miss Ma, Janet. Maybe eating one will help you remember her better."

Between sobs, Janet managed to nod. "Okay," she hiccupped, "I'll try one."

Relieved that the crisis had passed, Maggie finished getting the food on the table. Mr. Iverson hadn't said anything during the exchange, but Maggie noticed he blinked several times. *Lord, put Your healing hand on this family.* His chair scraped against the wood floor as he sat down.

When they were seated at the table and grace was said, the flapjacks and bacon disappeared before Maggie's eyes. She thought she had made enough to keep everyone happy while the next batch cooked. She couldn't have been more wrong.

Ted extended the plate to her. "Are there any more ready?"

Maggie handed him a full plate in return. "I just took these hot ones off the stove, but there are more on the griddle."

Janet faced the one pancake on her plate.

Placing a hand on the girl's back, Maggie stood behind her. "Did you taste it yet, Janet?"

"I need Romy to help me."

Romy leaned over and applied butter and syrup to her lone cake. The melting butter and syrup flowed in rivulets across her plate. He used her fork to cut it. "Okay, now you taste one bite."

Maggie was amazed he took the time to care for his little sister. She had known many young men who wouldn't pay attention to a five-year-old girl, much less cut up her pancake. He would be a good father someday.

Where did that thought come from? Maggie shook her head.

She watched as Janet put a piece in her mouth. A stray tear trickled down the girl's cheek. She shut her eyes as she chewed the pancake. Everyone waited for her response. "They taste like Ma's."

Her eyes grew as big as a pancake as she put the next bite in her mouth.

"You see, Miss Maggie is a good cook. God sent her here to make us flapjacks." Romy smiled at Maggie as the rest of the family chuckled in the background.

Ted soon held out an empty plate again. Maggie tried to keep up with the enormous appetites around the table. The pancakes weren't cooking fast enough to keep the plate full. She looked in the bowl to scoop out the next batch only to find the bottom looming up at her.

"Um . . . I'm getting near the end of the batter. I think I can only make four more." She looked up and saw five pairs of eyes peering at her. This wasn't good. The men didn't look a bit satisfied. "I can start another batch if you're still hungry."

"No, we don't have time to waste sittin' here waitin' for more food." Pa put down his fork with a clunk. "We'll have to last until dinnertime."

"I thought I made enough. I'm so sorry." Her hands shaking, Maggie could barely get the words out. "Next time I'll make more."

Her wonderful breakfast plan wasn't so wonderful after all.

Pa and three brothers left the kitchen. Harry stayed behind.

"I have to head out to work soon." He patted Maggie's arm. "Don't worry. They'll survive the morning. I'm full enough for sure."

Maggie smiled her thanks. "I'll get your lunch packed for you before you leave."

After Harry left for work and the breakfast dishes were finished, Maggie knew her real task of the day was staring her in the face. She needed to bake bread for this large family. She had done that at home under the tutelage of her mother many times, but never for this many people. She wanted to make sure everything was perfect, especially after the disappointing breakfast.

"It's time to bake bread, Sally. How many loaves did your mother make in a day?"

"I'm not sure, but I can show you where she kept the bread tins." Sally headed toward the north wall of the pantry. She showed Maggie the high shelf where the large bread bowl and pans were stored.

Maggie had to get the stepstool to reach the tins. She handed stack after stack of tins to Sally along with the heavy stoneware bread bowl. Counting the pans, she would be baking ten loaves. Would they eat this much every week? She would have to do some calculating to get the amount of ingredients correct for that much bread.

"Did all these bread pans fit in the oven at one time?"

"I think so." Sally picked up the loaf pans and placed them into the oven cavity. Only five would fit in at once.

"Maybe it's easier to make two separate batches." Maggie started gathering the ingredients.

"Here's where we store the flour." Mary walked over to the dark oak kitchen cabinet standing against the wall. It had two separate tin-lined bins that tilted out from the base holding a large amount of flour and sugar. When she opened the flour bin, a white puff of flour dust invaded the air.

"Thank you, Mary. I'll need more help in a couple minutes."

"What about me? How can I help?" Janet pulled on Maggie's apron.

Maggie wasn't sure how she would organize three girls and still get the bread baked. "While I get everything in the bowl, Janet and Mary can grease the pans."

Several hours later, Maggie finally placed the first five loaves into the oven. She hoped they would be baked in time for dinner. She glanced at her watch and saw she only had an hour before the men would be in for the noon meal. She would have to make a quick stew to go with the fresh bread.

"Sally and Mary, can you show me where the canned food is stored so I can see if there is any stew meat down there?"

The girls led her down the cellar steps to show her where the winter supply of food lined the shelves. Squinting in the darkness, Maggie was glad she had brought down the lamp from the table. The shelves were almost bare. Looks like she'd be busy filling them again during the summer months. She spotted several cans of stew meat. Avoiding spider webs, she reached for a quart jar.

"We can see if there are any more carrots and old potatoes still in the baskets." Sally stooped over a bushel basket full of sand. She dug her hands into the tan crystals and searched until she pulled out a large potato. Repeating the process, she plunged her hands in for more spuds. "The other basket was full of carrots. I'm not sure how many are still in there."

Mary copied Sally's motions to check that basket before Maggie turned to head up the stairs.

***

Romy followed his father onto the porch after washing up at the pump. The screen door slammed shut as magnificent scents coming from the kitchen assaulted his nostrils. His mouth begged to taste what his nose told him was waiting for dinner. Maggie must have managed to get the bread baked.

"That smells great!" Ted dried his hands and headed for the table.

Maggie glanced at them as she lifted the heavy pot off the stove. Romy eyed specks of flour on her nose. He had the urge to brush it off, but stopped his hand from doing something so foolish. He felt he should offer to help her with the kettle, but Jim stepped in and beat him to it.

The four men and three girls took their places while she filled the bowls with the steaming stew. Romy's brothers looked like they were more interested in the stacks of white bread in the basket than what was in their bowls.

"Please pass the bread." The chorus rang out from all corners of the table. The bread in the basket disappeared as suddenly as a box of doughnuts at a church picnic.

"Let's pray first," Pa said.

After the prayer, silence reigned around the table except for the clinking of spoons on the bowls. Maggie had probably worked hard this morning, but he was very glad for it. How could he tell her?

"Miss Maggie, this is sooo yummy." Janet voiced the opinion of everyone present as she rubbed her tummy. "Can I have another piece of bread?"

Several siblings echoed Janet's thoughts. "It sure is. Yes, very good meal."

Romy gained the courage to add his thoughts. "Thanks so much . . . for all your work this morning."

If only Maggie could read more into Romy's thanks since he wanted to say more, but couldn't find the words. How could he tell her the difference she'd made in the household already? Not only the fantastic food she'd prepared, but the peace that had settled around the dinner table. Could the rest of the family feel it?

His father nodded in approval.

Maggie concentrated on her bowl. "You're welcome. The girls were a big help to me getting this all finished."

Pa found his tongue, but didn't say what Romy expected. "We need to welcome our neighbors this afternoon. Romy, you and Miss Maggie can take a loaf of this bread to them and say howdy from all of us."

"But—"

While Ted and Jim winked at each other, Pa stopped Romy with an outstretched hand. Why him? He was the shy one.

"Ted and Jim can help me do what needs to be finished today. I want you to do the neighborly thing for me since I can't go myself."

That was the end of the discussion. Romy didn't have to bother wasting his breath anymore. He looked at Maggie out of the corner of his eye. "Can you be ready . . . by two thirty?"

Maggie looked at the rest of the loaves peeking over the edge of the pans on the stovetop. "It looks like the bread's all set to be baked, so it should be done by then. I'll put on a pot of beans to cook first, then I'll be ready to go."

A sigh escaped her lips as her shoulders slumped. She must be exhausted after all the work she did during the morning.

***

A couple hours later, Romy stepped into the house to see the remaining loaves of bread lined up like soldiers on a parade ground. A lone loaf, wrapped in a dishtowel, was separate from the rest. Probably the welcoming present for the new neighbors.

"Are . . . are you ready to go?" He called out to a seemingly empty house. Where was she?

He heard the squeak of the rocking chair in the living room and headed in that direction.

"I'm just sitting for a minute before we go." Wearing a navy skirt and blue blouse, Maggie closed her book and placed it on the floor. She stood as he walked toward her. The chair she had vacated continued to rock for a moment.

"Good book?" Romy smiled.

"Yeah. By Mark Twain. I just started reading it this morning." Maggie returned his smile. "Not too much time for reading these days."

She bent over and rubbed her back with her fingers. "I'm a bit stiff from standing on my feet all day."

The I'm-trying-to-look-peppy smile on her face never reached her eyes. Romy could see the exhaustion hidden in their depths.

"Their farm isn't too far down the road, so I thought we'd

walk." Amazing, he got the words out without stuttering. Maybe this was a turning point for him.

"I've got my shoes on, so I'm set." Maggie picked up the wrapped loaf as she passed the table.

They walked down the driveway in silence. His heart racing, Romy's mind came up blank. What could he talk about? Of course, his dry mouth didn't help things at all.

"The old Zimmerman place is the farm toward the left." At last he had found his voice again.

"Oh, that's not too far." Maggie straightened her shoulders and picked up the pace a bit. Then silence . . .

When they finally reached the door of the neighbor's house, Romy knocked. A good-looking young man with thick blond hair and blue eyes answered the door. Maggie's face brightened, as if the sun had come out from a cloud.

Romy's stomach dropped to his shoes. This wasn't good at all. Not only could he not find the words to say to her, but now this blond-haired blue-eyed chap would probably woo Maggie away from the family. Could things get any worse?

"I'm Maggie Ehlke and this is Romy Iverson. We wanted to welcome you to the neighborhood." Obviously, she had no problem warming up to this stranger.

"Well, thank you. It's nice to meet you." He stretched out his hand and shook Romy's. When he took Maggie's hand in both of his, he held on too long. "My name is Leon Winkler. I'm sorry my parents aren't home right now. They had to run to town for a few items. Come on in."

"That's fine, we just came over to introduce ourselves." Maggie's pink-tinged cheeks announced her interest in Leon without a word being spoken. She offered the bundle in her arm. As they entered the kitchen, she placed the wrapped bundle on the table. "Romy's father wasn't able to come himself, so he sent us over to give you this bread."

Leon picked up the loaf, unwrapping it. He raised it to his nose and inhaled slowly, a smile emerging on his clean-shaven face.

"Thank you so much. It smells fantastic. Ma hasn't had time to bake yet since we moved in three days ago. I'm sure we'll enjoy it." Grinning, he leaned up against the sink, never taking his eyes off Maggie.

"My pa owns the land across the road west of here." Standing with his hands in his back pockets, Romy joined in the conversation. He'd better not sit this one out since he could feel his blood pressure rising by the second. He didn't like the look Leon had on his face as he studied Maggie. The Cheshire-cat grin didn't impress Romy one bit.

Leon motioned for them to sit down. "We're trying to get used to farming. Pa inherited money from his father and wanted to start over somewhere else. We were at the auction a while back, and here we are." He gazed at Maggie as if she were a luscious strawberry.

"Yeah, we weren't surprised when Zimmermans had to sell off their farm." Romy glanced from Leon to Maggie. "Well, we're the closest farm to yours so come on over if you need help with something."

It was the neighborly thing to say, but he didn't know what Pa would think about the offer. Things were tough for everyone right now.

"I'll be sure to tell Pa about what you said. We may take you up on that." Leon responded to Romy's offer, but still didn't take his eyes off Maggie.

"Where did you live before?" It was as if Maggie wanted to lengthen the conversation as much as Romy wanted to end it. Now. And walk out the door.

"My pa used to be a teacher in La Crosse, Wisconsin, but lost his job last year. When he found out about the inheritance, we packed up and left."

"Oh, really. I'm from Wisconsin, too . . . or used to be. I grew up on a farm there, but had to move here in spring." Her eyes sparkling, Maggie laughed. "We have so much in common."

That was the last thing Romy wanted to hear.

CHAPTER 14

Maggie wrapped her arms around her midsection. The somer-saults being performed in there had to be tamed. What a dream come true. This handsome man, with a strong, distinctive nose and chiseled chin, lived next door. His piercing blue eyes bore into her.

"We'll have to compare notes sometime." Brushing his thick golden-blond waves off his high forehead, Leon winked at Maggie. His tanned face lit up when his lips tilted into a half-smile.

For a long time, she had prayed for a place she could call home. Maybe God had brought her to the farm in order to meet Leon, eventually marry him, and have a home to call her own. But she was being ridiculous and getting way ahead of herself.

"We need to get going now. It was nice meeting you." Romy rose and started for the door before they could say a polite farewell.

Maggie glanced at Romy. What was wrong with him? They weren't in a big hurry. If only she could stay longer, but Romy wasn't giving her that option.

She turned her attention back to her new neighbor. "I hope we can get to know each other better."

Was this too forward? Maggie bit into her lower lip.

Leon winked. "Oh, I'm sure we will."

Smiling, she followed Romy out the door. "See you soon."

Maggie waved as she stepped onto the porch. Scurrying

down the steps, she hurried to catch up with Romy. "Why did we have to leave so fast?"

The birds called their greetings to each other in the afternoon air, but Romy couldn't possibly have noticed. At the speed he was going, he wouldn't have seen a train coming straight at him.

"Pa needs me to help with the chores." He stormed ahead of her down the driveway and turned toward home, pumping his arms as if in a race.

"Well, you didn't have to be so abrupt with Leon and run out of his house." Why couldn't they have stayed and chatted with Leon longer? "I think you were impolite to act like that."

Sweat rolled down her back from the midday heat. Or was it the anger burning in her gut?

"I left because we did what we went there to do. We welcomed him and his family and offered to help if they needed something. Since we did what we were supposed to do, it was time to leave."

Her hand flying to her chest, Maggie stopped dead in the middle of the road. Had Romy just spoken to her in more than a clipped sentence? She would never have guessed he had so much to say to her in one breath.

But it happened when he was mad at her. Or, at least, it appeared that way. Why was he upset? Leon hadn't done or said anything to offend him.

Maggie scurried after him.

***

Romy glanced back at Maggie. He shouldn't have been so rude to her. She was trying to match his pace, so he shortened his steps to equal hers. But it didn't last. With his heart racing, his feet followed along. What was wrong with him?

Was it anger that drove him? What was he angry about? This stranger could talk to Maggie without difficulty, something Romy longed to do. Maggie almost threw herself at Leon. His blood boiled at the thought. They were both from Wisconsin. Perfect.

Leon seemed to be a guy who would do anything to get what he wanted. And from the way he looked at Maggie, Leon wanted her. Romy had known guys like him before. Did she have a clue how to handle them?

On the other hand, why should Romy care what happened to Maggie? The longer she lived with them, the more difference she could make, especially with his sisters. Beyond that, what did it matter to him?

Okay, he'd have to admit life would be better with her in the house. The fresh baked bread on the table was proof. The well-balanced meals were a huge improvement, but it was more. The thought of being in contact with her each day used to send shivers down his spine, but now after only a couple days, he could see how much she added to the family.

She not only helped the girls run the household, but also gave them the stability their lives needed since Ma's death. Janet had stopped crying all the time. Sally and Mary didn't seem so nervous anymore. Maggie managed to bring peace to his family. Her cheery smile brightened up their lives.

Was his fury caused by the fear of losing Maggie to someone else? Of course not. She didn't matter to him. It was just for the sake of his three sisters. If he kept repeating that, maybe it would be true.

The farther he walked, the calmer he became. Maggie was keeping pace with him now, but she puffed as she plodded along. He'd better take smaller steps.

"Thanks for going over there with me to welcome them." He tried to sound friendly, but probably failed since there was no responding comment.

As Romy headed up the driveway, he resolved to keep Leon away from Maggie, but only for the sake of the girls. He didn't want his sisters to suffer another loss.

***

The next morning, Maggie groaned when she pried her eyes open. She stretched and touched her feet to the floor, ignoring the dull ache in her legs. She wasn't used to being on her feet so much in one day.

She'd managed to survive the long day yesterday, but today she faced her first washday. If only she knew how the process worked in this household. The girls would have to answer lots of questions.

Maggie hurried into the kitchen to get started. A wave of heat pummeled her as she entered the room. Someone had made a roaring fire to heat the water. The large round wooden washing machine stared her in the face. Who had done half of her work for her?

"Good morning. The boys got the machine up from the basement for you." Romy checked a pot on the stove. "It's a good thing they carried pails of water up from the cistern last night. I started the fire so the water's almost hot."

"Uh . . . thank you for all this help." Maggie was stunned by what he had done and how much he had said.

"On washdays we always have oatmeal for breakfast to make things easier. We'll be in after chores." With that, he was out the door.

She froze in the middle of the floor with her mouth open. He had done all of this to make her laundry task easier. He remained a mystery to her—one day angry over nothing, and the next, very helpful. She sure appreciated the helpful side when Romy went out of his way to lighten her task.

Maggie stood with her arms crossed and her head tilted, eyeing the contraption she was supposed to use. She had never seen anything quite like it. When she was growing up, her mother had had a machine that ran with a two-cycle gasoline engine. On washdays, Pa would always have to hang around the house to help Ma kick-start the ancient machine, but this looked more antique yet.

Eleven-year-old Sally entered the room yawning. "What's for breakfast?"

"Romy said oatmeal is the usual for washdays, so I guess that's what we're eating." Maggie pointed at the appliance sitting in front of her. "How does this thing work?"

"The hot water gets dumped into this tub and then the soap. When the clothes are put in, someone pushes and pulls this lever for a looong time to wash the clothes." Sally was demonstrating the different parts as she talked. "Then you take this stick and lift out the clothes and put them through the rollers to wring them out. It's my job—turning the rollers. See, they come out here and fall into the rinse water. Then they have to go through rollers again after they're rinsed. Every washday Ma helps me rinse them before I turn the handle—" She stopped in midsentence.

Maggie put her arm around the girl and gave her a hug. "Oh, Sally, I know you miss your ma more than anything. You have those good memories to think of when you do." She clasped Sally's shoulders and searched her eyes. "Now you can be my right-hand man and teach me everything you know about doing this."

Smiling, she tried to get Sally to return her smile.

Mary entered the kitchen. "Oh no, it's washday!" The nine-year-old rubbed her arms. "My arms get so tired pushing and pulling the paddles."

Maggie groaned. This didn't help at all. What was she getting herself into? She knew this would be a long day.

During the next hour, Maggie scurried around getting the oatmeal ready for the men, at the same time preparing for the laundry process. She put the girls to work to make sure everything was ready. Even five-year-old Janet was given a task, setting the dishes on the table.

"Is the water boiling yet?" The door slammed after Romy burst through.

Maggie turned from the job of sorting the dirty laundry to see him open the lid on the pot. "Almost. As soon as we're finished eating, I can start the wash. By the way, thanks so much for getting the water boiling this morning. That was a big help."

Romy's head swiveled in her direction. "You're welcome. After we eat, I'll show you the ropes."

"Sally has been telling me all about it, so I'm sure we'll be fine." Maggie added another pair of socks to the whites pile. "You must have chores to do outside this morning. I'm used to washday at home, so I'm positive I can figure it out."

"If you say so . . ." Romy's lopsided grin told Maggie he didn't believe a word she said.

***

Maggie's head swiveled when she heard a knock on the door. Who would be here in the middle of the morning? Drying her hands on her soaked apron, she sauntered toward the porch.

What was Leon doing on the other side of the screen door? Was there a rock she could crawl under? Her damp hands reached for her frizzy hair. She must look a fright. Why did her hair always burst forth from its usual controlled bun on washdays? Her teeth came down hard on her lip.

"Hi, Maggie, sorry to disturb you in the middle of your busy day." Leon stood there looking dressed to perfection. The blue shirt he wore brought out the color of his eyes. His hair was combed back leaving a wave in the front begging for Maggie to run her fingers through. And here she was, Miss Frump Girl. Terrific!

"That's fine. I'm glad to take a break." She brushed her hair away from her face as best she could.

"We seem to have a problem. I have to take you up on the offer you gave us yesterday."

"Sure, I'll be glad to help in any way I can."

"We used all the chopped wood we brought. Now we need to chop some logs, but I can't find our axe. It must be buried on the trailer we haven't unloaded yet. Ma wanted to start cooking dinner and needed some firewood. Would it be possible to let us borrow an axe for the morning?"

How could a farmer misplace an axe when it was one of the tools of necessity? "I'd be glad to help you, but I don't know where the axe is kept. I just moved in myself recently."

"I didn't realize that. I guess we'll have to figure out something else, then." Leon turned to leave.

"Wait . . . I'll ask Sally and Mary if they know where to look. Come on in for a bit so I can ask them." She opened the door. Her rapid heartbeat pounded in her ears. They walked through the porch before stepping into the kitchen. "You'll have to excuse the messy kitchen. I'm in the middle of laundry."

Leon's smile calmed Maggie's nerves. "Don't worry about it. Looks like our house does lately. I'm used to it."

"Let's check with the girls."

During the next ten minutes, Sally and Mary looked from place to place for the axe. Maggie and Leon kept up a running conversation as they walked with them. Compared to Romy, this was so refreshing.

"There it is." Mary pointed to the axe resting against a stump in the shed. "Pa must have been planning to chop more wood."

Leon picked it up and slung it over his shoulder. "Nifty. Are you sure we can borrow it for the morning?" He put his hand lightly on Maggie's back to usher her out of the shed. The touch sent a current to her toes.

"I'll explain the situation to Romy when I see him. I'm sure no one will be chopping any wood the rest of the day."

***

Romy glanced toward the house as he walked between the

corncrib and barn. Clean white shirts were waving in the breeze from the clotheslines. He smiled. She actually figured it out. Maggie must have managed to do a couple loads of clothes. So much laundry had piled up from the month without Ma. He'd offered his help, but she'd turned him down cold. If she were going to be stubborn about it, he'd let her struggle by herself today.

The porch door opened as he approached the house. Maggie must have another load finished. Instead, he saw Leon emerge from the porch and wave before sauntering down the driveway with an axe over his shoulder. Romy covered the distance between himself and the house in the blink of an eye.

"What was he doing here?" He barked the question before he even spotted Maggie. His blood was near the boiling point just seeing Leon swagger down the driveway. The way he walked seemed to emit the attitude that he was better than the farmers who lived around here.

Maggie continued to feed the dark pants through the wringer as she glanced toward the door. She watched the large handle make its revolutions, squeezing the rinse water out of the clothes. "We're almost finished with this load, Sally."

She finally slanted a glance in Romy's direction. "I borrowed him the axe for the afternoon."

"What are you talking about? He lives on a farm. Can't he use his own axe?"

"They can't locate their axe right now since they just moved. Mary helped me find the wood axe, and I borrowed it to him."

Maggie's hair escaped the bun at the back of her head. Romy felt the urge to brush the tendrils of hair off her neck. Where did that thought come from? He dismissed it at once.

The pressure built up behind his eyeballs. He didn't have time for this on such a busy day. She wasn't making any sense. "You didn't *borrow* the axe since it was ours already. You mean you *loaned* him the axe."

"That's what I said." Maggie stood up with her hands on her hips, letting the pant leg drop back into the rinse water. "You sure are talkative today."

"I have the gift of gab." Romy crossed his arms over his chest with his chin jutting out. He wasn't going to let her get the last word.

Maggie tsked. "I was being sarcastic."

"No, you were being an annoyance."

"We always used the word *borrowed* like that at home."
Maggie started feeding the dangling pant leg into the wringer
again. "In German, *borrowed* and *loaned* are the same word. It's
how I grew up."

"Around here, the less German we hear the better. Pa was in
the Great War fighting against the Germans. He doesn't cotton
to anything German." Romy shook his head. "That's beside the
point. What else did Leon say?"

How come she got under his skin so easily?

Her smile threatening to outshine the sun, Maggie looked
like she was ready to strut around the yard. "He asked me to go
for a walk tonight."

"Swell. How in the world will you have energy to go for a
walk after washing all these clothes and cooking supper for us?"
How did Leon manage to make you glow with happiness when
he was almost a total stranger? But, of course, he couldn't ask
that question out loud.

"I guess you'll have to let me figure it out." Maggie stood up
as the last leg cleared the rollers and fell into the clothesbasket.
"It's time to hang out this load now, Sally. Then we'll have to
get dinner on the table."

Romy sensed he had been dismissed. He stormed out the
door, planning what he would say to her later.

***

"Is there room for these pants on the end? We're going to run
out of room on the clothesline if we aren't careful." Maggie
reached for the clothespin Sally was handing to her. "I'm glad
we have three loads finished already."

Her thoughts weren't on the clothes she was hanging up at
all. She was reliving the few moments she'd spent with Leon.
Maggie couldn't deny her attraction to Leon. Something just
clicked between them.

Jerking her thoughts back to the clothesline, she pinned
another shirt in place. What should she wear for their walk
tonight? Would she be finished with the supper dishes before he
showed up? Did he like her as much as she liked him? The questions tore through her mind as she put on the last clothespin.

"We'd better hurry to get dinner on the table." Maggie put
her arm around Sally's shoulder as they walked toward the house.

The afternoon flew by while Maggie finished up the laundry. With the help of Sally and Mary, she struggled to get the washing machine back down the stairs to the storage area in the basement.

She managed to wash her hands and face before supper to freshen up and be ready for the walk. Her best apron covered a blue-and-white-striped seersucker dress. She was all set.

Hurrying to get supper ready before the men walked into the kitchen, she managed to clean up the mess just in time. The stew she had started earlier in the day was simmering on the stove as the brothers came in the door.

When supper was on the table, no one complained about anything. What a relief. Maggie had cut corners on the meal during her busy afternoon. Her fresh bread from yesterday helped to keep the hungry men happy.

She glanced out the window for the umpteenth time while she washed the stew pot. Leon couldn't come yet. She had to put the finishing touches on the kitchen first. She didn't want to be caught with wet hands again when he walked up to the back porch. Was it silly to get this nervous for a walk down a country road?

CHAPTER 15

Romy slammed the milk pail onto the concrete floor of the barn, spilling some of the white foamy contents. The straw surrounding the pail absorbed the escaping drops.

"Whoa, brother, what's eating you?" Ted continued sweeping the lime on the walkways behind the cows, the dust crawling its way up Romy's nose.

"Nothing's wrong. I just don't understand females." Romy picked up the last empty pail, so he could finish milking the remaining cow.

Ted leaned on the broom. "Of course you don't understand women. You never talk to any of them. At the moment, which dame are you referring to?"

"The one in the house all gussied up for a walk with our new neighbor. How can she be interested in a guy she only met yesterday?" Romy pulled the milking stool into position by the Hereford. The cow bellowed as if it were impatient.

"How do you know Miss Maggie is stuck on him? She doesn't even know him."

"Did you see the way she was all dolled up in the blue-and-white dress at supper? After washing all day, she should have looked dead tired, but instead she looked so pretty." Romy plunked himself down with a thud. "You can't tell me you didn't notice it."

"I didn't try to notice, but I know what you're talking about. She really looked spiffed up."

The milk pinged in the empty bucket as Romy squeezed the teats. "How can I compete with him?"

"Well, telling her you noticed how swell she looks might be a way to start."

"I know, I know. I'm trying to talk to her more, but sometimes the words don't come out right." Romy leaned his head against the cow's flank.

"You should go in there now and tell her what you're thinking. It may be the best way to start." Ted leaned his broom against the barn wall. "I'll even finish milking Bess for you, so you don't lose your nerve."

"How can I explain why I'm in the house in the middle of chores?" Romy rubbed the back of his neck.

"Take the milk pail in and fill up the pitcher in the icebox as an excuse." Ted nudged Romy toward the door as an encouragement. "You know, she's done so much good for Sally and Mary since she moved in, and it's only been a few days. We need to be nice to her so she stays with us."

"You aren't kidding." But that's not why Romy wanted her to stay. She brought sunshine back into the house. He headed out the barn door. "I'll be back in a jiff."

Romy needed time to think. Why was Leon chatting with Maggie this morning? Why did he ask her for an axe instead of seeking out the men? He had no right.

Now wait a minute. Was this reaction based on anger? Or was it jealousy? He'd better figure it out soon.

At the very least, Romy had to protect her because she lived under his roof. He didn't want other men intruding in her life when this family needed her. It sounded good, anyway.

He took a deep breath. How could he tell her how nice she looked without sounding sappy?

His hand gripping the handle of the screen door, Romy saw Maggie bending over the table giving it a good washing. *Now or never.* At the squeak of the door hinges, she paused and glanced up. When she spotted him, her shoulders sagged and her hand continued its course along the edge of the table. Maggie didn't appear too thrilled to see him.

He blinked. "I'm checking to see if we need more milk in the icebox."

Did he look as sheepish as he sounded?

"I'm not sure. Sally put the pitcher away after supper." Maggie all but ignored him, her actions screaming an I-don't-care attitude. The scent of her lilac perfume invading his nose, she leaned over to wash the far side of the table, causing her skirt to hitch up higher.

Romy swallowed and proceeded on his mission. He opened the icebox before continuing. "You look like you're all ready for your walk. Where are you headed?"

That didn't come out right.

"I'm not sure. He only told me he wanted to go on a walk this evening." She turned her back and marched toward the sink.

"I didn't mean it like that." After filling the milk pitcher to the brim, he studied his hands. "I, um . . . I wanted to tell you . . . you look nice tonight."

Squeezing the dishcloth, her hands halted as her head turned in his direction. Romy watched to see how she would react.

At the sound of a knock, their heads swiveled toward the back door.

***

Maggie lowered her eyes, rubbing her forehead. Leon stood on the other side of the screen door. If Romy hadn't come in, she'd have been finished with her tasks and watching for Leon to come up the driveway. Bad timing.

She threw a glance in Romy's direction. His eyes bore into her. How could she respond to his comment when Leon was waiting? "Thank you. I have to get the door."

She grabbed a towel to dry her hands and sauntered into the porch. Why would Romy be in here complimenting her when he knew Leon was coming? Why would he be complimenting her when he was so angry this afternoon about the upcoming walk? He didn't even like her, did he?

Too many questions flew through her head. She couldn't begin to understand Romy, and she certainly didn't have time to figure him out now. Her teeth bit down on her lower lip.

And . . . her hands were wet once again when Leon was here. She swung the door open. "I'm sorry I'm not quite finished cleaning up from supper. Please come in."

"That's fine. You didn't know when to expect me." Leon followed her through the porch into the kitchen.

He stopped dead in his tracks when he noticed Romy next to

130

the icebox. "Hi, Romy."

"Hello, Leon." Romy's face matched the cherry-colored sunset. "I . . . I was just leaving."

"I wanted to thank you for letting me borrow your axe today."

"You're welcome. That's what neighbors are for."

"I leaned it against the outside wall." Leon stepped forward to shake his hand. "We finally found ours in the bottom of the last crate we unloaded. I can't imagine how it got so buried when we packed."

"I'm glad you found it." As he shook Leon's hand, he looked from Maggie to Leon and back to Maggie again without smiling. "I have to get back to the barn."

Romy didn't sound too neighborly. He scooted past Leon and headed out the door. Was he upset with her again?

After Maggie hung up the towel, she took off her apron. She brushed her hand over her hair to make sure it was still in place. "I'm ready to go now."

Winking, Leon scanned her from head to toe. His eyes sparkled as his lips tilted in a half-smile. "You look nice tonight."

Those were the same words Romy had said to her a minute ago. Whose were more sincere?

"Thank you. Shall we go?"

Leon opened the door and motioned for her to precede him. "I guess this isn't a very romantic place to walk with you."

He put his arm around her waist as the door shut behind them.

Smiling, she stepped away from him. "But we have a beautiful sunset to enjoy."

Starting down the steps, Maggie headed toward the driveway. The multicolored sky put on a wondrous performance for them. Crickets filled the evening with their harmonic melodies as the last of the birds bid each other a good night. She breathed in the fresh country air and let out a sigh.

"I agree with you there." Leon's steps matched Maggie's. "You never explained to me this morning why you've only been here a couple days yourself."

"I don't know if you've heard Mrs. Iverson passed away last month. It was a terrible shock. You haven't met the whole family, but Romy has six siblings. As you saw this morning, the three youngest are girls who could not take care of everything there was to do in the house. Last week, Mr. Iverson decided they needed someone to live here with them to do the house-work and take care of the younger ones."

"I didn't know. How terrible for them." When they reached the road, they turned toward the sunset. "But it doesn't explain why you ended up here in Iowa."

"There's another long story." Maggie glanced at Leon as she walked. His arm brushed against hers from time to time. She didn't mind.

"Since we have a long road ahead of us, I think we have time to hear the story." His wide toothy grin caused grasshoppers to riot in her belly.

"Up until Sunday, I was living at my sister's house in Dubuque. I moved in with her at the end of March because she had twins."

"Oh, that must have been when your parents sent you here from Wisconsin, since you said you grew up there."

"You're right. With my large family, someone had to leave. Not enough money." How had Leon remembered those details about her? She'd told him so quickly yesterday. She tried to thank him with her smile.

"Then why aren't you still in Dubuque? Those twins aren't very old yet."

"No, they aren't. And they're so cute now." A tear trickled down her cheek. "My brother-in-law and sister couldn't afford to feed . . ."

Her throat shut down. She couldn't even finish the sentence. Why did no one want her? It was all so unjust. She missed the children so much.

Leon stepped in front of her and wiped the stray tear away with his thumb. "I can't imagine how hard it was on you. Being sent away from your home twice in a four-month span."

He understood. He was the first person to know her pain. He reached for her hand and sheltered it in his. Maggie felt his strength flow into her. Her heart threatened to float away. She nodded because no words would come.

He released her hand, and they started walking again. "Did your brother-in-law lose his job since they couldn't afford you any longer?"

"No, no." Maggie shook her head. "He's a pastor. With his small salary, they depend so much on donated food from their members. I guess the members weren't giving like they used to. The church couldn't afford his salary last month. They don't even have enough food for themselves anymore."

She looked to her right and noticed Leon wasn't with her. She paused, spinning around to see him standing in the road looking like a cloud had descended on his head. "What's the matter?"

He shook his head and started walking toward her. The smile he gave her didn't reach his eyes this time. "Uh . . . Nothing. We better turn around and head back now."

What had changed?

Maggie nodded, noticing the approaching twilight.

"Anyway, you moved here recently, then?" Whatever had caused the cloud seemed to have dissipated.

"Yeah. They brought me here after church on Sunday." When Maggie glanced sideways, she noted the cloud had reappeared. Not wanting to spoil the moment, Maggie ignored it and smiled at Leon. "We're really in the same boat."

"Well, you grew up on a farm, at least, so you know a lot more than I do." He draped his arm around her shoulder. "Since we are both new, you'll have to agree with my idea. Friday evening after chores are done, we'll need a night of relaxation."

His arm felt uncomfortable. Should she let him do this? She enjoyed talking to him, but she didn't know him well enough for more. She stepped sideways. "What do you mean?"

"I'm sure we can find a dance to go to on Friday evening. There should be one somewhere in town."

"A dance?" Now Maggie stopped dead. "Mrs. Iverson died last month. We can't go dancing."

Leon turned and walked the few steps back. "Now, wait a minute. She wasn't your relative, Maggie. I'm not asking her family to go. I'm asking you."

"Oh, but . . ." She started walking again. "I can't do that so soon with you."

He snatched one of her hands as they walked. "What about a movie then? You'll be dead tired from a week of hard work and will need some time off."

His eyes persuaded her to say yes.

Leon glanced in her direction. "You may have to ask one of the boys where we could go, is all, since I don't know where the theater is. I'm new to the area . . . and so are you."

"I'll see if I can find out." By this time they were back at her driveway. Maggie paused. "You don't have to walk up to the house with me. I'm sure I'll be safe out here."

Did her smile show him her thanks?

"Okay. I'll say good night then and head home." Leon waved as he headed down the road. "I'll talk to you later about the movie Friday night."

Maggie hummed to herself as she ambled up the driveway. The evening air was feeling a bit cool, although she still felt the warmth of Leon's hand in hers. Even after her hard day, she wasn't a bit weary any longer.

A thought deep down asked about the cloud on Leon's face when she mentioned her brother-in-law's occupation and church on Sunday, but she pushed the thought away.

No other guy had understood her like Leon had. She'd led a sheltered life, helping Ma with Frank for so many years. The opportunity to mix with boys had passed her by. If only she weren't uncomfortable when he tried to put his arm around her. This was something new. Next time she would not step away like she did tonight. If there was a next time.

"What are you doing out here all alone when it's so dark?" Romy marched toward her. "Did he leave you to walk home by yourself?"

Romy did a superb job of getting his thoughts out when he was upset with her. Maybe she had to get him upset more often. She covered her mouth with her hand to stop the giggle that threatened to erupt. But of course, he couldn't see her expression in the shadows anyway.

"I told him he didn't have to walk me up to the house. It's perfectly safe out here." She ambled toward the retaining wall.

He spun around and kept pace with her. "Of course it's safe out here. That doesn't change a thing. Doesn't he know it's polite manners to walk a lady home?"

Oh, now Romy thought she was a lady. "Don't be so hard on him. I'm the one who said it was okay."

"Well, it's not okay with me."

"Why are you so angry?" Maggie glanced at him. She couldn't figure him out. A while ago he was complimenting her. Now he was rude.

He shook his head. "I'm not angry. I was concerned about you when you were gone so long. You must be exhausted after working so hard on the laundry all day. Plus, you'll have another long day tomorrow."

"I can take care of myself without you telling me what to do, Romy." With hands on her hips, Maggie didn't want to admit her legs and back were aching. She hadn't noticed until he mentioned it. She had to agree it had been a long day.

They climbed the few steps and headed toward the porch. Romy rubbed the back of his neck. "I'm sorry if I upset you. That's not why I came out here."

His swift change in attitude mystified her. Two minutes ago he was ranting—true, he was ranting against Leon, but he had been ranting—and now he was apologizing to her. She didn't know how to respond to this side of Romy. She gnawed on her lower lip.

He let out a sigh. "I thought I could lend a hand out in the garden tomorrow after breakfast."

He opened the door and motioned for Maggie to enter first.

"That would be helpful. I've been so busy the last couple days with baking and laundry, I haven't even thought about the garden."

She didn't know if she wanted to be so close to Romy for so long, but the garden was a large area. They could work there without interacting too much.

Maggie headed to her bedroom. "I'll say goodnight then."

***

"See you tomorrow." Romy turned to go outside. He couldn't stay in the house while she was still up and about.

He wanted to kick himself. Why did he go storming down the driveway to question her? It wasn't her fault his new neighbor left her to walk home in the dark alone. Even if the farm was in the middle of nowhere, it was unconscionable for Leon to let her walk alone. He replayed the conversation in his mind. Had Maggie really told Leon she could walk home alone? Did that get him off the hook for abandoning her? After all, they'd lived through the Roaring Twenties. Things were changing. Did that make a difference?

Maybe Romy was making this into a larger issue than necessary. Maybe he didn't want Maggie to be around Leon at all. Wasn't it ironic? For months he couldn't get his mouth to say anything to Maggie, and now he managed to talk to her, but it came out all wrong. All he wanted was to be her friend, at least for now. *Lord, help me to know Your will in all this and to say the right thing when Maggie's around.*

He would start again tomorrow and see if he could get on the right path next time.

CHAPTER 16

"I can't believe the size of this garden. Harry told me on Sunday that your aunts planted it after the funeral." Maggie covered her mouth with her fingers. Why couldn't the earth open up and swallow her on the spot? Her cheeks must be broadcasting her embarrassment. "I'm so sorry."

The birds in the trees twittered, filling up the awkward silence.

She looked across the space to see Romy's head bowed in the morning sunshine. Seconds passed. At last, he looked up. "It's okay. It seems no one wants to talk about what happened around here. Ma will never be forgotten, but we have to move on."

"Of course she'll never be forgotten. There are seven of you to carry her memories forward." Maggie's throat tightened when she noticed his eyes glistening with unshed tears.

"Did you know she died working out here? We were trying to get the ground ready for planting." He brushed a hand across face, but he couldn't hide the escaping tears.

If only she could take away his pain. How could he work out here now, only a month later? "I didn't know . . . you don't have to help me."

"No, no. I need to do this." Looking around, he grabbed a foot-tall weed and yanked. "I have to go on with my life. We've let this mess go too long. It will be hard to get the weeds out now."

Maggie couldn't argue with him there. Purple flowers burst forth from the thistles growing next to the sweet corn. The weeds overshadowed the vegetables in the garden.

She cleared her throat. "While we're talking about your ma, Mary and Sally brought up the subject on Sunday after I got here."

She'd like to spare him the pain, but she had to tell him. She leaned on the hoe.

Romy jerked to attention. "What do you mean?"

"Mary thought her heart was broken when she died. And as a result, she didn't love them anymore."

"Wha—"

She held up her hands to stop him. "She heard about the heart attack and came to the wrong conclusion. I assured them their ma loved them very much, but God took her before she could tell them."

She blinked to dismiss the unwelcome tears.

"I had no idea." He took off his hat and raked a hand through his hair. "Thanks so much for talking to them. I'm glad you're here to help them with their grief."

She had to continue. "I'm sorry to say, it sounds like your father isn't being very helpful for the girls. It's not good if she's never spoken about at all."

The cicadas serenaded them as the sun beat down on their backs. She longed for a breeze to stir the air.

He nodded as he returned to his task. "He's having a really hard time coping with all of this. Sometimes I feel like I'm the parent around here."

Her eyes widening, Maggie's hoe stopped short in midair. Romy had opened up to her? Had he made it over his self-imposed hurdle? If he could tell her what he was thinking, it would be easier to be around him every day.

In only three days, he had transformed from a shy turtle to a protective sheepdog. She approved of the new man much more than of the shy boy. If he'd been this way when she'd first met him in March, things would be different between them now.

She glanced sideways to see him wielding the hoe among the potatoes. The muscles in his arms bulged with each stroke. Her face burned. She had to stop thinking of him like that. After all, she had to think about Leon now. She turned back to the green adversaries and lost herself in her work.

He pulled on his hoe, fighting the growing foes. "I'll talk to the girls soon."

Maggie worked close to the peas. She nodded. Romy seemed to understand how important it was to help the girls over their pain. His compassion for his three sisters was evident. It's good someone took the time to care about what they thought.

Maggie breathed easier again.

***

Romy continued to hack away at the invading opponents in the garden. The disorder wouldn't be cleaned out in a morning, but they were making progress. This mess had been growing over a month. He removed his hat to wipe the sweat from his forehead.

"I'm going in to find the girls. They can help us out here."

He glanced at Maggie, who looked exhausted. The curly tendrils framing her face were damp. If only he could reach out and smooth them away for her. He had to stop thinking of her like that. "Do you want some water?"

Her half-smile broadcast the weariness she carried. "That would be wonderful."

"Why don't you rest until I bring the kids back?"

"I'm okay." She continued bending over the beans.

A moment later he hurried back with two glasses. "Here's some nice cold water."

"Thanks."

He handed the glass to Maggie. "The girls will be here in a bit to help."

Maggie downed it in gulps. "Thanks so much. That helped."

He watched a drip run down from the corner of her mouth. He squelched the urge to wipe it away with his finger. He'd better work harder so thoughts of her wouldn't pop into his head. She dried her mouth with the back of her hand.

"It's going to be a hot one today." Swallowing, Romy slashed at the weeds among the potatoes. "By the way, I have to help Pa cut the hay in the back forty this afternoon. I can't help too much longer."

"That's fine. I'll probably quit soon, also. I'll try to get more done after supper when it's cooler."

By then Mary, Janet, and Sally had arrived to help. Romy pointed toward the sweet corn. "You girls can weed the corn. Maggie and I have been working for a while already, so we'll only be working a few minutes. Let's see how much you can finish by then."

"Do I have to work, too?" Janet looked up at Romy.

"It won't hurt you to help us out for a bit. How about if you pick out the weeds from one row of corn? Then you can go play with Blackie." Romy turned back to the potatoes.

The five worked in different areas of the garden, rescuing the vegetables. The blackbirds in the willow trees called back and forth to each other while flies buzzed around Romy's head. A peace descended on him that he hadn't felt for the last month.

Maggie broke the silence. "Since you're going to cut hay this afternoon, what's the process here? I'm used to haying back home, but need to know what I'll be expected to do."

Romy smiled. She had no idea what she was asking. There was no way she could help get the hay in the barn. "The men can manage the work outside. There will be extra hands to feed for dinner and possibly for supper on Friday. Your task will be to get food ready to feed everybody."

"How many?"

"Usually we try to get about four or five neighbors to come. Then, when the hay is ready at their places, we go over there to help." Romy leaned on his hoe. He might as well give up any pretense of weeding.

"Oh, my. I don't think there will be enough flour to make pies for everyone. I'll probably need other things, also."

"No problem. Tomorrow morning right after breakfast, I have to run into town to the feed mill. I can take you along, and you can get what you need at the store."

As soon as Romy made the offer, he wanted to swallow his words. Maggie would be with him the entire twenty minutes alone in the truck. And back again. He would have to carry on a conversation about . . . What would he talk about? A lit box of firecrackers exploded in his stomach. Now wait a minute. He had just talked to her for a long time. He could do it again in the morning. He knew he could. He hoped he could.

Maggie looked down at her shoes. Maybe she was thinking the same thing he was. "Um . . . will it take a while at the feed mill?"

"It usually takes an hour." Romy's mind raced to formulate some kind of plan.

"Maybe there would be a bit of time for me to visit with Emma and the children." Maggie looked over at Janet amidst the corn. "Could Janet come with us and play with Lucy?"

The air rushed out of his lungs with relief at the suggestion. "That's a swell idea. We'll work it out somehow."

Sally came up and stood next to Romy. "While you two were talking so much, we worked hard and got the corn all done." She crossed her arms. Mary joined Sally and nodded her head.

Janet bounced up and down. "See my row." She pointed her chubby arm toward the corn.

"Good for you." He hugged each one in turn. "We'll quit for today since you worked so hard. Why don't you all go play with Blackie for a while until dinner time." He paused with his arm around Janet. "Be careful in the barn."

"Yeah, I know." Janet grabbed Romy's hand. "Ma tells us the same thing all the time."

She stopped short, as the color drained out of her face.

Romy's heart went out to her. He squeezed her hand. Ma's passing somehow slipped into every conversation. "You run and find Blackie now. I left an old bone of his on the corner shelf in the milk house. I bet Blackie would love to chew on it."

When would this heavy load be lifted?

***

Maggie stretched as she lay in bed on Thursday morning. She didn't have the luxury to lie around, but it sure wouldn't hurt to relax one more minute. This would be her first trip back to see Emma. It had only been four days since she had seen the twins, but she smiled in anticipation. Thank goodness Janet would go along to help bridge the gap between her and Romy, although the bridge might not be needed anymore. On Sunday, Romy barely spoke a word on the trip from town, but yesterday they'd talked ten minutes nonstop.

Maggie had to admit Neil and Emma had been correct back in March. They said Romy was a nice guy when you got to know him. She hadn't believed it at the time, but she'd underestimated him. He showed her his big heart this week and, without a doubt, he had empathy for his sisters. He knew what to say to them to make them feel special. She could see it on their faces. He would make a good father. When he found the right woman, of course.

She jumped out of bed and threw on her blue-and-white seersucker dress for her trip to town. She brushed her hair and decided to leave it in its naturally curly state instead of pulling it into a bun. After four days of hard work, she wanted to relax a little.

She hurried out to the kitchen to get breakfast started and almost ran into Romy as he came barreling down the steps in his barn clothes. She sidestepped to avoid him. "Good morning."

"Yes, good morning to you. We'll have to leave for the feed mill right after breakfast. How soon can you be ready?"

"I'm planning on making scrambled eggs and some of the sliced ham from the cellar to keep it simple." Maggie headed toward the cabinet to retrieve the black skillet. "Did you let Janet know she's coming along?"

"No, I haven't seen her yet this morning. I didn't want to tell her last night. She'd have been too excited to sleep." He made his way toward the door.

"I'll let her sleep a bit more and wake her up to tell her then." Maggie put her hand on Romy's arm to stop him. "Before you go . . . Um . . . Who will tell Mary and Sally? They aren't coming with us. I don't want them to feel left out."

She didn't want to break the news to them since she wasn't part of the family. "Do you want to ask your Pa while you're doing chores?"

Romy shrugged his shoulders. "Pa doesn't seem to care about little things around here lately." He put his hand on the doorknob. "I'll think about it."

Then he was gone.

Maggie scurried around the kitchen for the next hour slicing the ham, getting the coffee brewing on the stove, and retrieving the eggs out of the cool cellar. She came up the steps with only eight eggs left from yesterday.

Mary trotted down the stairs at the same time, almost bumping into Maggie as she opened the basement door.

"Good morning, Mary. I don't have enough eggs for breakfast this morning. Could you run out to the chicken coop and find a dozen more?" She reached for the basket and handed it to the girl, giving her a hug at the same time.

"Sure, Miss Maggie. I'll be back in a while." She let the door slam after her. Maggie smiled at the bang. The young girl was always so helpful. If only Romy could find a way to make it right with the two sisters since they couldn't go to town.

By the time Mary came in with the eggs, the table was set and everything else finished.

"Thanks so much." Maggie smiled at her. "Sally helped me get the rest ready. Maybe both of you can crack the eggs into this large bowl so we can get them started before the men come in."

She turned the ham in the skillet as the heat from the stove radiated throughout the kitchen.

"I helped, too." Janet added her comment to the mix.

Maggie put an arm around her shoulder. "That's true, but now you need to finish getting ready to leave." She glanced at the other two girls before whispering to Janet. "Remember I told you we were going to town to see Lucy this morning?"

"I'll hurry." She scampered off, nodding.

The door burst open as the four men entered the kitchen. The curtains on the windows fluttered with the burst of fresh air. The crowded kitchen suddenly felt much smaller with the addition of the men.

Maggie flitted between the stove and the bowl of broken eggs. "We ran out of eggs, so Mary had to go find more. That's why it's not ready yet." She chewed on her lower lip as she poured the yellow stream into the waiting black pan.

"Don't worry. I'm sure it won't take long to scramble the eggs." Romy looked at Mary and Sally. "Then Pa will have time to talk to the girls."

Mr. Iverson sat in his chair. "I'll need you two to stay here with me this morning to help me search for some honey while the boys are sweeping the hayloft. I found a hollow tree in the woods. Might have a bee hive." He put his arms around the two older girls. "You'll have to help me check it out and find how much is in there. We'll bring it home if we can."

The girls' eyes grew to the size of dinner plates. "What fun! An adventure!" Sally clasped her hands together in front of her.

"I guess it's quite an adventure." Maggie stirred the eggs to hurry them along.

Finally, their father was going to spend time with the girls. The joy on Mary's beaming face shouted her happiness. It appeared like this hadn't happened for the last month.

Maggie looked at Romy. "They won't get stung, will they?"

"No, they'll be fine if they go with Pa." He winked at her.

Maggie concentrated on the frying pan as the heat from her cheeks flowed down her neck. Was he flirting with her?

When the eggs finished cooking, Maggie scooped them into a bowl.

What was that wink all about?

This couldn't be happening right now. What about Leon? Two days ago, she'd walked out with Leon.

She didn't want Romy to spoil her time with the new neighbor. She and Romy had only been working together in the garden yesterday. That's all. She wanted to focus on Leon now, not Romy.

CHAPTER 17

As Romy scooped a forkful of eggs into his mouth, his mind recalled the amazing conversation with Pa before they entered the house. He'd been struggling since yesterday to find the best time to approach him. Finally summoning the courage to talk to him, Romy had said what was on his mind. "Pa, can I talk to you for a minute?"

"Sure, sure, go ahead. What's on your mind?" His father had stopped and turned toward him. The sun's rays peeked through the trees over his shoulder.

Romy had fidgeted with his hat. "Miss Maggie told me something yesterday I thought you should know."

Pa had tilted his head and waited.

Taking a breath, Romy had had to say it out loud even if it might hurt Pa's feelings. "When she moved in, Mary and Sally told her something about Ma's death. They thought Ma didn't love them anymore."

Pa's mouth had fallen open as his head jerked back. "However did they get such an idea?"

The words had come out in a mere whisper. Even the birds managed to sing louder.

"They must have heard someone say something about her heart attack. Maggie told me they thought Ma's heart was broken. In their minds, then, she couldn't love them." Romy had swiped away his unbidden tears.

Pa hadn't even bothered drying the tears streaming down

his cheeks. "They . . . they thought that?"

"Yeah. For over a month, no one took the time to find out what they were thinking. That's the hard part." Romy had swallowed past the lump in his throat. "I figured you'd want to know."

With his head bowed, Pa's shoulders had shaken as he wept without a sound. "How could I? I've been so wrapped up missin' your ma, I haven't seen what my girls are goin' through."

Pa crying? How should he react? He had put his arm around him. "Aw, Pa, it's been so hard on everyone. We need to be there for each other all the time."

Pa had stood still and stared into the trees by the garden. "I haven't been there for Mary and Sally, have I?" His eyes had bored into Romy, piercing him to his core. "What about Janet? She's even younger than the other girls?"

"Maggie didn't mention too much about Janet. She seems to be okay."

Pa had put his hand on Romy's shoulder.

"I'm so sorry for the way I've been actin'. I've been locked in my own world and so distant from all of you without realizin'. It must have been so hard on you and Harry to carry this family for so long. I'm sorry." He shook his head, but continued. "I miss Ma more than I can say. I miss her more than my life. However, I know I will have to go on with my life for the sake of the family."

Romy had exhaled and allowed his shoulders to slump in relief. Maybe Pa would be able to face life again and resume his role as the head of the family. "I know you wish Ma were still with us, but we've all got to go on. Pa, we all need you to be with us, not only the girls."

That was an understatement. Maybe they'd hit the bottom and could climb up to level ground now.

Pa had taken a deep breath. "I'm glad you told me about this. How do I make it up to them?" He had wiped his hand over his face. "How do I get to know them again?"

"How about spending some time with them? In fact, I'm going to the feed mill this morning. Miss Maggie is coming along to buy food for dinner tomorrow." Romy had headed toward the pump to wash for breakfast. He had pumped the handle several times until a stream poured out. "We'll take Janet with us to visit with Pastor's children. It would be great if you can find something to do with the two girls."

Pa had reached into the water coming from the spigot and scrubbed his hands. "Yeah. It would be a good time to be alone with them." He had looked at his son. "Now I'll have to think fast to figure out what to do."

"Well, you have about thirty seconds to come up with something before we get in the house." Romy had breathed in the fresh morning air. The birds had sung a merry tune to match his mood.

"Yup." Pa's smile had rivaled the streams of sunlight piercing through the trees. Ma must be looking down on them from heaven.

Romy drank another swig of milk. Pa's idea of hunting for honey was a doozy. That was really fast thinking. The girls would love it.

But why had he winked at Maggie?

He hadn't been flirting with her in the least. The color in her cheeks told him she thought otherwise. His heart had still been pounding after his conversation with Pa minutes before. The wink had happened without thinking. How could he make sure Maggie knew?

He scraped the last bit of eggs together on his plate. Was Maggie upset by his wink? He'd have time to find out on the way to town.

***

Maggie helped Janet climb out of the truck in front of Emma's house. The ride to town hadn't been the awkward silence she had experienced before with Romy. Janet had kept the conversation flowing from one topic to another. The youngster skipped up the sidewalk to the porch steps.

Maggie turned around to wave as Romy drove off. They'd decided Maggie could visit with Emma while he unloaded the corn at the feed mill. Then he'd come back to take her shopping, leaving Janet at the parsonage until they were ready to head back to the farm. She'd enjoy the time to visit with Emma and see the babies. She would skip up the sidewalk herself if she could. Instead she forced her feet to walk sedately up the steps to the front door.

"Let's both knock on the door so they hear us." Janet's little-girl smile beamed up at Maggie.

Maggie hoped the ensuing barrage of banging didn't wake the twins. She hadn't intended to be so loud. She put her hand on Janet's shoulder. "I think we can stop now and wait to see if they heard us."

After only an instant, the door burst open. "Who's pounding . . . ?" Cissy's eyes widened. "Well, hello to both of you. I never expected to see you here today when I came over to play with Lucy and Denny. They'll be so excited to see you, Janet. Ya know what I mean?"

Cissy's presence at the door surprised Maggie. This day got better all the time. She'd have a visit with her friend now, also.

"Is something wrong since you're here today?" Maggie could hear crying upstairs. "Are the babies sick?"

"No, no. I've been dropping by around this time every morning to give Mrs. Hannemann a hand. She's missed you something fierce." Cissy opened the door wider. "Come on in. Janet, run upstairs to surprise Lucy."

Janet took off, scurrying up the stairs. "Lucy! Surprise! I'm here."

"We won't have to worry about them the rest of the morning. Lucy was just moping around before, saying she didn't know what to do with herself. Now they can go play outside. Ya know what I mean?" Cissy turned toward Maggie. "How are you doing out on the farm?"

"I'll tell you all about it, but it sounds like Emma may need some help upstairs first. Let's go see those babies, and I can tell you both at the same time." Maggie headed up the steps, followed by Cissy.

As the rhythmic squeaking of the rocking chair soothed Timmy, Maggie described her busy life to Emma and Cissy. She stroked his head while she rocked him. For the first time in days, Maggie shed her anxiety as a tree sheds leaves.

"Now wait a minute." Cissy interrupted Maggie midsentence. "You didn't tell us the best part. Harry told me you went out walking with a new neighbor a couple days ago. What's with that?"

Maggie touched her throat where heat climbed under her collar. "Oh, it was nothing much."

"Level with us. What is this all about?" Emma burped Tina on her shoulder. "If my sister is out walking, I need some information."

"Oh, for pity's sake. A new family moved in next door to the Iversons. Mr. Iverson told Romy and me to take a loaf of bread over to his house as a sort of welcoming gift. I met him then, and went for a walk with him the next night."

"Come on, Maggie. Details." Cissy's fingers wiggled in a come-hither motion. "What's his name? What does he look like? What did you talk about? Do you like him? If his pa bought a farm, he must be rich. Ya know what I mean?"

Maggie held up her palm against her friend's outburst. "Wait a minute. One at a time. His name is Leon Winkler. We get along very well. It seems we never run out of things to say to each other, so I enjoy being with him."

Rubbing her forehead, Maggie closed her eyes. "Oh my goodness!"

"What's eating you? You look like you've seen a ghost." Emma stopped rocking.

"I completely forgot."

"What did you forget?" Cissy almost climbed down Maggie's throat.

"Leon asked me to go to a movie tomorrow night after supper. I was supposed to talk to Harry, or someone, to find out where the theater is. Here it's Thursday already, and I never thought of it."

"Well, that's not such a tragedy." Cissy shrugged her shoulders. "You just thought of it now, and I can certainly answer the questions you were supposed to ask. I don't think it's a problem at all."

"I'm glad I thought of it now. Leon's counting on me to get the information." She looked at Cissy. "So, where is the theater in Dubuque?"

"It's downtown on the corner of Eighth and Iowa Streets. It used to be called the Grand Opera House when it had live productions going on in the building, but now it's called the Grand Theatre since it shows movies. It was a couple years back when it was renovated and changed to show movies instead of plays. To get there you just have to go down Central Avenue, the road you come in from the Iverson farm. Then you turn right one block to get to Iowa Street, and then go to Eighth Street. Ya know what I mean?"

As usual, Cissy gave Maggie more data than she had asked for. She was always good for a wealth of information. "Thanks,

Cissy. I'm sure we'll be able to find it then. I wonder what's showing tomorrow night."

"We can look in this week's paper." Cissy looked at Emma. "Mrs. Hannemann, do you have the latest *Telegraph Herald* around?"

Emma's face turned a nice shade of pink. "We can't afford the newspaper anymore, so I don't have one."

Ignoring the color of Emma's face, Maggie stared at her sister. Things must be tougher for them than she had thought.

"No problem. I'll run home and get ours." Cissy headed for the door. "I'll be back in five minutes."

She turned and ran down the steps.

"While she's gone, let me know how things are going here." Maggie continued to pat Timmy, hoping he'd go to sleep.

Emma fidgeted with Tina's blanket lying on her lap. "Maggie, before we start on that, I'd like to tell you something."

By the look on Emma's face, this must be serious. Maggie swallowed past the lump in her throat. "What is it?"

"I don't know if I ever told you about Freddie."

"Who?" Slanting a glance at Emma, Maggie searched her brain trying to figure out whom Emma was talking about.

"Freddie, Freddie Neumann. I probably never spoke about him before." Emma's cherry-colored face gave her away.

Something secretive from her past? Maggie covered her smile behind her fingers. This ought to be interesting. "No, I don't recall that name."

"During my year of teaching in Racine, I spent time with Freddie. He was a very nice young man whom I dated several times."

"Before you met Neil?" Maggie couldn't hide the grin any longer.

"No, no. Neil was my pastor so I knew them both at the same time. Freddie lived next door to the family I boarded with. He took me around, showed me the town when I got to Racine. He taught me the Charleston and other dances. We had fun double dating with Vivi and her boyfriend at the time."

Maggie couldn't contain herself any longer and started sniggering. "This is getting better all the time."

"Shhh! You'll wake Timmy at that rate." Emma shook her head. "I'm telling you all this to warn you about Leon."

"Warn me?"

"Yes, young men can pay you all the attention in the world to turn you head, but if they don't have similar values to you, as far as God is concerned, you shouldn't give them the time of day. Take it from me." The scowl on Emma's face broadcast her earnestness.

"Don't worry about me, Em. I'm sure Leon goes to church." An uneasy feeling started deep in Maggie's gut, but she ignored it completely.

"Well, my advice is to have a conversation with him soon to make sure you are on the same road to heaven. But that's enough of that for now." Emma filled Maggie in on all the events with her children since Sunday. "I miss you so much. I find I don't have enough hands to get everything done in one day."

"Is that why Cissy is here?"

"She comes for an hour or so in the mornings and then after the children's naps in the afternoon. It gives me the extra hands I need around here during the busy times."

"I would have loved to stay."

"I wish you could have, but we are getting so low on food these days. And God has been testing us since you left." Emma laid the sleeping Tina in the crib.

"What do you mean? Did something happen in the congregation?"

"No, no. Last weekend the local authorities raided Hooverville and now . . ."

Maggie shook her head. "Wait a minute. I don't know what you're talking about. Hooverville?"

"That's right. Juneau, Wisconsin doesn't have one of those." Emma stifled a laugh with her hand. "I guess I'd better explain then. During these hard years, shantytowns have been growing up where homeless people gather and try to survive. Usually small shacks are built of whatever materials they can come up with—stones, cardboard, some wood—whatever.

"Too often the Hoovervilles, as they're called, are overrun by drunkards and hoodlums. The police come in and chase them out for a week or so, which is what happened last weekend. It doesn't help much because all the poor people have to go back there again when they can't find any other place to go."

"Well, how did that affect you?"

"Any time the shantytown is raided, we get the fallout for

weeks. The poor find every church in the city and try to get help there. Neil has been sending people to our house for sandwiches every day this week. We try to help as much as possible, but we need to keep food for our own children. We pray God sends help to these unfortunate people soon. It's so depressing to have to tell them we can only give them a sandwich, or a glass of water."

Maggie finally put Timmy in his crib. She turned to hug Emma. "I'm sorry to hear you had a trying week."

"We know we are here to do whatever we can for them. God has placed us here for these hard times." Emma wiped a tear from her cheek.

"I think God has sent me to the Iverson's for a specific purpose, as well. I can see I need to be there to help the girls." She told Emma about her conversation about their mother.

"I'm sure God wants you out there for many reasons."

Maggie heard Cissy coming in the front door.

Tapping Maggie on the shoulder, Emma whispered, "Let's go downstairs since the twins are asleep."

As they trotted down the stairs, they met Cissy in the hallway.

"I got it." Gasping, she sounded as if she had run the entire way. She opened the paper to the correct page. "*Red Dust* is playing right now. It should be a great movie to see. Clark Gable is in it."

"Clark Gable?" Where had Maggie heard that name before?

"You've never heard of him? I just *love* him. He's sooo handsome—a real sheik." Cissy folded her hands under her chin, looking as if she would swoon.

Laughing, Maggie shook her head. "I haven't gone to a movie very often. Haven't been in years. No time to get to town when I lived on the farm."

"Well, then it's about time you saw this one. I saw him in *It Happened One Night* a year ago or so. He's really a good actor."

"I'll have to tell Leon about it."

"I've got a keen idea." Cissy's eyes beamed. "When I see Harry at dinner this noon, I'll mention you and Leon are going. Maybe we can double up for the movie. Harry is making money now, so he should be able to come up with the dough and spend twenty cents on movie tickets."

What had Maggie gotten herself into now? What would Leon think if Harry and Cissy tagged along? On second thought, maybe it wouldn't be bad if they went with another couple. Maggie didn't know Leon very well. She'd let the guys decide what to do. "Harry can talk to Leon about it tonight. I'm not going to worry. I have too much else on my mind today."

Maggie heard a truck approaching. All three women turned toward the window.

"Romy must be back from the feed mill." Maggie headed toward the door. "Are you sure it's okay to leave Janet here to play while we go shopping?"

"Absolutely. Lucy will stay busy then." Emma gave her a quick hug. "You don't have to hurry back on my account."

"I'm sure we won't be too long. I have so much to do at home to get ready for feeding the haying crew for dinner tomorrow noon."

Cissy waved as Maggie walked out the door. "I'll see you tomorrow night for the movie. We'll have a swell time. Ya know what I mean?"

Smiling, Maggie skipped down the steps toward Romy's truck. Somehow Cissy always managed to get in the last word.

Focusing on the task ahead of her, Maggie glanced at the man sitting behind the steering wheel. She didn't have Janet as a buffer now.

Would the silences be eternal again?

***

Romy studied Maggie as she strolled down the sidewalk with her skirt swishing to the rhythm of her hips. He'd like nothing better than to have their budding friendship grow into something much deeper. He'd have to be patient with her since she was living in their house. Things looked different than they had only last Sunday.

He hopped out to open the door for her. "Ready to go?"

"I'm not positive my list is complete, but I'm ready." Maggie climbed into the truck before he closed the door behind her.

He ran around to the driver's side. "I'm sure you have the staples like flour and sugar on the list. We'll have to buy items for tomorrow as well. What are you planning on serving?" Romy pulled away from the curb.

"I'll cook two chickens and find potatoes from the basement and lettuce from the garden. The peas looked ready to pick, also. I'm not sure about dessert."

"There are strawberries in the garden. They should be ripe. Do you know how to make strawberry pie?"

"Of course. Sounds like a great idea. I'll make some in the morning." Maggie cleared her throat. "I wanted to ask you on the way into town, but didn't want to bring it up when Janet was with us. What did you say to your Pa this morning? I was surprised at the plan he had for Sally and Mary."

Romy recounted his conversation with his pa. "I had no idea what he was going to suggest until it came out of his mouth. He hasn't gathered honey for a long time, so it will be a real adventure for the girls. Most of the time when he goes out to look for honey, he never finds any. So this was basically a way to spend time with them."

"I'm glad he had a change of heart. God works miracles every day."

He agreed with her when he saw the radiant smile on her face. A miracle was happening in his heart, too.

CHAPTER 18

Maggie jumped out of bed Friday as soon as she heard the early morning twitter of the songbirds. She had so much to accomplish before dinnertime. Her head was bursting with to-do lists. At least the strawberries and peas were picked yesterday after the trip to town. If only the overnight stay in the cool basement had kept them fresh.

The lettuce had to be crisp for dinner. Sally would have the task of cutting it later in the morning.

Mary and Janet would be sent down to the root cellar to dig potatoes out of the bushel baskets full of dirt. It was a good thing they were stored that way to keep the potatoes fresh longer. They weren't as spongy as Emma's.

Her biggest hurdle would be getting the chickens ready to roast. She'd been part of butchering many times at home, but she'd never be able to manage without the help of Ted, or maybe Jim. She could never catch the chickens, running around the coop. Somehow, those screaming maniacs always managed to avoid her.

Most of all, she could *not* manage to cut off their heads when they were thrashing around and making such a racket. She needed a strong arm to help her with the task.

With the lists organized in her mind, she slipped on her shoes and headed toward the kitchen. She tied her apron strings as she turned the corner. Spotting Romy across the room, she smiled a greeting. "Good morning."

His arms loaded with wood, he motioned to his brother who followed him into the kitchen. "Put your bundle in the woodbin, Ted."

Glancing her way, Romy nodded. "I made sure you'd have enough wood to get all the baking done this morning. I'm sure you won't run out now."

After he had heaped the woodbin until it looked like a volcano about to erupt, he flashed her a self-satisfied smile.

Mirroring his smile, her heart warmed as they made a connection with their eyes. Hummingbirds bombarded her stomach. That wouldn't do at all. She was going to a movie tonight with Leon. She had to think about Leon, not Romy.

Maggie took a deep breath. She'd better think about the task before her. "Thanks much for the help. By the way, do you know how many extra men will be here for dinner?"

"Pa asked Mr. Winkler and Leon since they live closest to us, along with . . ."

Maggie swallowed twice as Romy rambled on. Leon would be here for dinner? He was helping the Iversons with the haying? Would he make a comment about going to the movie during the meal? She had talked to Harry last night, but no one else knew about it.

What would happen when Romy found out? Would there be a scene at the table? She had to stop worrying so much. *Lord, help me through this day.*

Nodding, she brought her mind back to what Romy was saying. " . . . our neighbors to the west, Mr. Wellington and his two sons, Gilbert and Melvin. Nine in all, with Pa and the boys."

He inched toward the back door. "I have to get the chores done so we're ready by nine o'clock when the hay is dry."

"Can I ask one quick favor?" Maggie caught her lower lip between her teeth.

"Sure."

"Can either Ted or Jim help me butcher the chickens right after breakfast? I need to get them in the oven." She shivered as a chill flowed from head to toe. She had so much to do. How would she accomplish everything she needed to do before noon?

"How about if they both help you? Then the chickens will be ready in time."

"Thanks. I can't manage all by myself, I'm sure." She headed toward the cupboard to pull out the iron skillet.

"No, I'm sure not with so many to feed." Romy's smile followed him out the door.

After breakfast Maggie hurried to clear the table. "Mary and Sally, we have lots to do this morning. I'd like you two to clean up the breakfast dishes. Then I can help Ted and Jim kill the chickens."

"Sure, Miss Maggie." Sally pulled out the dishpan. She was always so willing.

Maggie found the largest kettle in the cupboard. "We'll need this full of boiling water. I'll fill it at the pump." She headed for the back door and almost collided with Ted.

"Miss Maggie, I'm so sorry. I was just coming to get . . ." He pointed to the kettle in her hands. "You might as well give me the other one, too."

"Thanks so much for helping me with this."

Stepping around her, he reached for a second pan on the shelf in the porch. "My pleasure. We'll probably use more than one pot of water this morning. I'll bring them back shortly. Is the stove nice and hot?"

"I'll add the extra wood right now." Maggie opened the lid on the stove and grabbed firewood from the Mt. Vesuvius woodpile. "I'll meet you outside."

She wasn't looking forward to this.

The three of them spent the next hour getting the chickens ready for the roasting pan. Jim fed the flock cracked corn so it would be easier to catch the chosen ones. Maggie supervised the choice of the chickens, but Ted had to snatch them in the coop. He managed to grab one by the legs and drag it to the chopping block.

Jim stood by with axe in hand, waiting for the perfect moment. "The trick is to lay the head of the chicken on the block and stroke it to calm it down."

He demonstrated on the first victim. When the chicken lay calmly as if in a trance, whack, off came the head.

Maggie laughed out loud when Ted released the legs. The headless chicken flopped around the barnyard until it finally collapsed. "I guess that's what you call 'running around like a chicken with its head cut off.'"

After the second chicken was butchered, the real work began.

"I'll go get the kettle of boiling water." Ted headed toward the house while Jim got out the galvanized bucket for scalding. Ted poured the boiling water into the bucket. Jim grabbed the chicken by the legs and dunked the body up and down in the water.

Maggie and Jim stripped the smelly, wet feathers off the fowl. Then she helped him singe the pinfeathers, taking care not to burn the carcass. When both chickens were completed, the boys carried them into the kitchen.

"I can finish now. Thanks so much for all your help." Maggie laid the chickens on the cutting board.

"Are you sure you can gut them by yourself?" Ted held his dirty hands away from his clothes.

"Yeah, I've done this many times at home."

"Well, make sure you get the gizzard out carefully since I always claim it first." Ted gave her the Iverson smile she'd seen many times on Romy's face.

"Okay, I'll be careful." She grinned in return. "Thanks again for the help."

A truck pulled into the farmyard.

"Looks like we better get going." Jim led the way out the door with Ted right behind, letting the screen slam after them.

"Euw, I hate gutting chickens." Mary wrinkled her nose at the prospect.

Maggie found the sharpening steel and pulled the knife back and forth over it until the knife was honed to a fine edge. "Since you cleaned the kitchen so well, Mary, you and Janet can go upstairs and dust mop the bedroom floors while Sally and I work on the chickens."

This wasn't Maggie's favorite part of the job either, but she would have to face the task and get it done.

She took the sharpened butcher knife and cut through the rear end of the chicken. Swallowing hard, she put her hand into the cavity and pulled out the innards. Yuck! Sally helped her find the edible parts. They cleaned up the rest of the chicken and prepared it for the roasting pan. Both chickens squeezed into the same large black roaster. The job was finally finished just in time to put them into the oven.

Maggie and Sally washed their hands at the outdoor pump.

"I'm glad that's done. Now I have to concentrate on the strawberry pies. I'd like this dinner to be perfect for all those men."

Or, for one of those men. But which one—Romy or Leon?

***

Romy breathed a sigh of relief as he climbed down from the hayloft. At long last, he was released from the hot airless space where hay dust managed to crawl up his nose. It seeped into every crevice of his body, threatening to suffocate him. He coughed, struggling to fill his lungs with fresh air. Oh, for a drink of cool water to wash away the dirt in his throat.

"I'm ready for a break." Gilbert jumped down the last step of the ladder. "Sure is tough work. When the hayfork dumps the load into the loft, the dust just gets to me." He coughed as if to emphasize his words.

"I know what you mean. I always thought the fork sticker had the hard job of clamping the hayfork at the right time, but I think I changed my mind after being up in the loft." His cough matched Gilbert's.

"Oh, for the days when we were younger and in charge of getting the horses to pull the loads up with the pulley. Working out in the air was so much better than up top."

"I hear you there. Let's wash up for dinner and get a drink." Romy led the way out of the barn toward the pump.

He undid the hooks of his bib overalls and stripped off his shirt on the way. The dirt on his arms stopped where his shirt-sleeve ended, making it look like patches on a Guernsey cow in the pasture. Time to wash up and be presentable for dinner. He slapped his pants repeatedly with his shirt and raised a cloud of dust.

When they reached the pump, Romy pumped the handle. "You go first."

Gilbert stuck his head under the cold running water and tried to wash off dirt down to his waist. "Brrrr! But it feels exhilarating."

Romy handed him the towel and proceeded to wash when Gilbert pumped. The cold water drenched his hair and poured over his shoulders. His energy returned as the dirt washed away. He grabbed the cup hanging from the nail and drank until his throat was as cool as a brook. "I wonder how Leon did out on the wagon this morning."

Gilbert finished drying off his arms. "Melvin reported he could hardly keep upright when the horses pulled the wagon.

Takes a while to get used to."

Romy shook out his shirt before slipping it on again. "I bet he's exhausted already. The morning was long enough for me. Let's go see if dinner is ready."

As they headed for the house, Pa and the rest of the men rounded the corner of the barn. They looked as tired as Romy felt. "Gil, you can wait out here until everyone is washed up. I'll go check on the situation in the kitchen."

Romy opened the porch door and was greeted by the tantalizing aroma of roasted chicken. His stomach responded with a growl. "Sure smells great."

Maggie, with tendrils of curly hair framing her face, looked up and beamed at him. "I think your stomach agrees. Are the rest coming soon?"

Her glad-to-see-you smile warmed his heart. "They're washing up right now. Is dinner almost ready?"

"I have to mash the potatoes and cut the chicken yet. Everything else is finished." Maggie handed a large bowl of lettuce to Sally. "Can you put this on the table, please?"

"Pa can cut up the chickens while you mash the potatoes. I'll go get him." He headed out the door again.

After several minutes of chaos, the meal graced the table. The men shuffled around to find places to sit. Maggie stood back. "The girls and I will eat after you're all finished."

She reached over Romy's shoulder and placed the large platter of chicken in the center of the table. Out of the corner of his eye, Romy saw Leon wink at Maggie before she turned and walked back to the stove. Romy's stomach burned deep within him. What was that all about? Was Leon flirting with her?

They had only gone on a walk down the road. No reason to wink. Romy glanced at Maggie, her face a pretty pink hue. What was she thinking?

Romy shook his head. Had he missed something?

After saying grace, Pa handed the peas to Mr. Winkler. "I think we made good progress this morning."

Melvin scooped potatoes onto his plate. "How much longer will it take this afternoon?"

"Oh, we should be all done in two or three hours. Don't ya think?" Pa poured gravy over his potatoes.

Leon blinked. "It'll take hours to finish?"

Everyone paused and peered at him.

"What's your hurry, Leon? That's only the middle of the afternoon." Mr. Winkler took a drink of lemonade.

Jim's eyes held a mischievous glint. "Maybe he needs to take a nap before we're done."

The men exploded in a loud guffaw. Maybe some of the other men agreed with Romy's notion—Leon wasn't ready for farm work.

"Thanks a lot." Leon scowled at Jim before he continued to eat. A moment later he set down his fork. "I have to get home and get the chores done early. Maggie and I are going out on the town tonight."

What? Eight heads turned and eight pairs of eyes stared at Maggie. By the color of her face, Romy imagined she wished the floor would swallow her whole. Leon continued, "Harry and I are taking the girls to a movie."

Romy's food threatened to erupt all over the table. When had they planned this? Harry hadn't mentioned anything to him, but that probably wasn't too surprising. Is that why Leon had winked at her before?

Hadn't Maggie and he been getting closer lately? Oh, how wrong he'd been. The tasty dinner just lost its appeal.

***

Maggie's hand stopped short with a plate of bread halfway to the table. Why had Leon told everyone? She was embarrassed enough when he winked at her. Then he announced their plans to the entire room. Was he trying to make her self-conscious? The men looked at her as if she were a caged animal at the zoo. She didn't like it one little bit.

Her eyes were drawn to Romy. All she could see was the top of his head as he studied his plate. She shouldn't care what he thought about tonight, but she and Romy had become friends during the week. She didn't want to upset their fragile relationship.

Trying to take a deep breath, she found her lungs wouldn't cooperate. "I haven't even heard the plans for tonight, so thanks for sharing them."

Somehow she forced a smile on her face and kept on filling the bowls as they emptied.

"Looks like he's sharing 'em with you now." Jim scraped the last bit of chicken off his plate.

Ted laughed and slapped Leon on the back. "Everyone will know sooner or later anyway."

Maggie might agree with that statement, but Leon didn't have to embarrass her in front of all these men. Would Romy have done something this brash?

Leon glanced her way as she brought the coffee pot to the table, but didn't say a word.

Biting her lower lip, Maggie's motions seemed exaggerated in the silence. Could Leon detect her annoyance? No words came out of her mouth. She could feel the eyes of the men follow her around the kitchen.

She moved around the table serving the strawberry pie while trying to ignore the strong musky odor mixed with the smell of new mown hay. Her nose twitched as she served a piece to Ted.

"This pie is delicious." Mr. Wellington took another bite.

Looking at Maggie, Mr. Iverson wiped his face with a napkin. "I agree with you there, George. I hope you made extra for later."

Thank goodness for Romy's Pa. He managed to change the subject when the air was tense.

She smiled her thanks. "There's an extra one sitting in the pantry."

The meal, in any case, was a success. If only Leon hadn't blurted out their plans. She was excited about going with him tonight, but she didn't appreciate his timing. Would this ruin everything?

"So what's playing at the theater this week?" Gilbert forked another bite of pie into his mouth.

Why couldn't the subject be dropped? This should be discussed with Leon later. He replied, jumping in with both feet again. "Harry says we're going to see *Red Dust* with Clark Gable tonight."

Ted dismissed the suggested title with a wave of his hand. "That's too bad. I've heard that's a movie dames like to see."

Melvin chimed in. "Yeah, that Clark Gable guy is a real sheik. The gals really go for him."

"I bet Cissy had something to do with persuading you to go tonight." Jim put his fork on his plate and leaned back in the chair.

Several people agreed with Jim, commenting at once and nodding their heads.

"Is Cissy his girlfriend?" Leon leaned his forearms on the table.

"Oh, yeah. Wait until you meet her." Romy finally joined the conversation again. "You'll never forget her."

Was he angry or jealous? Maggie had no idea.

Chuckles flew around the table as the older men rose and started out the door. Mr. Iverson closed the conversation in an instant. "Back to work."

Maggie had to face the confusion they left behind—in the kitchen and in her mind.

CHAPTER 19

Leaning against the stone wall adjacent to the driveway, Maggie waited for Leon to arrive. She had been mighty glad to see the last of the neighbors drive down this same road after the haying was finished. There was no way she could have fed them another meal.

As it was, the family had to be satisfied with cold sausage and cheese sandwiches for a quick meal at supper. Maggie couldn't have managed cooking anything else. At least no one had complained. Her legs ached from standing all day, preparing dinner and then cleaning up the kitchen disaster after the men returned to work.

Watching a dark green car approach, Maggie pushed off the wall and smoothed out her black skirt. Leon turned into their drive and stopped next to her.

He hopped out from behind the wheel. "Hi there. Are you as tired as I am?"

Nodding, she pushed random curls behind her ear. "I sure am. Seems like I've been on my feet since sunup."

"Exactly. My legs are still wobbly from riding on that swaying wagon in the field." He mimicked his tipsy wagon ride. "I'm so glad that we'll be sitting at the theatre tonight."

"I know what you mean." Maggie looked at the watch pinned to her blouse. "Harry got home late from work, so he's not down yet. He'd better hurry since we still have to pick up Cissy."

"Ah. Here he comes now." Leon pointed toward the house.

Trotting down the hill, Harry slipped his arms into the sleeve of his suit coat. "Sorry I'm late. I couldn't believe how much rock I had to move at work. We built the retaining wall along the park road. Man, am I tired."

"Maggie and I said the same thing about making hay here. I haven't worked so hard in my life." Leon wiped a hand across his brow.

"Yeah, Ted and Jim told me about your conversation at dinner today." Harry glanced from Leon to Maggie. "I heard you got razzed about the movie tonight."

Her cheeks turned to fire for the second time in one day. It was still a sore spot. Had she forgiven Leon for embarrassing her? She wasn't sure. Harry didn't have to remind him, though.

"I'm sure sorry I brought it up that way." Studying his hands, Leon fidgeted with the car keys. He glanced at Maggie. "You didn't appreciate it either, did you?"

"Well, to be honest, it wasn't the best timing. Not with all the men there."

"I realized that after it slipped out of my mouth." He took a step toward her. "I hope you can forgive me."

At least he had apologized. Now she should put that behind them and go forward. Giving him a half-smile, she nodded. "Sure."

Harry rubbed his hands together. "Since we're out of that sticky situation, I think we should change plans for the evening."

"What?" Both Maggie and Leon asked at the same time.

Harry shrugged. "If they teased you about going to a movie, we'll do something different."

Maggie glanced at Leon before focusing on Harry. "What are you talking about?"

"While I was at work today, I heard they're dedicating a band shell in Galena this weekend and have a band playing tonight. Let's go there instead."

"Galena? That's way over in Illinois." Leon leaned against the stone wall. "We planned on going to a movie."

"Actually, Galena's less than twenty miles away. Besides, I think the movie sounded stodgy. We'd have to leave now to get to Galena in time, but I say we hit the road."

"I told Leon I couldn't go dancing since your Ma died a

month ago, so that's not a good idea." Maggie hugged her handbag to her chest.

Harry paused with arms outstretched. "Dancing? Who said anything about that? This is a concert. I don't think there's anything wrong. We'll only be listening to music."

"Well, what about Cissy? Does she know?" Maggie wasn't convinced yet. Harry's Pa and Romy thought they'd be going to town, but instead they might be traipsing across the river to Illinois.

Harry waved his hand as if dismissing the thought. "Aw, don't get balled up about Cissy. She'll think it's a swell idea."

***

As Maggie and Leon waited for Harry to emerge from Cissy's house, Maggie toyed with her purse. "Leon, I hope you're ready to meet Cissy. Let's just say she likes to talk."

That was an understatement, but he'd find out soon enough. She watched Cissy bound down the stairs to the sidewalk.

"The Iverson boys mentioned Cissy this afternoon while we were working. I'm anxious to experience this."

Harry hurried to open the car door as Cissy approached the vehicle.

"Hi there, Maggie." Cissy scooted into the back seat followed by Harry. "I've been thinking of you all day. How did you manage to get the chickens butchered? How did the pies turn out? Did you survive your dinner with all the men?" Before Maggie could get a word in, Cissy glanced in Leon's direction. "Oh, you must be Leon. I'm sure glad to meet you. I've heard so much about you from Harry here. Ya know what I mean?" She rubbed her hand along the seat cushion of the 1934 Plymouth sedan. "I love this car."

This was Cissy in her full glory, but of course Maggie couldn't say it out loud. "Leon, this is Cissy."

Smiling, he nodded toward the back seat. "Nice to meet you."

Maggie rolled her eyes as she peered at Leon. "I agree with her. This is a great car. When did your folks get it?"

"Shortly after my dad heard he had an inheritance, they went shopping. My ma fell in love with the dark green color. It only cost six hundred dollars, so they picked it up." He looked out the front window again. "How do we get there?"

Harry pointed toward the left. "It's easy. Go down Main

Street to Highway 20, then east to Galena."

"OK. Sounds good."

Maggie turned in her seat to chat with Cissy. "Did Harry have a chance to mention our change of plans?"

"Absolutely! He told me all about it before we left. I think it's a nifty idea. I haven't been to Illinois for so long even though it's just across the river. You'd think there would be no bridge going over the river since I never get over there. But, of course, people travel on that bridge every day between Dubuque and Illinois. It was built back in the last century so it's quite old already. Ya know what I mean?" Cissy poked Maggie on the shoulder. "Now, tell me all about your day."

Maggie took a big gulp of air. Listening to Cissy always took her breath away. "I can tell you it's been hectic."

She proceeded to relate details of the last twelve hours. "We finally finished washing . . ."

Cissy flicked a hand as if to dismiss Maggie's monologue. "I'm so excited about going to a concert in Galena. And it's in a new band shell. Is that one of the ones the WPA is building, Harry?"

"I think so, but I'm not positive."

"I just love to sit and listen to bands in a park. It's so romantic sitting out under the stars." She glanced in Harry's direction. "Did you say which band is playing?"

"According to the guys at work, Tommy Dorsey will be playing tonight and tomorrow afternoon for the official dedication concert."

"Oh, I've heard of the Dorsey Brothers Band. They play big band music, something like jazz. I love listening to that type of music, but of course, to some people that music is way too immoral. I've heard my ma's friends from church talk about it, like it's music written by the devil himself. Ya know what I mean?"

Leon glanced in the rearview mirror. "Are you serious?"

"Well, I wouldn't put it quite like that, Cissy. I do know that many people in our church look down on modern music." Maggie didn't want Leon to get the wrong impression. She hadn't had time to find out if he was a churchgoer yet.

Cissy patted Maggie on the shoulder. "You're right. I'm not sure it's the music itself. I think it's more like the lifestyle that the musicians lead when they're traveling the country, playing concerts. Bad reputation. Ya know what I mean?"

Maggie glanced over her shoulder. "That's being judgmental, Cissy."

"Maybe. But wait until you hear this story." Cissy rubbed her hands together and scooted forward in her seat. "I heard that in New Hampton, west of here, a huge scandal hit the town when a young girl ran away to marry a band member. They say that the girl's family was devastated that she up and disappeared a couple weeks ago.

"When the band was playing in the town, the clarinet player saw her sitting in the audience and immediately fell in love with her. He managed to talk to her after the concert and somehow persuaded her to run away with him. A couple days later she disappeared and caught up with him in the next town he was scheduled to play in. Can you believe that?"

"Oh, how dreadful for the family. And they were Lutheran?"

"You betcha. It caused a ruckus in town. They talked about the girl for weeks after. It made headlines in the newspaper. Of course, I think it's such a romantic story. Ya know what I mean?" Cissy scooted back in her seat.

"You can pipe down now, baby." Harry gave Cissy a peck on the cheek. "I think we've had an earful of your story for the evening." He nudged Leon's shoulder. "Isn't that right?"

Leon grinned. "Well, it does seem to be a tall tale to me."

He looked in the rearview mirror trying to connect with Harry.

"Yeah, it's hard to believe that the entire town was put out by one girl's disappearance." Harry patted Cissy's knee. "I think you're stretching the facts a bit there."

Cissy dove back in. "Well, my neighbor's cousin told me all about it so I know it's true. I'm not pulling your leg, Harry."

Maggie turned in her seat. Just in time to witness Cissy's elbow connecting with Harry's side.

Rubbing his ribs, Harry turned toward Cissy. "We were just teasing you. You didn't have to get your nose out of joint and jab me with your elbow."

"Maggie, you have to be on my side against these hard-boiled guys." Cissy tried to nudge Harry a second time, but he captured her hands to prevent any further attacks.

"Cissy, stop beatin' your gums." The grin on his face showed Harry wasn't serious.

Maggie chuckled. Sounded like her siblings back home.

They could be downright rude, but still be teasing.

Glancing out the window as they crossed the bridge, Maggie watched a steamboat float south on the Mississippi River. She'd never been in Illinois before. It was the last thing she had thought she'd do this evening.

***

After the last song ended, Leon pulled Maggie to her feet. She brushed her skirt to get the wrinkles out of it. "That concert was fantastic. I'm glad you suggested we come tonight, Harry, but it's so late now."

Leon folded the blanket they were sitting on. "It won't take that long to get home from here."

Maggie nudged his arm. "I'm so exhausted I don't know if I'll be able to stay awake on the ride home. You may have to poke me to keep me awake."

He clasped Maggie's hand and strolled toward the parking area.

"I'll have to get Cissy to do it since she's already had her practice shots on poor Harry's ribs." Leon winked.

"Oh, baloney. Poor Harry, indeed." Cissy cocked her elbow as if she would give Harry another prod as they walked in front of Leon and Maggie.

Harry rubbed his side. "Don't you dare. My ribs can't take it anymore. You're a real live wire tonight. What's eating you?"

"I keep thinking of that gal running away and marrying a band member. I can't help myself." She put her hands under her chin, letting out a long sigh.

"Well, don't get any romantic ideas there." Harry opened the car door and helped Cissy into the back seat.

Cissy leaned forward and poked Maggie's back. "Hey, I have to tell you about an interesting thing I read in the paper this week. Did you ever hear of the Cassville Ferry north of here? No, of course, you haven't. You just moved to Iowa. Harry, have you ever heard of it?"

"I know there's a car ferry that crosses the Mississippi River some miles up north. I'm not sure how many people from here use it since we have the bridge. What about it?"

"It's become a fad to make a day trip of driving north and taking the ferry over to Wisconsin. Then drive down the Wisconsin side of the river and come back to Dubuque by the end of the day. All the rich young people are doing it. Doesn't it sound like a swell idea? It's too bad we don't have dough to spend on such a trip. Ya know what I mean?" Cissy leaned back in her seat.

Leon glanced in the rearview mirror toward Cissy. "I can probably use my folk's car again if we wanted to try to do it."

"Really? That would be nifty. I'd love to take a drive up the river and back again. We could pretend we're puttin' on the ritz. Maggie and I could get all dolled up, and you guys could get on your swanky duds." Cissy smoothed her hair as if she were already pretending. "Ya know, we could pack a picnic lunch to make it cheaper. I don't think the car ferry would cost *that* much. What other costs would there be?"

"Baby, you're forgetting the petrol. Can't go anywhere without gas."

"Well, of course I didn't forget it." Cissy laid her hand on Harry's arm. "We'll have to think of something. I don't want this plan to fail."

"I can't help out there. I'm only getting room and board at the Iversons', so I'll have no way to come up with any cash." Maggie didn't want to admit this to Leon, but everyone might as well know now. "I can supply the food for the picnic, perhaps."

"I'll help with the food, too. We gals have to stick together."

"Harry, if you can come up with the cash to pay the ferry fees, I'll ask my parents to spring for the gas money."

"Attaboy, Leon. I'm sure I can save some from work to buy the ferry tickets."

"Don't forget about the toll bridge. We'll need money to cross the bridge from Wisconsin back into Iowa. That would take the cake. If we got all the way almost back to Dubuque, and then didn't have enough to pay the toll for the bridge. Ya know what I mean?" Cissy laughed out loud, but no one else joined in.

"Cissy, you slay me sometimes. Of course, we'll have enough for the toll. It only costs twenty-five cents." Harry touched her knee. "So, when would we try to do this great adventure?"

"That may be the hardest part—coming up with a date." Leon parked the car in front of Cissy's house and turned in the seat to face Maggie. He held her hand, rubbing his thumb across her knuckles.

"It has to be a Saturday or Sunday since I work all week." Harry folded his arms across his chest.

Leon shook his head. "I think I have to rule out Saturdays. I'm sure I can't get away because of all the farm work."

"I don't think Sundays are a good idea. We couldn't get started until after church. It would be too late by then." With Leon rubbing her hand, shivers ran up Maggie's arm. She wasn't even sure she could think straight. "That rules out every day of the week."

They all sat in silence for a minute. Would their big plan ever happen?

Cissy clasped her hands together excitedly. "How about Independence Day? It's only a week away. Harry shouldn't have to work, and farmers usually take the day off to celebrate. What do you think?"

"Absolutely. That's a swell idea, Cissy." Harry hugged her.

Maggie wanted to do the same thing. Maybe this would work. Lots of details to work out before then. She pulled her hand away from Leon, placing it in her lap.

"We'll count on it and get the rest of the plans figured out when I see you next time." Cissy scooted toward the car door. "I better let you all get home tonight."

"I'll be right back after walking Cissy to the door." Harry opened his door and hurried around the car, opening the door for her.

"Great. Don't take too long spooning with her." Leon grinned as he put his arm along the back of the car seat.

"Thanks a bunch." Harry laughed before he slammed the door.

Leon's fingers twirled the hair dangling in Maggie's nape. "I had a great time tonight."

She glanced in his direction. Tiny butterflies chased each other down her spine to her toes. "I did too. Thanks so much for taking me."

He looked toward the porch. She followed his gaze and saw Harry and Cissy immersed in a strong embrace. Turning back to Leon, Maggie could now share her opinion about her friend. "Cissy is quite a character. She loves to talk about everything."

The twinkle in his deep blue eyes showed his agreement. "Yes, I think Harry has his hands full with her." His lopsided grin was infectious.

"Actually, I think they're made for each other." Maggie's smile matched his.

"I'm looking forward to our trip back to Wisconsin." Leon tucked a strand of hair behind her ear.

A tiny butterfly floated about in her stomach. "Sounds like a real adventure."

She couldn't utter another word as his eyes searched the depths of her soul.

"I didn't think I'd be back there so soon." He trailed his finger along her shoulder. A tremor slid down her arm, ending at her fingertips.

"Me neither. I'll have to write to my parents and tell them about it." That was an intelligent comment. If only he would stop touching her so she could think clearly again. "We'll have to do more planning before the Fourth."

"I'll be happy to meet with you to plan the details."

What did Leon mean by that comment? What was he hinting at?

"I'll look forward to it." She might soar all the way home, at this rate. She'd never felt like this before.

Harry opened the car door and slid into the back seat, breaking the spell. "Let's head home."

***

Romy paced back and forth in the kitchen. He looked at his watch for the umpteenth time. "The movie started at seven o'clock, so should have been done by nine. They should have been home by nine thirty at the latest, and now it's close to eleven."

He hated talking to himself. Glancing out the window, he searched the driveway. "Yeah, that's right. What is taking them so long?"

He hated it even worse when he answered himself. Did they get into a car accident? Did someone force them off the road? Was Maggie hurt?

"Now wait a minute . . . they were with Cissy and Harry. Maybe he persuaded them to stop for ice cream or something. Stop this, Romy." Here he was doing it again. He headed into the living room to sit and read a book. After looking at the page for two minutes without comprehending a word, he walked back to the kitchen.

When he reached his destination, he saw headlights heading toward him. Finally they were home.

Harry bounded in the door an instant later. "What are you doing up yet?"

"Uh, I just came in from checking the livestock for the last time. Where's Maggie?"

"Yeah, sure, you were checking the livestock." Nodding, Harry smiled. "Maggie will be in shortly. She has to say good-bye to Leon, doesn't she?"

Romy swallowed. What was wrong with him? Why was he torn up inside knowing Maggie was outside—in the dark—with Leon? "I didn't mean it that way. I don't care if she says good-bye to Leon."

As long as she didn't kiss him. He forced himself not to look out the window.

"Hey, wait until you hear about the nifty excursion we talked about." Harry looked toward the door when Maggie burst into the room, her cheeks a vibrant pink. "I was just telling Romy about our swell plans."

Romy glanced from Maggie to Harry. "What plans?"

Why were her cheeks so flushed? Had she kissed him? He had to concentrate on what Harry was saying.

"On Independence Day, the four of us are going to drive up north, cross the Mississippi on the car ferry, and then come back to Dubuque via the toll bridge. We'll pack . . ."

"You're what?" Romy interrupted his brother. Maggie will spend a whole day with their neighbor? How could he stop this folly?

"We're going to Wisconsin for a picnic. Then, we'll head back down here." Maggie's smile told Romy all he needed to know. "We don't have all the details figured out yet, just the basics."

"How can you just take off and leave us for a day?" Romy knew he wasn't being reasonable.

"Oh, come on, bro. After two and a half weeks, don't you think Pa will gladly give her a day off?" Harry stood with arms akimbo. "I'm sure he'll be fine with it."

Maybe Pa would be fine with it, but Romy didn't feel fine at all. He was getting closer to Maggie all the time, and now Leon had come into the picture and ruined everything. "We'll talk about it in the morning."

He wasn't going to give in to the interloper without a fight.

CHAPTER 20

Maggie glanced around the organized chaos in the pantry. Not much time to finish packing the picnic lunch. Leon would be here soon. She paused when the back door slammed.

"Miss Maggie!" Mary raced into the kitchen. "The pigs broke through the garden fence and are eating the green beans."

"Run and find Romy or Jim and tell them." Maggie threw down her to-do list and tore out the door. She ran around the corner of the house. Two weeks of hard work. Had it all been a waste of time?

She had worked to get the garden back into shape after all the neglect. When she had watered the cucumbers yesterday, everything had looked terrific. The peas still produced, the green beans had started to blossom, and the corn was knee high, just as it should be. She'd been trying to figure out when canning season would start, and now three pigs were rooting around in the beans. She dashed toward the fence and waved her apron. "Shoo, shoo."

The fence closest to the ravine was broken down. Must be how they got in. How would she get them out without letting them trample all the other vegetables? The hogs lifted their heads when she shouted. They turned tail and darted for the strawberry patch on the other end.

"No, not the strawberries!" She shouldn't rush toward them, chasing them the wrong way. She stopped and took a breath.

"Miss Maggie, hold on." Romy and Jim ran full speed toward

her. "We need to lure them out of the garden, not chase them."

Romy pointed toward the corncrib. "Jim, go get some corn."

"Will do." His brother changed directions.

"I'll open the gate and see if we can coax them out of there." Romy slowed his steps as he approached the fenced-in garden.

Maggie twisted her hands in her apron while she waited for the brothers to work their magic. Her blue-and-white dress flapped around her legs in the breeze. When they succeeded, she scurried through the gate to inspect the damage.

"I think we can prop up most of the beans." Romy bent down to push dirt around the base of the stripped stems. "Looks like they ate some of the leaves, but I hope the plants will bounce back."

"The strawberry plants are pretty much ruined." Maggie tried to salvage some. "I hope the sun won't wilt them too much. At least they're done producing for this year."

"Yeah, by next year the new plants will replace the damaged ones." Romy stood and brushed off his overalls. "I'll get the garden fence fixed tomorrow since we're going into town for the celebration today."

Maggie turned in the direction of the house. "I still have to finish packing for the picnic."

She brushed her hands down her apron, sparing the dress that had looked so clean and neat a half hour ago.

"Oh, yeah. Well, I hope you have a lovely adventure."

Somehow Maggie didn't think he meant it since he spoke through clenched teeth. He turned his back and stomped to the barn. He didn't have to be so snippy about the picnic. He acted as if he were jealous or something. Preposterous.

Back in the kitchen, she studied her list. She had to forget the garden for the rest of the day. Taking a breath, she let it out bit by bit. "Now, where are those plates? I had a stack all ready to pack."

After all the planning she'd done for this picnic lunch, now she was behind. Leon would be here soon. She spotted the plates hiding under the tablecloth and put them into the basket.

Harry came in from outside. "I heard about the garden fiasco. Don't worry, we've had this happen other years, too."

Maggie's shoulders fell. "I know. I've been trying to keep the garden growing even with the water shortage this year. We need as many vegetables preserved as possible before winter.

I'm just afraid they've ruined the beans."

"We'll have to pray they survive."

Dropping her chin, Maggie sighed. She hadn't remembered to do that during the crisis. *Lord, forgive me for not turning to You first. Please bless the produce in the garden because we need the food to feed this family.*

"Are you about ready?" Harry snatched a cookie from the covered bowl.

As she slapped his hand, she smiled. "Can you get the pan of cold chicken out of the basement? Then I'll be all set."

Harry glanced out the door in time to see Leon's car pull up. "Good thing 'cuz here he is."

Harry disappeared down the basement steps.

***

"Here's where the pigs broke out of their pen." Romy, ignoring the pungent odor emanating from the enclosure, pointed to the broken boards at the corner of the fence. "I'll get a hammer to patch this hole. Jim, you stay here and make sure there are no more escapees. I'll be right back."

Romy headed to the shed to find the appropriate tools. When he heard a car approaching, he slid a glance in the direction of the driveway. Leon was here with his fancy car. Romy clenched his teeth. How was this plan one bit reasonable?

Leon would spend the whole day with Maggie, which is exactly what Romy wanted to do. He'd never even been up north to cross the Mississippi on the ferry. His heart longed to travel, so why couldn't he at least be going on a trip like this?

Envy overtook any sane thoughts he had about Leon. Not good. *Lord, forgive me for my jealousy. Help me to think positive thoughts about the situation and keep Maggie safe today on her trip.* Taking a big breath, he felt the tension flow out of him.

Maggie bounded out of the house with a tablecloth on her arm. She tucked stray strands of hair behind her ear. "Hi, Leon. We've got beautiful weather for our adventure today."

The smile on her face was a kiss of sunshine to Romy. If only her smile were directed his way, he'd be a happy man. Grabbing his tools, he walked back toward the pigpen, the peace from his prayer flying away. He had to stop wallowing in self-pity.

He tortured himself with questions. Why Leon? Why does she light up for him? Why doesn't she see me like that?

Romy pounded a board back into place. Ten nails for one small board. Guess he had overdone it a bit. No problem there. He needed to pound something.

His irritation was irrational, but somehow he couldn't stop himself. How could he find a way to spend more time with Maggie? If he came up with something, he was sure she'd start smiling at him the same way. After all, they'd been getting along very well before Leon took her out a couple weeks ago.

Janet appeared at his side as he pounded another nail. "Whatcha doin', Romy?"

"I'm fixing the fence so the pigs don't get out again."

"That'll make Miss Maggie happy. She was sad when the pigs wrecked the garden."

"Yeah, I know." His sister always had a way of bringing life back to basic truths. If only life were so simple.

"We'll all be happy 'cuz then we'll have veg'bles for dinner later. I love corns on the cob." Janet rubbed her tummy.

"I do, too." He measured a space where a board needed to be replaced.

"Can I have corns for my birthday dinner?"

"Well, your birthday is three weeks away. I don't think the corn will be ready to eat by then."

Janet rubbed the toe of her shoe in the dirt. "My birthday will be sad anyway 'cuz Ma's not here."

Romy's arm froze in midair. Maybe things weren't so simple for the five-year-old. After laying the hammer down, he took her in his arms. "Oh, Janet. We'll have lots of sad days because Ma isn't with us any longer, but we'll have to try to be happy somehow anyway."

He put her at arm's length and looked into her eyes. "You think of something fun you'd really like to do for your birthday, and I'll see if we can make it happen."

"Okay, let me think." She walked ten feet away and sat down by the corncrib. "I'll think over here."

"Let me know when you have an idea. I'll keep working." His face broke into a smile as he focused on the task before him. This shouldn't take too much longer.

While she thought on her problem, he'd think of a way to spend time with Maggie. *Lord, if it be Your will, I'd like to get to know her better. Help me to carry out Your will for my life even if it doesn't include Maggie.*

Janet skipped across the space to the fence. "I'd like to spend my birthday with Miss Maggie, making her happy since she's made me happy again."

"That's a wonderful idea." Was this the answer to Romy's prayer? "What do you want to do to make her happy?"

"Well, she was so happy after the movie last week, maybe we could go to a movie on my birthday."

Romy almost choked. Even Janet saw how happy Maggie was after her date with Leon. "Well, she actually didn't go to a movie. They changed plans and went a concert instead. Does that matter?" Leon probably made her happy, not the concert.

"No, I still want to go to a movie." Janet sat down beside him. "Lucy was telling me about a movie with a little girl with curly hair." She put her hand under her chin. "I can't remember her name."

"Do you mean Shirley Temple?" Her movies had been all the rage the last year or so. He'd never seen one, but Cissy had gushed over how cute she was on more than one occasion.

Janet's head bobbed faster than a bouncy Ping-Pong ball. "Yeah. That's her name. Can Miss Maggie and me and you go to one of her movies for my birthday?"

Hoorah. He'd jump up and down if he could. Here he had the answer to his prayer—and it was a birthday present for his little sister. Maggie couldn't say no to Janet. "Well, we'll have to wait until she gets home tonight to ask her, won't we?"

Now he had a reason to spend time with Maggie. He'd enjoy planning this birthday outing.

***

Maggie looked out the window as the four friends sped north following the Mississippi River. The rolling hills and verdant pastures were more beautiful than anything she'd seen before. They reached the pinnacle of a steep incline, giving her a glimpse to the east across the river valley. "Oh, my! What a view. You can see so far into Wisconsin."

Leon took his eyes off the road. "And how. I had no idea this drive was so picturesque."

"That's why I wanted to bring you two up this road. It really is quite a sight. I love this drive even though we haven't been up this way for such a long time with the Depression. Ya know what I mean?"

Cissy's hand came over the seat back pointing out the window. "I've always said I'd love to be a farmer's wife up on these high bluffs. But maybe the weather gets nasty way up here in the winter since there's no protection from the strong wind. I've never thought of that before."

"I'm surprised you haven't thought of that. It seems like you think of everything." Harry was such a tease with Cissy. Maggie turned around in time to see him grab Cissy's wrist before her hand could strike his arm.

"Quit pulling my leg all the time, Harry." She leaned back in the seat and crossed her arms.

"What's your beef? I was trying to compliment you." Harry's grin gave him away. "You're so much fun to tease."

"That's right, Harry. A gent should always flatter his girl." Leon's smile smoothed things out. Maggie hoped her friend would take the hint and calm down.

Cissy gave Harry a dirty look before settling into silence.

"How much farther do I have to go?" Leon glanced at Cissy in the rearview mirror. "I don't want to miss the turnoff."

"Well, you have to drive through Balltown first. That's where Breitbach's Country Dining is. It's the oldest restaurant and bar in Iowa. I've eaten there. It's really good. You'd love the fried fish they have. Too bad we don't have time to stop to eat.

"My folks drove us there for their twenty-fifth anniversary party. We had such a grand time with some of their friends. Of course, that was before the bad economy ruined everything. Ya know what I mean?"

"Cissy, that's not telling us how to find the ferry." Maggie couldn't believe how fast she changed topics of conversation.

"Oh, yeah. Then after a few miles, we'll have to keep our eyes open for Turkey River Road. It's a tiny gravel road leading down to the boat landing on the river. My pa has driven past that road more times than you could mention. We always have to turn around and go back when my ma screams at him as we drive past. Ya know what I mean?"

Cissy kept up her chatter, but Maggie's ears finally tuned it out. They drove through Balltown, located on the highest bluff of the drive. She enjoyed the changing scenery and looked for Turkey River Road. She pointed as the car drove past the turnoff. "There it is."

"See, I told you a person misses the road no matter how hard you're looking for it. As I said, Pa always misses it no matter how much Ma shouts at him. It's always so funny when that happens. Now here it happened to us, too. I knew it would. Ya know what I mean?"

Maggie shook her head. Sometimes Cissy's dialogue almost drove her batty. Too many words. In spite of that, she couldn't help grinning. What an enjoyable day!

"Attagirl! You're always right, Cissy." Harry's chuckle was contagious.

When they pulled up to the landing, Maggie saw the ferry sitting at the dock. "Perfect timing. Let's hurry so we don't miss the boat."

Driving toward the ramp, Leon stuck his head out the window. "How much to cross the river?"

The attendant, dressed in a gray uniform, pointed toward the landing. "If'n yur crossin' on foot, it's ten cents, but if'n yur takin' the car over ta' Cassville, it'll be fifty cents."

"We're taking the car on the ferry." Leon stuck his hands in his pocket.

"No, Leon. I'm paying for it." Harry's arm came across the back seat with two quarters in his hand.

"Thanks."

"Well, then, drive right over there, sonny, and turn yur car off. Ya all can git out and walk around since it's 'bout a half-hour trip."

Following his directions, Leon drove onto the six-car ferry. The sun's heat poured over her when Maggie emerged from the car. Removing her hat, she shook her head to release her curls. Joy pulsed through her veins. "I'm going to enjoy the sunshine while we're on the boat."

"That's a great idea." Cissy followed suit.

Maggie walked to the railing and looked across the river. The ferry pulled away from the dock, starting its journey to the other shore. As it picked up speed, the wind whipped through her hair. She hadn't felt this free for a long time. She leaned over the barrier to watch the rippling water spread away from the boat. If only she could capture this moment.

Her body tensed when an arm slid along her back. She found herself enclosed in Leon's arms as he grasped the railing on each side of her. His breath tickled her ear as he whispered. "I like it when the wind blows through your hair."

She tried not to lose the aura of serenity his closeness threatened. She took a deep breath and let it out slowly. Turning her head, she watched the Iowa shore recede. "Isn't it beautiful?"

"I agree, but I'm looking at you more than the scenery." He bent his head closer, his lips skimming the back of her neck.

Swallowing, Maggie's stomach hardened. She was fond of Leon, but not when all the other passengers on the boat could see him nuzzle her. She wasn't comfortable with that.

She ducked out from under his arm and walked toward Harry and Cissy on the opposite railing. Grabbing her hand, Leon followed her.

"Cissy, I'm so glad you suggested this trip. I'm really enjoying myself." Maggie would stay close to them from now on. She didn't want to be embarrassed in front of strangers.

"I know. I just love this ferry ride. I'd do it every week if I lived closer. Wouldn't that be a grand idea, Harry? Let's get married and live in Cassville and ride the ferry every week during the summer. We could buy a small house and live right along the river bank." Cissy threw back her head and laughed.

Harry's head snapped back, his eyes bulging. "Baloney! That's the silliest thing I've ever heard."

"What? The marrying, or the living here?" Cissy didn't stop laughing.

Harry cleared his throat. "I refuse to answer on the grounds that it might incriminate me."

Maggie and Leon joined Cissy in laughter.

***

"What a memorable day." Leaning her head against the back of the seat, Maggie was tired, but refreshed at the same time. After dropping Cissy off in town, Maggie wanted to keep the memories of the boat ride and picnic lunch fresh in her mind.

Dusk descended in the July sky. Crickets sang their evening song in the nearby ravine. Leon pulled into the farmyard to drop off Maggie and Harry.

"And how, except for Cissy's corny idea to live in Cassville just to ride the ferry." Harry emerged from the car.

"So the suggestion that you get married wasn't the stupid part. Hmmm." Leon opened Maggie's door.

"Now I can report that to Cissy." Maggie's smile matched her joy.

"No comment." Harry headed up to the house with the picnic basket.

Leon turned to Maggie. "Thanks so much for the tasty lunch you brought." They had eaten the noon meal at a park in Cass-ville before starting back toward Dubuque. He lifted a finger and traced it down her cheek. "I enjoyed it as much as I enjoyed being with you."

A tremble zinged across her face, mirroring the movement of his fingertips. She stepped toward him since they were alone in the dark. "I had a great time, too."

"When will I see you again?"

Soon, if she had much to say about it.

CHAPTER 21

"They're home. They're home!" Janet bounced up and down when she saw the car lights illuminate the driveway.

Romy watched as she ran from the living room window toward the back porch. "It's about time."

The sun had dipped below the horizon. At least now he could stop his pacing.

"What did you say, Romy?"

"Nothing." He looked down at Janet. "Let's go see if they need help carrying anything into the house."

They headed through the porch and out the screen door, letting it slam behind them.

"Harry, do you need any help with your basket?" Janet skidded to a halt in front of him.

"No, but Miss Maggie might have more to bring in." He nodded toward Leon's car.

Romy glanced their way in time to see Leon run his finger down Maggie's cheek. Clenching his fists, Romy took a deep breath. He'd better not make a scene, but then Maggie stepped closer to his neighbor. He'd better act fast. "Janet, why don't you run and tell Miss Maggie your suggestion."

Romy put his hand on her back to encourage her along.

"Okay." She skipped down the three steps by the retaining wall without any further encouragement. "Miss Maggie!"

Janet reached Maggie's side and slipped her arms around Maggie's waist. In the shadowy light, Romy watched Maggie

CONNIE CORTRIGHT

jerk her head around. She had interrupted their conversation. *Good timing, Janet.*

Maggie made a quick recovery and put her hand on Janet's back. "What are you doing up so late?"

"Pa and Romy let me stay up late just so's I can tell you the surprise."

Disappointment was written all over Leon's face even in the dimness of the car's headlights. He shrugged and looked at Maggie. "I guess I'll let you go, then."

Romy smiled. Maybe his plan would work.

"Thanks again for driving today." Maggie put her hand on his arm, but then turned back to Janet. "What surprise are you talking about?"

Romy's shoulder muscles relaxed for the first time all day. He smiled and waved at Leon. "Good night."

Maggie didn't even glance in Leon's direction as he slammed the car door. He must have been picturing a much cozier end to his day. Romy stifled his laughter and trotted down the stone steps to the driveway.

"My birthday surprise, Miss Maggie." Janet bounced around Maggie, resembling a yo-yo.

Maggie looked at Romy, but continued talking to the girl. "I didn't even know your birthday was coming up. When is it?"

"She'll be six in three weeks," Romy said before Janet could open her mouth. "We were talking about how to make it special this year." If only Maggie would understand the reason without saying it out loud.

The bounce left Janet and her shoulders sagged. "Yeah, it will be sad 'cuz Ma's not here anymore."

Maggie stooped down and circled Janet's waist with her arm. "Tell me your idea, then."

She was so good with the girls. Her love overflowed to Janet, who desperately needed a woman's love in her life. She'd make a good mother someday. His heart warmed at the thought.

"I want to go with you and Romy to a movie." Janet pressed her finger under her chin. "What was the name, Romy? I forget."

With fingers touching her parted lips, Maggie's eyes widened.

"Janet wants to go to a Shirley Temple movie with us on her birthday." He looped his thumbs in his front pockets and leaned against the nearby stone wall.

184

"Yeah, she's got yellow curls." Janet used her hands to demonstrate.

"You and me . . . ?"

"I'll explain later." Romy turned his attention to his little sister. "Now you have to head to bed, young lady. Pa said you could stay up only to tell your surprise."

"Okay. I'll go tell Sally and Mary all about it." She ran up the stone steps and darted for the house.

"Goodnight, Janet." Maggie blew her a kiss.

***

Maggie rubbed her forehead. Can anything else happen today? All she wanted to do now was lie in her bed and replay every minute of her wonderful day with Leon. Now she had to listen to plans about the birthday party. Her head started to spin.

She turned back to Romy to repeat, "You and me?"

"Janet has it in mind to see a Shirley Temple movie since Lucy was talking about her." He meandered toward the house.

She matched his stride. "So I gathered, but why you and me? Doesn't your pa want to go with her?"

Would Romy be comfortable spending an evening with her and Janet?

"I talked to Pa about it. He's not interested in seeing a kid's movie. He said the whole family could go, but he wasn't sure the other brothers would want to go either. So he suggested it be a girls' day out." Romy's mouth quirked in a half grin.

Maggie shook her head. Still didn't seem right to her. "Oh, it makes sense that the sisters go with Janet, but why me?"

"Since you were so upset about the pigs getting into the garden this morning, she wants to make you happy." Romy's smile spanned his face. He reached for the screen door handle. "Of course, you need someone to drive to town. She wants me to go along with you."

"That's sweet." She slid a glance in Romy's direction. "I made too much of the pigs this morning. After it was all over, it didn't seem like such a tragedy."

Romy swung the porch door open, allowing Maggie to enter first. "I'm glad it didn't ruin your entire day."

Stifling a yawn, she turned to him. "When exactly is her birthday?"

She had no energy to plan another outing tonight.

"It's almost a month from now, so we don't have to plan anything tonight." He must have read her thoughts.

She rubbed her forehead again. She couldn't think straight anymore. "Good to hear. I'm exhausted right now."

"She was just so excited to tell you tonight. I didn't want to disappoint her." His eyes twinkled in the lantern light hanging on the hook. In the glowing light, his angular nose and sturdy jaw took on a soft appearance.

Maggie's stomach quivered, as if filled with the same tiny moths flying close to the lantern's flame. "Very thoughtful of you. I'm glad she told me. We can keep her excited while planning for the big event."

She sent him a thank-you smile. Romy was being very considerate of his sister's feelings.

"I'm sure this birthday celebration is the exact thing Janet needs." Romy rubbed his hand down his pant leg.

"I couldn't agree more."

Would this get too confusing? Maggie's day with Leon, basking in his attention, had been memorable. But now her stomach rolled at the thought of planning this party with Romy. Spending time with two different men didn't happen often. Not in her lifetime, at least. The next three weeks would be very interesting indeed.

***

After Maggie took her leave and headed through the kitchen, Romy drew in a deep breath, trying to slow his heart rate back to normal. Needing some fresh air, he turned and headed back outside. Standing so close to her in the dim light had been agonizing. He had wanted to take her in his arms and hold her, but of course, that was impossible.

Could he be content with the planning phase of this adventure? For now, at least. He had to keep in mind that the goal was to get closer to Maggie.

Harry burst out the back door. "I saw Maggie head in to her room. She sure was beaming. Did you give her one on the kisser?"

"What are you talking about?" Would Harry ever stop pestering him? "Of course I didn't kiss her."

"Ya coulda' fooled me the way she looked—all goofy."

"We were talking about Janet's birthday celebration. She

wants Maggie and me to take her to a Shirley Temple movie for her birthday."

"Attaboy. Now Maggie will have to spend time with you."

Romy swallowed. "I suppose I shouldn't ask what happened on your picnic today, but I'd sure like to know."

He needed to stop being so jealous of Leon. If only he could follow his own advice. Maybe it was time to admit Maggie was more important to him than just about anything else.

Harry stuck his thumbs in his pants pockets. "I think Leon got a little too fresh with her."

Romy's stomach burned deep within. So much for not being jealous. "Was he trying to neck with her?"

"No, nothing so serious, but at one point on the ferry he had her locked in his arms against the railing. Next thing I knew she came running over to us. She didn't leave our side after that. She's no pushover."

Romy let out a breath. "Good to hear. Maybe he pushed his luck a bit too far."

"Could be."

Combing his fingers through his hair, he looked at his brother. "I have my work cut out—to get her to fall for me instead of him."

✳✳✳

Maggie heard a knock on the porch door as she washed the last of Saturday's supper dishes. Who could it be? She wiped her hands and headed out onto the porch. Leon stood at the back door with his hat in his hand. Dressed in a tan shirt with brown tie and slacks, he looked like he was ready for a night on the town. Oh, great. Once again, he'd caught her in the kitchen with her hands wet.

Her heart pounding, she rubbed her hands down her apron. If only she didn't look so disheveled. "Leon. What a surprise."

"I have to apologize for showing up on your doorstep without any warning. I finally found some time after my busy week to call on you." Leon twirled his hat in his hands.

Maggie raised her hand to try to get her hair under control. She untied her apron and hung it on the hook inside the kitchen door. "I wish I'd known ahead of time so I wouldn't look so frazzled."

"I was wondering if you'd come walking with me for a bit." He held out his hand to her.

She grasped it, letting the screen door slam behind her. Isn't this what she had hoped for since their trip up the river? Her thoughts had been reaching across the road during the week wondering what he was doing. Now, here he was, and she looked awful.

"I can only walk with you a short time. Since it's Saturday night, I have to help the girls with their baths before church tomorrow morning." His hand was warm, but it didn't reach her heart tonight. He could have somehow given her a warning, so she could have at least combed her hair.

"Oh, well, at least come and sit on the wall with me." Letting go of her hand, he walked down the few steps to the driveway and followed the retaining wall toward the road. "Let's sit here."

He leaned against the stone wall while she sat on it.

"I've missed you this week." Leon gazed into Maggie's eyes.

"I've missed you, too." Was that the honest truth? Maggie pushed that thought deep inside her head.

Leon reached for her hand again. "Maggie, I'd really like my parents to meet you. They're home right now. Would you walk over there with me, so I could introduce you to them?"

Was he kidding? Meet his parents the way she looked? Biting her lip, she pulled her hand away and reached for her hair again. "Now? I was working in the garden this afternoon. You should have given me a warning."

"I'm sorry I didn't. I understand. We'll have to plan it some other day at a better time. I want you to know how special you are to me. I don't care how you look when I see you." Grasping her hand, he squeezed her fingers.

Goosebumps ran up her arm. She longed to hear words like this from a man she could care about. She certainly did care for Leon, didn't she? Maybe this was the beginning of a lifetime relationship. Part of her heart struggled against that thought. "We'll have to make those plans soon then, I guess."

She heard someone whistling near the barn and turned to see Romy walk out the door. He stopped whistling as soon as he saw them. She lifted her hand to wave at him, but changed her mind when she saw the dour look crossing his brow. Why was he so moody?

Turning back to Leon, Maggie smiled. "Maybe you could

come to church with us tomorrow, and then I could go meet your parents afterward."

The croaking frogs filled the tense silence.

"Um . . . I . . . We can't tomorrow." Pushing away from the wall, Leon meandered a few feet away. "We've already planned to go out of town."

"Oh. We'll have to figure out something next week then." She stood up. "I need to get back in the house to help the girls."

Leon closed the distance in three strides. Grasping both of Maggie's hands, he pulled her toward him. "Okay, I'll see you soon."

He kissed her on the cheek, turned and walked down the driveway.

She wanted to sit down and ponder what had just happened, but couldn't take any more time out of the Saturday routine to think about Leon and her future. She brushed her hand over her cheek and sighed.

CHAPTER 22

The hot sun beating on her back, Maggie brushed the back of her hand over her damp forehead as she worked in the garden, picking green beans for their dinner tomorrow. As she searched to find the hiding vegetables, the scratchy green leaves reached for her hands and arms. Romy stood in the next row plucking another handful of the green pods.

Since July Fourth, the heat-filled days seemed to sap the entire family's strength, particularly the young girls. The only bright spot Maggie could remember the past three weeks was the occasional discussion of Janet's birthday.

More worrisome yet was the strain on Mr. Iverson's face from watching the crops shrivel up day after day. No rain to nourish them. She dropped several beans in the dish. "Your pa looks so worn out. What's going to happen if this drought continues much longer?"

"There's nothing much we can do about it except pray. Church will probably be full tomorrow for that very reason." Romy looked toward the field. "The corn should be shoulder high by now and starting to tassel out. Look at it. It's not much more than knee high. The leaves are curled up tight."

"I know. Watering the garden is the only thing keeping the vegetables alive. Thank goodness Jim and Ted can do this for me. I don't know what we'd eat next winter if the garden didn't produce crops." She moved more leaves to look for beans.

"Last month *Wallaces' Farmer* had an article about some

LEAD ME HOME

farmers down south who packed up and moved to California
because their crops failed. The magazine also said they've had
lots of dust storms down there making things worse."

Without a doubt, Romy had gotten over his shy streak during the last five weeks that Maggie had lived on the farm with
him. She enjoyed his friendship, working side by side with him
in the garden. If only he'd perked up before Leon came along.

"I haven't seen it this dry—ever." Maggie picked up the dish
and tucked it under her arm.

"Sometimes it's really tough being a farmer." Romy shook
his head. "I'm sure it's killing Pa to watch his farm wither away
to nothing."

"Good thing we know God is in control of our lives. I don't
know how any of us would even get out of bed every morning
without that."

***

The next morning, Maggie ran her brush through her stubborn
curls. Tiny drops of perspiration rolled down her forehead in
the airless humidity. She was trying to hurry so she'd be ready
for church on time.

Maybe Leon would come calling this afternoon. She hadn't
seen him since their talk by the stone wall a couple weeks ago.
He had mentioned meeting his parents, but nothing had been
planned yet. After that evening, she thought there might be an
understanding between them. Then for two weeks there had
been no word from him. He must be very busy with the farm.

She buttoned her navy skirt and pinned her hat over her
unruly curls. She'd better get out to the kitchen to make sure
the girls had their hair combed.

Minutes later, Mr. Iverson walked into the kitchen. "You've
only got one more minute to get ready. Since we have to take
the truck today, Romy is getting it out of the shed."

Squatting in front of Janet, Maggie smiled at her. "We'll make it."

He glanced down at them. "Good thing you have Miss Maggie to check you over before you walk out the door, Janet." He
rumpled her hair with his hand and smiled.

"I know, Pa. I missed the top button the first time. It was all
crooked."

"There, that's much better." Maggie hugged Janet and stood
up. "Do you want to sit by me in church today?"

Janet's face lit up. "Do you mean I can sit by Lucy and the babies?"

Finding it hard to disconnect herself from Emma's family, Maggie had sat with them every Sunday since she moved out to the farm. But no longer. She'd make the transition to the Iverson pew today.

"No, I meant I'll sit by your family today so you can sit next to me. My sister told me last week that she didn't need me to do that any longer. She's arranged for Cissy to take my place." Sighing, Maggie knew it was time, since she seemed to be a permanent addition to the Iverson family, but deep down it still hurt.

"Oh, okay. I'll sit by you in church." Janet's hand grasped Maggie's as she leaned against her.

"Romy's here with the truck, so let's load up." Mr. Iverson plopped his hat on his head. "Miss Maggie will ride in front with us. The rest of you climb in the back. Make sure you boys let the girls sit up front so their hair doesn't blow around so much."

Maggie scooted onto the seat, squeezing in between the two men. "At least it's a nice sunny day today."

At least she knew the trip to town wouldn't be a silent agony any longer.

"Well, that's nothing new. It's sunny and hot all the time." The sunshine didn't cheer Mr. Iverson up at all.

They turned toward town and increased their speed.

"Look, there's Leon walking along the road." Romy rolled down his window as the truck pulled to a stop.

"Wonder if he needs a ride." Mr. Iverson leaned forward in the seat.

"Hey, Leon, want a ride to town? We're on our way to church." Romy pointed in the direction they were headed.

He held up his pole. "I'm going to see if the fish are biting. I'm not about to waste my time in church on such a beautiful day."

Leaning forward to peek past Romy, Maggie gasped. Her heart thundered in her chest. Fishing on a Sunday morning? She hadn't heard him talk about God before, but he certainly knew about her faith. Was that why he was avoiding her?

Leon's eyes bulged, resembling a lizard's. "Uh . . . hi, Maggie. Uh, have a good time at church."

"We'll see you later." Romy sped up and left Leon standing with his mouth open.

Head bowed, Maggie hid her face in the palms of her hands. If only she had listened to Emma's advice weeks ago.

***

Romy tried not to let his glee show on his face. From Maggie's reaction, she hadn't known about Leon's contempt for church. This would be the advantage Romy needed to try to win her away from his neighbor. Leon had just handed him a gift.

"That was interesting." Romy stared out the front window before turning toward her.

Lifting her head, Maggie glanced at him. Through pursed lips, she spoke in terse words. "It certainly was. I assumed Leon had faith in God like I do."

"I suppose we can't figure he doesn't believe in God just because he's not going to church." Romy glimpsed her face before gluing his eyes to the road again.

"If he does, he sure has a strange way of showing it." Pa said out loud what Romy was thinking.

"I agree with you there, Mr. Iverson." Maggie closed her eyes.

If only Romy could reach out his hand to comfort her. He squeezed the steering wheel tighter to stop from doing something foolish. Leon's actions didn't surprise him in the least. But by the look on Maggie's face, she was devastated.

When they arrived at church, the family tumbled out of the truck. Before Pa could round everyone up and head into church, Mr. Handzel, Mr. Bartell, and Mr. Wellington surrounded him. Romy shook his head. They hadn't even waited until church was over. Out of the corner of his eye, he noticed Maggie wander off to talk to her sister.

"Albert, did you hear the news from Fayette County?" Mr. Handzel tucked his thumbs in his vest pockets.

"What're you talking about, Jack?" Pa rested his hand on the tailgate of the truck.

Mr. Handzel pointed to Mr. Bartell. "Dick heard five farmers in Fayette have called it quits and packed up."

"Haven't heard that." Pa rubbed his chin.

"Yup, it's even drier to the west than it is here." Mr. Wellington shook his head. "Don't know what'll happen here if we don't get some rain soon."

"God knows. That's about all we can say." Pa pushed away from the truck.

"I suppose we better get into church and do some mighty hard praying, then." Mr. Handzel headed off toward his family.

"Let's go, kids." Pa directed the family toward the church door.

Pastor's family was gathered at the bottom of the steps. Maggie had a baby in her arms. "I'm going to hold Timmy today, but after this Cissy will help Emma with the babies in church. She wasn't feeling well today."

"Goody. I get to sit by one of the babies." Janet laughed as the baby grabbed her finger.

"Would you rather sit with Mrs. Hannemann then?" Romy asked.

"No, she'd rather I keep Timmy with me." Maggie transferred Timmy to her other arm. "She said that Lucy and Denny would not be sitting by me from now on, so they might as well start today."

"Enough chattering. Let's go sit down." Pa led the way up the steps into the sanctuary.

Romy sat between Janet and Mary to make sure he was close enough to Maggie in case she needed an extra hand. Janet had squeezed into the pew right after Maggie, managing to get the spot next to the baby.

The baby cooed now and then during the service, making it hard for Romy to concentrate. He drew his attention back to Pastor Hannemann when he read the sermon text from Hebrews 12:9-11: "Furthermore we have had fathers of our flesh which corrected us, and we gave them reverence. . . . Now no chastening for the present seemeth to be joyous, but grievous; nevertheless afterward it yieldeth the peaceable fruit of righteousness unto them which are exercised thereby."

Romy could see the entire congregation sit up straighter as Pastor read this text. He was sure every person wanted to absorb what the pastor had to say.

"Dearly beloved of the Lord Jesus Christ, it is no secret that we have been experiencing hard times, times that none of us has lived through before. Many of us have witnessed how friends and family have been forced from home because of broken finances, unable to support those they love. We all go about our lives working our hardest in what we do, but so often it hasn't brought in enough to feed our families.

"Yet through the words of His apostle, our Lord is telling us that He loves us. That through these hard times, He is chastening His believers. Chastening here means teaching us, not punishing us. We must see His fatherly hand, training us so that we learn to lean on Him, to trust in Him in all our ways. St. Paul tells us in Romans that our tribulations produce patience; and patience, endurance; and endurance brings us hope. The hope of His love in our hearts by the Holy Ghost!

"And although we may not see clearly now how this can be, yet we must cling to our hope which is in Jesus. God, who has so loved us that He gave His Son into death for our salvation, will not leave us or forsake us."

As Pastor continued, Romy felt himself relax. These were the words he needed to hear during this long dry summer. He was glad that he could share this time of worship and comfort with Maggie. He slanted a glance in her direction to see her reaction.

Maggie had her hands full with the baby, but he hoped she was listening. Was she thinking of the troubling incident on the way to church? How did people like Leon deal with life during times like this without a thought for heavenly guidance? If they were rich, they might not have the same cares. But when the hard times did arrive at their doorstep, how would they cope?

Romy sighed. He and his family were in God's hands. They needed to trust that everything would turn out for their good no matter what came tomorrow. They could cope with hard times knowing that God was leading them on the journey home.

CHAPTER 23

"Please pass the empty chicken platter." Maggie pushed herself away from the Sunday dinner table and walked toward the stove to refill it. Even though her stomach churned at the thought of seeing Leon on the road, she had to look normal, keep going through the motions. If only she could stop thinking about it. She scooped the last chicken leg onto the platter.

Fishing on a Sunday morning? What would she say to Leon? She'd give him a chance to explain. She couldn't jump to conclusions. Her heart was still beating, even if it felt like a lead weight.

Pasting a smile on her face, she turned toward the family. "Would someone like more chicken? There's plenty left."

"Sure thing. This is really great, Miss Maggie." Ted grabbed the full plate from her hands.

"Yeah, this is so yummy." Janet rubbed her belly.

"It's time for the weekly planning." Mr. Iverson looked at his almost-grown sons. "Anyone have something to add to the list?"

Romy glanced at his little sister. "I know one thing that's coming up. Janet, do you know what that is?"

"Uh-uh." She shook her head as she picked up her milk glass. "What, Romy?"

"Your birthday, silly." Sally poked her youngest sister for emphasis.

"My birthday? When is it?" Janet set her glass down.

Tension leaving her shoulders, Maggie smiled. Something to take her mind off of Leon, at least. They'd been hinting about the party for weeks now, but Janet didn't understand the day was almost here.

"It's on Tuesday." Mary said.

"Are we going to the movie like I wanted?"

"That's what we're planning right now, so let's wait to find out." Mr. Iverson pushed his chair back and rested his coffee mug on his knee. "What else is going on besides Janet's celebration?"

"How are the oats doing? We usually start cutting about this time." Romy reached for the last cookie on the plate.

"I was discussing it at church this morning." Mr. Iverson took a sip of the black liquid. "The fields are so dry, I'm not sure if we'll get much of a crop, but we still have to harvest as much as the Lord has given us."

"Do you use a reaper and thresher to harvest oats like at my Pa's farm in Wisconsin?" Maggie curled both hands around her mug.

Mr. Iverson glanced at her. "Yup. I imagine it's pretty much like your Pa's place. The reaper will cut and bundle the oats into shocks in the field. Then when it's our turn to have the thresher come to our place, we'll thresh it and store it in the granary. Your job that day will be to feed the crew."

"Do we know when we're scheduled for the machine?" Romy gazed at his pa.

"I think the thresher will come here on Friday or next Monday. We'll be heading over to the Wellingtons on Wednesday, and I think the Handzels are on Thursday. Of course, there's always the chance of breakdowns which will put us behind."

"Do you know if Winklers are included in the rotation?" Maggie set her mug down. Would Leon be coming? He had some questions to answer. Maybe on Friday.

"They don't have any crops to harvest this year, so the thresher isn't scheduled to go to their place." Mr. Iverson put his cup on the table.

She swallowed. "That will make the scheduling easier then. When do you start working on the oats?"

When would she confront Leon?

"We'll use the reaper on Monday and Tuesday." Romy leaned back and crossed his arms.

"That should work, son." Mr. Iverson looked at Janet. "Tell you what. How about if Romy helps me on Monday and Tuesday, then on Wednesday evening he can take you and the girls to the family movie night for your birthday? That's only one day late."

"Family movie night?" Maggie looked from Romy to Mr. Iverson.

"Several years ago, a little town north of here started showing free movies on the side of a building downtown. They set out benches for people and sell popcorn and soda for a nickel. It's great fun for the family. The stores stay open, so it helps out the rest of the town, also. We've gone up there on occasion," Mr. Iverson nodded his head.

Janet's face glowed until a sudden cloud took her smile away. "Romy, me, and the girls? What about Miss Maggie? I told her I wanted her to go, too."

Maggie held her breath, waiting for his decision. Maybe Mr. Iverson wouldn't go along with the plan. She wouldn't want to disappoint Janet.

"If you'd like Miss Maggie to go, that would be fine." Janet's father stroked her long hair. "Since it's a family movie night, we could all go if you want."

"After working all day, count me out. There is no way I'd go if it's a Shirley Temple movie." Jim slumped down in his chair and crossed his arms, looking none too happy.

"Same here," chimed in Ted.

The sunshine smile returned to Janet's face. Maggie grinned in response. Mr. Iverson had interacted more often with the girls during the last couple weeks. Compared to the first day she'd arrived on the farm, the entire family treated each other with more love and respect now. Her prayers had been answered.

"Well, we don't know for sure if it's a Shirley Temple movie like you want, sweetie. Harry said he'd check in the paper tomorrow morning to see what's playing for movie night on Wednesday." Janet's pa winked at her.

Maggie started stacking the dirty plates into a pile. "That sounds good to me. That will give me Thursday to get ready for the threshers on Friday if that's when they come."

"We have two days to plan my birthday. Romy, can you help me this afternoon?" Janet wiggled like a fish flopping on dry land.

"I will if you sit still for the rest of our dinner."

***

Three days later, Romy massaged his sore back when he finished milking the last of the herd. He'd been assigned to do the
morning chores, but at least he didn't have to work at the Wellington farm all day. Before he and the girls could head to the
movie, he'd also have to see to the evening milking alone, but it
sure would be worth it.

The last two days tuckered him out, working with the reaper
sunup to sundown bundling the oat shocks. With the frequent
breakdowns, they didn't manage to finish until after dark last
night. Pa wasn't happy at all. At least the moon helped them
complete the job in the cool of the evening. His two younger
brothers were so exhausted that they had had to be dragged out
of bed this morning.

"I'll gladly do the chores by myself if I can spend the day
with the girls and Maggie." He slapped the cow on the rump.
"You know how lucky I am, don't you, Bess? I'm going to enjoy
this day just fine." Whistling a tune, he picked up the stool and
headed toward the milk house.

Thirty minutes later, he pulled open the screen door and let
it slam behind him. "I brought the fresh milk in for dinner." He
set the can on the table and looked around for any sign of life.
"Where is everyone?"

Silence was his only answer.

He poured the milk into the pitcher and set it in the icebox.
Where could they be? He headed outside again looking for the
girls. When he walked around the corner of the house toward
the garden, he saw four back ends draped with skirts—ranging
in size from Maggie to Janet.

"There you are. I've been looking for you." He strolled
toward the garden fence.

Maggie straightened up first, holding her bulging apron in
front of her. She brushed stray damp curls off her face with the
back of her free hand.

"We're trying to get the cucumbers picked. I'd like to get
them in the crock today." She walked toward the waiting container and dumped her full apron into the basket. "I'll make sure
we have an early supper for the men. They'll be starving. Then

we can head out to the movie."

"I'll help you ladies with the cukes then." Forgetting his aching back, Romy crawled over the fence and went to the other end of Janet's row. "We should be able to get these done in time."

"When does the movie start?" Mary moved to the next plant and bent over.

"Not until it's almost dark since it's outside. Harry found out *The Little Colonel* was playing tonight. How lucky can we be?" Waving away a pesky fly buzzing close to his ear, Romy stooped to search under the prickly leaves.

"Does it have the little girl with bouncy hair in it?" Janet asked.

"Sure does."

"What's a colonel?" Janet stopped working and looked at her brother.

"A colonel is a person in charge in an army."

"How can she be in the army if she's a girl?"

"She's called the little colonel because she's so much like her grandfather, who was a colonel in the army." He tossed a cucumber into the basket.

"That's a silly name for a girl." Mary tugged at a large one by her feet.

"It's just a nickname, like we call you 'sweetie' sometimes."

Maggie looked at the watch pinned to her blouse. "We'd better get back to work here, or we won't finish in time to see this great movie. Girls, make sure you look under all the big leaves to find the small cukes. They like to hide."

"Yeah, I like the baby pickles the best anyway." Sally brushed aside the leaves.

"How can we get all this done in time to go?" Thunk. Romy dropped another one into the container.

"We only have to wash them and get them in the crock. Then I'll mix up the brine and pour it over. I'll need to weigh them down and cover the crock with a towel." Maggie stood up and put her hands on her lower back. "Oh, that reminds me. We also need to cut lots of dill."

Romy's palms got sweaty as he watched her bend this way and that, emphasizing her curves. His feelings for her were deepening each day they worked side by side. He needed to find an errand to do—fast.

"I'll take care of that." He pulled his folding knife out of his pocket. "I'll get the crock out of the basement, too."

Maggie had been such a blessing to their household. He didn't know how the family would have pulled itself back together without her. *Lord, show me if she's the one for me.* Maybe she would stay in the family—permanently.

***

Maggie washed the last supper plate and handed it to Sally.

"We're about finished here. Mary, can you run and ask Romy if the car is packed?" She squeezed out the dishcloth and turned to wash the kitchen table.

She spotted the five-gallon crock sitting in the corner of the kitchen covered with a towel. Good thing they'd finished filling the crock with brine before suppertime. Romy had helped the younger girls scrub the cucumbers out by the water pump as she and Sally had mixed up the pickling solution.

When she had seen him with Janet and Mary, her heart had warmed faster than pancakes in the oven. He was always so kind and patient with his sisters. If only Leon had more qualities like this.

As Maggie sponged down the table, her hand stilled. Could she ever find a man like Romy . . . now, wait a minute . . . why not Romy?

But what about Leon? Maybe his fishing trip on Sunday was an answer for her. She placed her hands over her jumpy stomach as her mind flip-flopped between two very different men. This was much more complicated than she had ever imagined. What to do? What to do? But she didn't have time to dwell on it now.

The screen door slammed as Mary raced back into the kitchen. "He says there are three blankets, a jug of water, and five glasses in the trunk." She counted off the objects on her fingers. "Do we need anything else?"

"Let's take some cookies in case anyone gets hungry." Maggie handed Sally an empty cookie tin. "I think some are left in the jar in the pantry."

Sally licked her lips. "Oh, yummy. That's a great idea."

The smell of vanilla filled the pantry as they placed the cookies in the tin.

"I think we're all set then." Maggie followed Sally out the door.

The girls piled into the back seat so, of course, Maggie slid into the front seat with Romy. She smiled at the thought that she didn't have to hug the door today. The awkward silences between them no longer existed, so she'd enjoy her evening with Romy.

Leon forced his way into the back of her mind as they started down the driveway. *Lord, please help me get through this evening. I'm so confused. I don't know what to do anymore.* For tonight anyway, she'd force any thoughts of Leon to the background. "So where did you say we're going?"

Before Romy headed out onto the road, he glanced her way. His piercing brown eyes bore into her for an instant. She couldn't look away. Forgetting Leon for tonight might be easier than she imagined. She cleared her throat to break the spell.

He swung his eyes back to the front window. Did he feel the pull, also? "We're going to the town of Sherrill north of here."

"I've never heard of it." Of course, she didn't know too much about Iowa, so that probably wasn't surprising.

"That's because it's so small. It has a large church on top of the hill and a couple stores."

"Where do they show the film?" Maggie fidgeted with the strap of her handbag.

"They put up benches in the parking lot of the Behr General Store and show it on the side wall."

"Why the blanket, then?"

"Well, there are hills around the area. I thought the girls would rather sit on the ground instead of benches."

"That's probably smart, so Janet can curl up on the blanket if she falls asleep."

"Thus, the extra ones." Romy smiled at Maggie.

She couldn't wipe the responding grin off her face as her pulse raced. Focus on something else. Time to include the girls again. The three in the back seat jabbered away, ignoring the conversation in the front. She turned around. "Did you girls ever go to an outside picture show before?"

"Oh, yes. It's lots—"

"Yeah, I like the part where you can—"

"I always fall asleep." Janet's mouth turned down. "But it's fun before that."

Maggie relaxed and enjoyed the rest of the ride with the descriptions flying up from the back. A lightness filling her, she had a feeling of déjà vu from her childhood.

"Here we are." Romy pulled the car to a stop on a sloping street. "It looks like we'll have to walk a block or so." He handed a blanket to each girl. "Sally, you lead the way with your sisters. Miss Maggie and I will carry the rest."

"Let's go." Sally took Janet's hand and started down the hill.

Romy's smile spread across his face. "Our adventure begins."

"This does look like fun." Maggie saw the crowd filling up the benches as they approached the store. The red brick church stood as a sentinel on the crest of the hill, overlooking the festivities.

They spread their blankets on a sloping lawn close to the parking lot. Drops of perspiration coursed down Maggie's forehead in the sweltering heat. Tiny insects, reflecting the setting sunset, looked like shooting stars racing through the sky. People strolled down the sidewalks, window-shopping and chatting with neighbors.

"This reminds me so much of my hometown in Wisconsin."

"I've always liked coming to this little burg. Do you miss your town?"

"Not really. I miss my family, though." She glanced at the crowd milling around. "It's nice to be in a place where everyone knows each other."

"Well, that describes this place." He looked at the vendor selling popcorn. "Don't you think Janet should have popcorn for her birthday party?"

"Absolutely." Maggie's excitement grew, as if it were her own birthday. This was Janet's party, for Pete's sake. At least it was a night away from daily routine.

But she didn't want to get too caught up tonight with her mind pulling her toward Romy when things weren't settled with Leon. Romy wouldn't read too much into this event. Would he?

"Girls, come here."

The three ran toward Romy, after staking out their corners on the blanket. "What?"

He stretched out his hand and motioned for them to follow suit. "Here's a nickel for each of you to get popcorn."

"Yea!" The chorus rang out.

"Don't you and Miss Maggie want some, too?" Janet clutched the nickel in her small hand.

"We'll get some a bit later." Romy glanced at Maggie as he spoke.

"Okay. I want Miss Maggie to have a good time to-night."

Stooping to Janet's level, Maggie hugged her. "I'm having a good time already. It's your birthday party, so you need to have fun."

The girls ran off to stand in line by the vendor.

"Let's explore a while." Romy held out his hand toward Maggie.

She couldn't take it. It would be making a commitment to him, in a way. After all, they were in public in broad daylight. She tucked her hands in her pocket and followed him down the road. "Good idea."

Twenty minutes later Maggie heard someone shout, "Time to start!"

The crowd wandered back to their seats.

"Where are the girls now?" She scanned the area, searching for them.

Romy pointed toward the blanket. "There they are. Let's grab a bag of popcorn and head back."

He steered her toward the vendor with his hand on her elbow. "This looks great."

She pretended her heart didn't give a quick little kick against her ribs as the warmth of his hand spread through her.

After paying the nickel, they strolled toward the sisters. Maggie's shoulder bumped against Romy several times, but he didn't seem to mind.

"Looks like you girls are all set." Her pulse racing, Maggie sat behind Janet. If only her voice sounded normal. Would Romy sit by one of the other girls?

No, he lowered himself to the blanket right next to her. Gazing at her, his eyes twinkled in the fading light. She couldn't help but reflect his wide smile with her own.

He offered her the newly purchased bag. "We have to share the popcorn."

"Thanks." Unable to pull her eyes away from him, she grabbed a few pieces from the proffered bag. It was as if an unspoken tender moment stretched between them.

"When's the picture show going to start?" Janet licked her buttery fingers.

The moment disappeared into the darkening sky. Maggie sighed.

Romy rubbed Janet's back. "Very soon, little one."

"What's it about again?"

"Shirley Temple—that's the girl with bouncy curls—will be a little girl who doesn't like her grandfather at the beginning of the movie. Then—"

"Oh, it's starting." Mary pointed to the large screen as it began to flicker with the black-and-white movie.

"This is so great." Sally couldn't sit still.

People sitting on benches filled the parking lot. The surrounding grassy hillside covered with blankets looked like a patchwork quilt. Reflecting the light off the huge screen, all eyes focused on the flashing images. The quiet symphony of cricket calls echoed from the surrounding woods. What a perfect end to a lovely day.

Snickers from the crowd grew loud when the sound didn't work properly. The movie characters formed words, but the sound of the voices came seconds later. Before too long, it was synchronized.

Maggie was mesmerized at the outset. She'd heard so much about the girl actress, but had never seen one of her movies. Leaning back, she braced herself on her arms.

Romy copied her stance almost immediately. Her breath froze when his hand covered hers. Relaxing, she took pleasure in the warmth of his hand. After all, it was dark now. Her heart pounding in her chest, she kept her eyes glued to the screen as she watched the little actress dance across the stage.

What was happening in the movie? No clue. Her mind could only absorb the connected hands between them.

Maybe this was God's answer to her inner conflict.

CHAPTER 24

Maggie lay in her bed staring at the ceiling. She had so much to do for Friday that she needed all the rest she could get, but sleep wouldn't come.

Maybe it was the to-do lists going through her head. She'd have to be up before dawn getting organized for the noon meal—preparing chickens, peeling potatoes, baking pies. How would she get it all done in time?

Maybe it was because her thoughts kept returning to the events at the movie. She had tossed and turned for hours replaying the scene. The warmth of Romy's hand covering hers had spread from his fingers, up her arm, and into her heart.

Her stomach rolled beneath her ribs. She'd had a wonderful evening with Romy, so was it time to forget Leon? A couple weeks ago she had thought she'd found her life partner. She had almost been ready to plan her future life with Leon.

Now she didn't feel that way at all. How could she be so fickle?

Leon had demonstrated his first priority wasn't God. That was loud and clear on Sunday morning. He never came afterward to explain his actions. Never came to answer her questions. She couldn't commit her life to someone who didn't agree with her about faith. That wasn't being fickle at all.

Lord, be with me as I walk down this uncertain path in my life. Lead me in the direction You want me to go. You have placed Romy in my life. He has become special to me. Help me to know if this is the correct path.

Romy had demonstrated his love for God over and over by the way he treated her and his sisters. Maggie had to admit Emma and Neil were both right about Romy. He was a good man after he got over his shyness. The more she got to know him the more she liked him. It was time to admit this now. Tucking an arm beneath her head, Maggie smiled.

But what about the girls? Pulling the sheet away, Maggie sat up. How would Janet react if Maggie and Romy learned to love each other? When the time came, would Sally and Mary understand why Romy was more important to her than they were? Maggie couldn't let the girls down now that they had such a close bond. Tossing and turning, Maggie's night of sleep evaporated.

***

Romy whistled as he walked toward the house for breakfast. When was the last time he had felt this happy? Last night was a breakthrough for him. Had Maggie felt the spark, too? She hadn't pulled her hand away during the movie. He'd never felt this way about a woman before. From now on he could show his feelings to her more each day.

He opened the back door and headed into the kitchen. "Good morning."

Three pairs of eyes turned in his direction, but the ones he was hoping for, didn't look at him. Maggie continued stirring the eggs on the stove. Hadn't she heard him?

"Good morning, Romy." At least Sally smiled at him. "Breakfast is almost ready."

"Do you want me to put the syrup on the table?" Mary held out the quart jar toward Maggie.

"That would be great, Mary." Maggie flipped the bacon in the pan. "Could you pour some in the small pitcher?"

She spoke to Mary, but not him. What was up? Maybe if he talked to Maggie directly she'd acknowledge him. "I brought in some fresh milk, Miss Maggie. Do you want me to fill the pitcher in the ice box?"

She shrugged. "That's fine."

What's wrong with her? She should be smiling and happy to see him. He might as well be a statue, the way she ignored him.

Was she mad at him for holding her hand last night? His shoulders sagged.

The rest of the family rushed into the kitchen and sat down. Romy poured milk into the pitcher and set it on the table. Maybe he could get into her good graces by helping her serve the food.

"Can I help you?" Romy stopped himself from putting a hand on her arm. She had to pay attention now.

She glanced sideways at him. "The eggs can be served."

At last, he was getting somewhere. He scraped the eggs into the large bowl. Their hands touched when he placed the pan back on the stove. He turned to see if she had a reaction.

Instead of a smile on her lips, they were glued in a pinched line. How had things gone from wonderful last night to don't-touch-me today? His mouth matched hers as he held his tongue. He couldn't react in front of the family.

"Did you have fun last night at the movie?" Jim snatched a piece of bread off the plate.

"Oh, yeah." Janet's eyes opened like windows. "It was so fun. The little girl danced in such a pretty dress."

The entire table joined in the laughter. Romy shot Maggie a glance to see her reaction. Her face matched Cissy's pink finger nail polish from last Sunday. Yet Maggie didn't look his way. What was going on in that head of hers? What if he told his last-night story about holding her hand? What color would her cheeks be then?

Chaos erupted as the older girls explained their exciting evening at the same time.

"Miss Maggie, wasn't the movie grand?" Janet spoke up when there was a lull in the conversation.

Romy whipped his head in her direction. Ahhh! Her cheeks matched the red-checkered curtains blowing in the breeze. At least someone got a reaction from her.

"Uh . . . Sure, it was terrific." Her voice spoke the words, but her face didn't mirror the statement. There was no smile anywhere around.

Did she even have a clue what the movie was about? He sure didn't. His mind hadn't taken in most of the action on the big screen. He had been concentrating more on her fingers lying under his on the blanket. Did she regret what he had done? How could he find out?

The conversation flew over Romy's head until his father spoke. "The fair is coming closer. Are you boys planning on entering any pigs or calves this year?"

Every other year, the last week of July had become the highlight of the summer. Ma had always entered her baked goods while the boys took livestock. This year was different since they had not been to any 4-H meetings since before Ma died.

"Yeah, I suppose." Jim put another bite of egg in his mouth. "I could take my two feeder pigs."

"I'm planning on taking my calf. I've tried to keep her clean so she can go." Ted grabbed a piece of bread.

"Well, then we better make sure the animals are entered in time." Pa drank a sip of coffee and pushed his chair back. "Romy'll have to make sure the paperwork is all done correctly since I've never done it before."

Another occasion for Ma to be missed.

"That means we'll all be going to the fair next Wednesday since it's the day the animals are judged." Romy turned to Maggie to explain. "We always make a day of it. Pa and the boys will take the truck, and I'll drive the rest of the family in the car. Of course, Harry's working in town, so he's left out of this event."

"I love going to the fair." Janet's arms flew so wide she almost tipped her milk over.

"First you love the movie and now the fair." Mary poked Janet. "You have to make up your mind."

"Can't I love them both?" Janet's lower lip poked out.

The fair was something to think about for the coming week, but Romy wouldn't let the issue with Maggie just disappear.

***

Maggie stretched to pick the apple hanging out of her reach. Would she have to go to the shed to find a ladder to get this job finished? She didn't have much time. Baking three pies this afternoon would be a real challenge for her as it was. The threshing crew was scheduled to come for dinner tomorrow. There was no choice in the matter. She'd probably have to hide the pies in the basement, so they would survive with the hungry men in the house.

"What was that all about at breakfast?" Romy's voice boomed across the lawn.

She started at the sound and watched him stomp toward her. Rubbing a sweaty palm on her skirt, she swallowed. "What do you mean?"

"Are you mad at me for last night?" He stopped mere inches from her.

"Mad at you? What makes you think that?" She dropped an apple into the basket at her feet.

"You practically ignored me the whole time I was in the house for breakfast." Romy crossed his arms over his chest. "I thought we had a great time last night—at least I did. Then you ignore me. What am I supposed to think?"

Maggie's insides jumped a time or two. If only she didn't get so nervous in confrontations. She bit her lip.

"I . . . I didn't know what else to do?" Amazing. She couldn't get her words out when talking to him. Their roles were reversed. How ironic!

"You'll have to explain that statement." Romy shook his head, but didn't uncross his arms. She hadn't planned on making him angry.

"I lay awake last night thinking how wonderful the evening turned out. Then . . ."

His tone softened as he reached toward her. "I did, too. That's why I couldn't believe it when you ignored me."

She struggled to get the words out. "I didn't know how to act in front of your family. When you held my hand . . ." The dam of words burst open. "It felt so right to me last night, but I don't want the girls to know about us—or—especially your pa. I just thought I had to hide my feelings, and the only way I could was to ignore you."

"I suppose that should be good news for me, but I'm having a hard time coming around to your way of thinking. Why can't we act like we like each other in front of the family? Why's it so hard?" Romy rubbed the back of his neck.

He didn't get it. Maggie shook her head. Men. "Can you imagine the teasing we'd have to endure from Jim and Ted? What would your pa think? What about the girls? They trust me now. Life can be normal again for them."

"That doesn't have anything to do with the way you and I feel about each other. I thought our relationship had changed last night. I was ready to ask you to be my girlfriend this morning."

How could she make him understand? "Janet might feel like I would be abandoning her if I was your girlfriend—like I don't love her anymore."

"I don't think Janet would think that." Romy took a step away. "Why would she think that? I think you're worrying too much."

"Maybe she wouldn't, but I'm not sure I want to chance it at this point."

He turned his back and stared across the field. "In other words, you'd choose Janet and the girls over me."

Maggie's throat tightened with raw emotions. "Of course not, I don't . . ."

"Well, it sounds that way to me." Facing her again, he stared down at his empty hands. "When you decide I'm more important than they are, let me know. I'll get Jim to help you pick the apples."

With his shoulders sagging, he plodded away.

Maggie watched him leave with tears threatening to over-flow. That's not how she imagined this day would go. Last night, she'd found peace in her heart coming to the realization Romy was special to her. The weight in her middle threatened to double her over. *God, what just happened?*

She couldn't find the apples through her tears.

CHAPTER 25

"Where are they?" Romy, dressed in his gray suit, paced back and forth. Maggie must be in the house yet, combing the girls' hair. He'd retrieved the car from the garage minutes ago. Now they needed to get going. Pa and the boys would be waiting for them at the fairgrounds.

He leaned up against the fender, his dark gray fedora in his hand. What a week. He took a deep breath and slowly let it out. He'd been going non-stop since last Thursday. Friday had been exhausting with the threshing crew. Over the weekend, they had scurried around getting the animals ready for the fair. Monday and Tuesday were taken up getting the straw into the barn.

Thankfully, Pa told everyone today would be a day off, except for Harry, of course. The only tasks they'd have to do would be the morning and evening chores. It was about time. It'd be great to catch a nap sometime today. Ha! What a joke. That wouldn't happen at the fair.

"We're ready." Mary tripped as she ran out the back door. "Janet couldn't find the ribbons that matched her dress. We had to search everywhere before she finally found them under her bed. Miss Maggie wasn't too happy."

Not surprising. She hadn't seemed too happy all week. They'd treated each other the same way as they did in June— with awkward silences. Romy could feel himself reverting to his former self and didn't like it. He placed his hat back on his head. "Well, I'm glad you're ready now."

Maybe he had been too harsh last week. She just didn't make any sense that day in the orchard. Women. Why would a friendship—or possibly more—affect Janet and the girls? They would probably be thrilled if things went the way he hoped. Maggie would be a permanent part of the family then and never leave. If only Maggie could understand that.

Minutes later, they were on the way to Dubuque with the girls settled in the back. Janet leaned over the seat and tapped Romy on the shoulder. "What are we going to do all day at the fair?"

"Well, I suppose we'll go to the barns to see the animals the boys entered. I think the pigs and calves are judged this morning."

"But Romy, that's so boring," Sally complained.

"We need to be there for our brothers." Romy glanced at Janet. "Sit back, young lady, so you don't bang your chin if we go over a bump."

She slid back on the seat. "What about after this afternoon?"

Romy looked in the rearview mirror and caught Janet's eye. "Are you really asking if we'll be going on any rides?"

"Yes, oh, yes!" Mary jumped in first.

"I'm sure there will be some time to ride the merry-go-round."

"Oh, Miss Maggie, you need to go with us." Janet slid forward again. "It's so fun."

Maggie reached over and pushed her back in the seat. "I can see that, Janet. You sure are excited about it."

"Will you ride with us? I like riding on the yew . . . yewcorn. You know the creature with one horn." Janet demonstrated her thoughts.

"You mean the unicorn, silly," Mary said.

"Yeah, that one." Janet patted Maggie's arm. "Will you go, too?"

"Of course, I'll ride on the carousel with you." Maggie sent a smile in Romy's direction.

If only that smile indicated that Maggie was coming around again.

"Which is your favorite?" Mary broached the question.

"I guess the horses." Maggie turned a little, so her knee rested on the car seat.

Romy glanced down. As she looked into the back seat, the

hem of her blue-and-white dress pulled back a bit, revealing her knee. He drew in a quick breath and forced himself to concentrate on the road ahead.

"Then you and Romy can have a race with your horses 'cuz his favorite is horses, too." Janet clapped her hands.

Romy laughed. "I'm sure my horse will be faster than yours."

The pink hue of Maggie's cheeks enhanced her half-smile. Romy grinned. Things were looking up. Maybe this day would turn out better than he'd imagined.

***

"It's almost time to go home." Maggie herded the girls through the midway. The game and food booth vendors vied for their attention. "We need to meet your pa in the pig barn."

What a nice day they'd had. But she was getting exhausted from all the walking. Trickles of perspiration ran down her back while they stood in the piercing sun. The stifling air made breathing a chore today.

"Just one more ride before we have to leave." Mary folded her hands under her chin. "Please."

Maggie looked at the watch pinned to her dress. "We have a half hour, so I think we can get in one more ride. What do you think, Romy?"

"Absolutely. We haven't ridden on the Ferris wheel, yet. That's my favorite." He walked next to Maggie while the girls bounced ahead of them.

His arm brushed against hers as they walked. Was that on purpose, or a coincidence? If only it was on purpose. He had been his usual self all day. Maybe she'd been too harsh on him last week.

If only she didn't have this unreasonable fear in her gut about having a relationship with Romy. She couldn't explain why she thought it would never work out, even to herself.

They strolled past a game booth. "Step right up and win a necklace."

Maggie could see the glittering jewelry sitting on top of posts in the display. "Toss a ring around the post and win the prize," the vendor cried out.

"Oh, Romy, win a necklace for me." Janet bounced on one foot tugging his hand.

"I guess I could try." He turned in the ticket and reached for the five rings the vendor handed him. He tossed one ring. It landed between three posts. "Too bad."

"You'll do better next time." Mary clasped her hands together.

The second and third rings hit posts but slid down the edge to the table.

"Come on, Romy. You can do it." Sally tugged on his sleeve.

The fourth ring slipped over a corner of the post but tumbled off after a second.

"I only have one more." He looked at Janet. "Maybe you better blow on this for good luck."

Janet puckered up her lips and blew for all she was worth. "There, now you'll do it."

Maggie held her breath as the ring flew through the air. It glanced off a post and veered toward the left, landing around the adjacent one holding a bracelet.

"Yea!" The cheers went up from the sisters as they bounced around like popcorn.

The man handed the bracelet to Romy. He looked at it and held it up to Janet's wrist. "It's too big for you, Janet. I'm sorry I didn't get you a necklace."

"It's okay. It's really pretty." A smile filling her face, Janet touched the colored stones. "I know. You can give it to Miss Maggie since it's as pretty as she is."

"Now that's a great idea." He opened the clasp and held the bracelet toward her. "And you're right about it being as pretty as Miss Maggie."

"Thank you." Blinking, Maggie stretched out her wrist. As the clasp closed, Romy's gaze locked with hers. She grinned into his coffee eyes and was lost in their depth. His heart was exposed for the world to see. She dropped her gaze.

How could he still feel like that after the way she'd treated him? Would his sisters notice that she was staring at him? She rubbed her fingers around her new jewelry. If only she didn't have to worry about the girls.

The five approached the Ferris wheel platform. They wouldn't all fit in one car. She pointed toward the ride. "Why don't I sit with the two younger girls, and you and Sally go in the next car?"

She could read disappointment in Romy's face. "That would be great."

His words didn't match his slumped shoulders as they reached the front of the line.

"Step right into the next car." The barker ushered the three girls into the waiting seat and closed the safety bar.

"Wait . . . I was going to ride with Janet and Mary." Maggie leaned toward the closed bar.

"No, no . . . you young lovers need to ride in the next one." The operator moved the lever forward. The girls swung up and away.

As Maggie tried to draw in a breath, she slanted a glance toward Romy. His face matched the fire truck they'd seen earlier. Young lovers indeed. She'd ignore what the man said. That little girl was more important right now. "Has Janet ever been on one of these?"

Romy nodded. "Yeah sure, she'll be fine."

The next car pulled to a stop, and the barker raised the safety bar. She had no choice but to follow his direction to stay near the girls. She sat down and scooted to the far side. Romy followed and raised his arms as the man closed the bar.

"Don't worry about the girls. They love this ride as much as I do."

The car started to swing as it moved back and upward toward the top of the wheel. Maggie glanced over the edge of the swinging car. She had a view of the entire midway crowded with people. None of it mattered right now.

"How often have they ridden on this?" She had only been on a Ferris wheel once in a great while.

"I suppose Janet hasn't had too many rides since she's only six." Romy glanced toward the girls' car.

"That's what I thought. Will she be scared of the height?" Stretching her neck to see their car, Maggie bit her lip. She couldn't see if the girls were okay. "I wish he hadn't done this to us."

Romy put a hand on her arm. "Relax. You don't need to worry all the time."

The heat from his hand seeped through the sleeve of her dress. They rocked back and forth when the car stopped to let in more people.

"I know. I worry too much sometimes." She gave him a half-hearted smile before wringing her hands.

***

Romy watched Maggie study her hands. He had no clue what she was thinking. He wanted her to enjoy their moment together. They had not been alone today at all. Now it was handed to him on a platter. He had to make the most of it.

The Ferris wheel started rotating again.

"What was it like growing up in Wisconsin?" He looked at Maggie to see if this sparked something in her eyes. If only he could keep her mind off the girls.

"I had two brothers older than me, so I pretty much was stuck . . ."

A piercing scream brought Maggie's conversation to a standstill. Romy's eyes glanced at the car ahead of them. Was that Janet?

Maggie's eyes mirrored his own, as the knuckles of her hands clutched the locked bar in front of her. "I thought you said Janet liked this ride. What have we done?"

The Ferris wheel picked up speed now that all the riders were in place. Up, around, down. The wheel turned faster. The screaming changed into sobs as Maggie's face blanched.

"I'm not even sure that it's Janet." Romy forced himself to remain calm as his pulse increased its tempo.

Maggie peered over the front of the seat at the car below them. "Who else would it be? We should have never let that man split us up like this."

"Even if she's a little scared now, she'll be fine when we're back on the ground."

Maggie shook her head. "But, Romy, this is what I was talking about in the orchard last week. Will Janet trust me again after she got so scared without either of us around to assure her she'd be fine? This is a disaster."

"You're worrying too much again. There's nothing we can do until the ride's done, and we can give her a hug. She's not going to get hurt. Sally will make sure of that."

While the wheel circled around and around, Romy glanced toward Maggie in time to see her retreat to her corner of the seat. Was this going to ruin all the progress he'd made today smoothing over the past week's misunderstanding?

The car stopped abruptly on the top of the arc. As it swung back and forth, Romy got a magnificent view of the surrounding area. He could see the entire fairgrounds, past the carnival games, and over the animal sheds. The bluffs of Dubuque stood out in the western horizon.

"Hey, look. There are clouds forming in the west." He pointed toward the bluffs. "Maybe we'll get a bit of rain this afternoon."

Maggie peered at him from her side of the car. "I can't even think that far ahead. My mind is filled with the fact that Janet is sitting in the next car terrified to death."

"Maggie, you need to stop jumping to conclusions." He observed her hands as they fidgeted with her purse. "Janet will be fine. Just think what the possibility of rain could do for the crops."

She turned her head westward. "Well, I will agree that the garden needs rain, but Janet is more important to me right now."

Romy crossed his arms over his chest. Why couldn't she get over her anxiety? There was no point ruining the day with fears that might not even be true.

The car continued on its downward rotation toward the next stop. Finally, it was their turn to disembark from the car. Maggie practically flew out of the seat and searched the area for the sisters.

Janet was standing with the other two, smiling as if nothing had happened. Maggie squatted and put her arm around Janet. "Are you okay, honey?"

Mary's arms waved to match her enthusiasm. "Didn't you hear her when we went so fast?"

Sally exploded in laughter. "Of course they didn't. They were talking too much."

"Yes, I heard her crying." Maggie stared at Sally. She hugged Janet closely. "Were you very scared? I was so sad that I wasn't with you."

Janet face scrunched up as if she didn't have a clue what Maggie was talking about. "Scared? Crying? That wasn't me."

Mary tugged on Maggie's arm. "I think that was the little boy in the car ahead of us."

Maggie's eyes glanced up at Romy. Smiling, he quirked his brow at her and nodded. He'd been right all along. He didn't have to say anything to make his point. Maggie's cheeks turned a glowing crimson.

Janet tugged on Maggie's arm. "I had soooo much fun. Can we do it again?"

"Not today. We have to go meet Pa now." Romy pointed west. "It looks like it might rain. We need to get on the road."

"Okay. I'll go tell Pa all about our ride, then." Janet skipped ahead with Mary while Romy and Maggie followed with Sally.

As they trailed the girls toward the cow barn, he spotted a couple striding toward them. The young man, with blond hair falling across his forehead, was involved in a conversation with the young lady draped on his arm. They made a handsome couple, with her long flowing curls.

As they got closer, the hair on the back of Romy's neck rose. He felt Maggie falter at his side. He glanced again at the couple, now less than ten feet away. Leon. He placed a hand on the small of Maggie's back.

"Keep walking," he whispered in her ear.

Maggie bit down on her lip. "I'm not sure I can." The smile glued on her face belied the frown furrowed on her forehead.

Leon glanced at them and stopped. "Well, hello." He stretched his hand toward Romy.

Romy reciprocated and reached out. "Hello, Leon." How awkward. As far as he knew, Leon had not talked to Maggie since that Sunday morning weeks ago. What was going through her head?

Leon put his arm around his companion's shoulder. "I'd like you to meet my friend Betty. Betty, these are my neighbors Romy and Maggie. They live across the road from Pa's farm."

As if there was nothing embarrassing about introducing a current girlfriend to an old girlfriend. Was that what Maggie had been to Leon? Her blushing face hinted that Romy had guessed correctly.

Romy covered for Maggie. "Nice to meet you, Miss Betty." His hand resumed its place on Maggie's back, staking out his territory in front of Leon. "I'm so sorry we can't stay to visit. My sisters have run ahead of us, so we need to keep up with them before they get lost." Good excuse. He needed to extract Maggie as soon as possible.

"That's too bad. We'll have to get together sometime, so you can get to know my neighbors better, Betty." Leon raised his hand to wave as he steered her down the path.

"Bye." Romy waved before heading toward the barns. Hard to be polite, when he was burning inside. Rubbing his hand up and down her back, he whispered close to Maggie's ear. "Are you okay?"

Romy turned toward his sister and gave her a slight push. "Sally, why don't you run ahead and make sure Janet and Mary find Pa and the boys."

Maggie closed her eyes. "I . . . I didn't know what to say to him." Her teeth clamped on her lower lip.

"That's fine. It must have been uncomfortable for you." He was reluctant to break contact with her. "Have you talked to him at all since we saw him going fishing?"

"No. That's what was so awkward. He never explained himself. It's not like I pine for him or anything. I couldn't be with a man that didn't put God first in his life." She looked at Romy, her eyes beckoning him. Was she trying to tell him something? "It surprised me when I saw them, that's all."

He shook his head as they continued toward the cow barn. *Lord, help her to get over her needless fears about having a relationship with me.* What more could he say?

***

Maggie watched out the car window as they sped down the road toward the farm. She breathed deeply, trying to relax. She closed her eyes, replaying the scene with Leon and his new girlfriend. Her face must have been all shades of red when she'd recognized Leon walking toward her and Romy. She'd wished there was a rock close by to crawl under. *Thank You, Lord, for having Romy by my side to rescue me from that embarrassing situation.*

How had she ever believed for one minute that Leon was the man for her? He'd proven weeks ago that God wasn't important to him, and now he'd proven she wasn't important either. God was great. He'd shown her the truth before she could do something stupid.

Romy had been so understanding of her predicament. How did she ever think that he was callous? He was one of the sweetest men she'd ever known, but she couldn't act on her feelings toward him. If only she didn't have this anxiety deep inside.

She glanced into the back seat where silence reigned among the three sisters. They must be exhausted. They were the reason she still pulled back from Romy, but was her anxiety unfounded? That dilemma would have to be solved later.

Maggie turned toward Romy. "It was a great idea to start home ahead of the men so I can make supper. Did your pa say when they'd be home?"

Her hair attempted to escape her bun as the wind whipped through the open window. She tugged at the escaping curls trying to control them with her fingers. Romy glanced her way from time to time, as if he wished the wind would continue to blow her hair as much as it wanted.

"I imagine they'll stay at the fairgrounds until all the animals are fed and settled for the night."

"I won't have to hurry to get the meal ready then."

Maggie glanced toward the west. The dark cloudbank towered over the lower gray puffs nearer the ground. They grew more menacing by the minute.

"Wow, the clouds are moving in faster than I thought they would." She turned back to Romy. "Will we get home in time?"

CHAPTER 26

"I'm sure we'll be fine. The clouds are getting darker, but we only have a couple miles to go." Romy glanced at the western sky.

"Look, Sally, the clouds are getting so spooky." Mary's shrill voice couldn't mask her fear.

"They aren't spooky, Mary, but they sure are getting darker. Romy, does it mean we'll get lots of rain?" Sally poked Romy in the back.

"Let's hope so." He looked out the left window. "They're really rolling in here."

The clouds piled high on each other, billowing into dark threatening gray columns. The sun, still shining on their car, caused a sharp contrast with the approaching squall. He sped up to outrun the storm.

"I'm glad we're almost home. I've never liked to be out in storms." Maggie's pale face emphasized her words.

"Were you scared when you were a little girl?" He smiled hoping to help take her mind off the clouds.

"My bedroom was in the corner of the house with windows facing both directions. When it stormed at night, the lightning lit the room as if we were outside. My sisters and I always dove under the covers, but even that couldn't shut out the brightness." Her fingers were white where they gripped the door handle.

"I can see you never got over it." Romy's hand covered hers

to comfort her.

"Oh, I'm much better now, but I still don't like them." She plastered a watery smile on her face, but her damp eyes were overly bright. He had the feeling she wasn't being honest with herself.

The storm marched closer, obliterating the sunshine and surrounding them in an eerie darkness. The tall weeds at the side of the road twisted, trying to escape the wind bearing down on them.

"Hey, the sky looks green over there." Janet brought everyone's attention back to the horizon. The layer of clouds nearest the ground broke open into a greenish wall.

"I've never seen a sky look like that before." Romy couldn't take his eyes off it.

"Is it a tornado?" Maggie voiced his thought.

He searched the sky. "I don't see a funnel cloud anywhere."

Sally sat on the edge of her seat. "What is it, then?"

The green wave rolled closer with the speed of a train. He managed to slow the car down in time to turn into the driveway. The blustery wind pummeled leaves against the windshield.

He flicked a glance at Maggie. "It might mean hail is coming."

"Let's get in the house then before it gets here." Maggie grabbed her purse and gloves. She looked into the back seat. "Gather up your things, girls, so we can run."

Romy's eyes glanced in the mirror and saw the girls whispering frantically to each other. He couldn't hear what was going on since he was concentrating on getting the car safely up the driveway in the increasing wind.

When he brought the car to a stop, the back door flew open and Janet and Mary dashed out into the wind. "Wait! You can't go out in the storm!"

"Blackie . . ." That's all they heard from Mary as she grabbed Janet's hand and headed toward the back of the house.

"Girls, come back here." Maggie shouted after them, but to no avail.

"Where did they go?" He turned to the back seat at the same time as Maggie. Rain started pelting the front window. It blew in the open car door, soaking the back seat in an instant.

Sally, sitting by herself, tried to pull the door shut. Romy reached over the seat, grasped the door handle, and slammed it. "Janet remembered she tied Blackie up to the garden fence to keep the rabbits away. She persuaded Mary to go with her to find Blackie." Tears slid down Sally's cheeks. "I tried to tell them they couldn't go out there, but they wouldn't listen."

While the wind buffeted the car to and fro, torrential rain and hail bounced on the roof of the car.

"You and Sally run into the house . . ."

Maggie shook her head. "No, I'll come with you."

Romy grabbed her shoulders firmly. "Listen to me. I need you to get Sally into the house and go down to the basement. Then I'll know you, at least, are safe. I'll go find the girls."

No time to argue right now.

He opened the car door and held tight, preventing it from tearing off the hinges. After slamming it shut, he started the trek across the lawn toward the garden. He stumbled as the blustery weather pushed him forward. How did the girls manage this? He could barely keep his legs moving in the right direction.

He glanced over his shoulder to make sure Maggie and Sally were progressing toward the house. Through the rain, he could see they were out of the car. They staggered toward the porch, clutching each other.

Hail poured down on his head and shoulders as he once again turned toward the garden. The wind whipped the trees into a frenzy. Small branches flew past him, hitting his arms and legs. Still he struggled on. He wiped the rain out of his eyes and spotted the girls clinging to a fence post. The wet lump between them must be Blackie. Oh, why had they done this?

"Romy, help us. We can't get Blackie to move." Mary tugged on the dog's collar.

He had to shout at them to make himself heard. "You and Janet head back to the house. I'll bring Blackie with me." He helped them to stand and grab each other, stabilizing them in the storm. He gave them a push to start them in the direction of the house. Struggling against the wind, they stooped over to keep moving forward.

"Come on, you mangy mutt." He hoisted the soaked dog into his arms. This was not a little dog to be carrying in this squall. He strained every muscle to haul the animal to the house.

A thunderous roar pierced his ears. CRAACKK!

***

Maggie spotted Mary and Janet clinging to each other in the wind. She tore open the porch door and ran across the short distance to help them out of the torrent, gathering them in her arms. The hail pummeled the three huddled together. Would they make it back to the house?

By now her hair was plastered to her head. Brushing the strands out of her eyes, she glanced toward the garden. Romy slogged toward them with Blackie in his arms.

A crack split the air followed by a whoosh. Romy disappeared.

Time stood still. Maggie's blood froze in her veins. A piercing scream filled her ears even though her throat was paralyzed.

She turned toward the house and saw white-faced Sally screaming. In an instant, she found herself surrounded by three girls clinging to her.

What had happened? She twisted around and squinted through the wall of water. All she could see in the spot where Romy once stood was green leaves and crushed branches. The old oak tree had split in two, with half fighting to stand against the wind and the other half burying Romy on the lawn.

The weight of the world descended on her shoulders. How could she support the girls when he needed her help? *God, help me!*

Calmness settled around her in the chaos. The storm was passing. The wind and rain diminished to a mild summer rain.

"Girls, we need to pray for Romy." She pried them off her. *God, help them, also.* "Father in heaven, You know what's happened to Romy. Please protect him. Help us to find him. Bring him back to us safely. Amen."

Three amens answered back. The fear in their eyes had vanished. *Thank You, God.* Now she had to keep a clear mind.

"Romy! Romy! Can you hear me?" If he responded, she would know a little more. The wind rustled the mound of leaves. Nothing.

Soon the girls were echoing her. No response.

"We need an axe. Sally, do you know where your Pa keeps it in the shed?"

Sally gulped down a sob. "Yeah."

"Run and get it, but be very careful carrying it back again."

Maggie searched the faces of the two younger girls. "We have to try to move as many leaves as we can until she gets back."

The three tore at the leaves and branches as fast as they could. Tears rolled down Maggie's cheeks, taking the place of the pouring rain. They were only able to move the smallest branches.

"Ow. My hands hurt." Janet looked at her hands. They were bleeding where the leaves made tiny cuts.

"I know, honey, mine do, too. But think of Romy lying under here somewhere." Maggie gave her a quick hug and urged her back to work.

"Here's the axe." Sally dragged it across the soaking grass.

"Okay. I'll try to cut the larger branches so we can pull them away faster. You all stand back until I can make some progress."

She managed to lift the axe and cut some of the smaller branches without too much problem. The clothesline ropes were wound up in the branches. The tree had swallowed up the clothesline pole as well as Romy. Was this good news?

"You pull away the ones that I chopped. I'll go over there to start on the big branch." She wielded the axe as best she could on the larger branch. Where were Romy's pa and brothers? She could use those strong backs to handle this axe. In her drenched dress, she shivered.

Little by little the large branch gave way. With a final chop, the branch was severed. It still wouldn't budge.

"Sally, come help me pull this away." The drizzling rain made her hands slippery. Maggie rubbed them together, trying to dry them off so she could get a grip.

She and Sally pulled with all their might. The branch finally gave way, causing both to almost end up on their backsides in the soaked grass. As soon as the leaves were moved, Blackie trotted out from the green jumble looking a bit tipsy.

Janet spotted the dog at once. She dove at him and almost tackled him in her arms. "Oh, I'm so happy you're all right." She sunk her face in his wet fur.

"Girls, if Blackie made it out of there, we need to work harder to find Romy."

Maggie found herself on her hands and knees pulling at anything she could reach. The other girls followed her example. Finally, they pulled a branch out of the way to reveal one of the clothesline posts.

Standing to assess the situation, Maggie saw the top clothesline pole was holding up the main branch of the broken tree. It sheltered the ground under this pole. *Lord, please let Romy be in the shelter of Your arms.*

"Romy . . . Romy, can you hear me?" Maggie held her breath while she waited for a response. The girls, sensing the importance of the moment, stood like statues.

Maggie was ready to start tearing at the branches again when she heard a faint moan coming up from the mass. She fell to her knees again. "Romy, are you okay?"

This time she heard a distinctive grunt in answer.

"I think we're almost there, girls. Try to work a little more."

As they were using their last bit of effort, Mr. Iverson drove into the driveway. The brothers were out of the truck in an instant.

"Where's Romy?" Ted sprang to Maggie's side.

She had no resilience in her anymore. All she could do was point toward the pile of leaves while tears trickled down her cheeks. The three girls clung to her again, sobbing for their lost brother. Their fight was over, to be taken up by the men now.

Mr. Iverson, Jim, and Ted hauled on the branches like madmen, calling to Romy from time to time. The three made more headway than Maggie could have done in an hour.

She stood and watched as if frozen to the spot. What had she said to Romy last week? How could she have possibly thought the girls' opinion about them was more important than Romy?

She knew now she'd been wrong. The girls would have to get used to it. He was worth fighting for. Would she be able to tell him? She would welcome the teasing of his brothers if only Romy could be by her side. Was it too late now?

The men stopped what they were doing and leaned over. Had they found him? Maggie eased closer to peek over Jim's shoulder.

They stepped back, dragging Romy across the grass. Blood ran down the side of his head. With his arm twisted under his body, he shook his head and blinked in the light.

As much as Maggie wanted to spring on him and engulf him in her arms, she held herself in check while the others ascertained the extent of his injuries.

"Romy, what hurts?" His pa stooped over him, wiping the leaves out of his hair.

"My head feels funny." Romy moved to untangle his arm. He rubbed it.

She knelt on the ground next to him. Thank God, it mustn't be broken. Maggie reached out and grasped his hand. His eyes widened as he glanced up at his brothers. Did he think she'd let him go again after this scare?

"Do you think you can sit up?" Mr. Iverson looked him over, head to toe.

Romy nodded.

With a brother on each side, they helped him to a sitting position. He wobbled, but didn't fall over.

The three girls in the cheering section clapped and hopped in circles.

"What happened in there?" Jim still had his hand on Romy's shoulder.

Romy surveyed his surroundings. "When I heard the tree crack and saw it heading for me, I dove under the clothesline with Blackie, hoping it would save my neck."

"Thank God you did." Maggie squeezed his hand. "The biggest branch was leaning on the top clothesline pole, so God kept you as safe as you could be."

"I think I'm pretty much in one piece except for my head." He put his hand on the bump, touching the seeping blood.

"Let's get him into the house." Mr. Iverson stood while the brothers hoisted him into an upright position. "Do you think you can wash up his cut, Miss Maggie, while we make sure everything is okay? We have to go check the barn and animals."

Exactly what she was hoping to hear. Time to talk to him alone. "Absolutely. Sally can help me if I need more hands."

The boys stumbled closer to the house with Romy between them. He put one foot in front of the other, but didn't walk on his own power.

"Where should we lay him, Pa?" Ted looked over his shoulder for direction.

"It'll be too hard to get him up the stairs to his own room. Sally's bed is the closest, so put him in there."

They got through the kitchen and dining room before laying him on his sister's bed. He collapsed onto the bed and closed his eyes.

After the men left the house, Maggie sized up the situation. "We need to wash the dirt off his face and arms before we look at his cut. Sally, you sit with him while he rests, and I'll go get the supplies."

When Maggie returned, his eyes were open again. They met hers when she entered the room and didn't look away.

"How are you feeling?" She sat on the edge of the bed.

"I've been better." He rubbed his forehead, leaving a smudge.

"We need to get you cleaned up." She carefully cleaned off the gash on his head. "We don't want that to get infected."

"I'm sure it will be fine." He lay still while she swabbed his forehead.

Maggie stood up. "Sally, I'll hold up his arm while you clean it as best you can."

She grasped his hand to raise his arm and was surprised when he squeezed her fingers. She stood to hold his arm in place and allow Sally to bathe it. The entire time his young sister used the washcloth, he searched Maggie's eyes and gripped her hand. The heat surged between them. What was he trying to tell her?

"Did you have fun at the fair, Sally?" Maggie talked to the girl, but stared at Romy the entire time.

Sally threw Maggie a sideways glance as she kept rinsing. "Well, yeah. We talked about it in the car."

"I thought the best part of the fair was the amazing view from the top of the Ferris wheel." Maggie set his arm back on the blanket. "Let's do the other arm."

"I thought you didn't like the Ferris wheel." Sally continued her ministrations.

"That's not the case. I just didn't like the idea of Janet being separated from Romy and me."

Romy was staring at her now. She was talking absolute nonsense, but she couldn't say anything important with Sally standing right there. His eyes never left her face.

"There, you're almost yourself now." She patted his hand on the blanket. "Sally, go tell your pa that Romy is doing better now, so he doesn't worry."

"Okay, Miss Maggie."

After Sally left the room, Romy pulled Maggie down to sit on the edge of the bed. "What was that all about?"

"I had to find an excuse for her to leave, so I could talk to you."

"That's not what I mean, and you know it."

"Romy, I'm so sorry about what I said to you last week." Her eyes filled with unshed tears. He tried to say something, but she placed her fingers over his lips.

"I need to finish . . . I thought I had lost you. I don't know what I'd have done. I'll be happy to endure teasing by your brothers, as long as I can have you by my side."

"What about the girls?" Romy didn't move an inch.

"I realized you're worth fighting for. They will just have to get used to the idea, one way or another."

He was going to kiss her. The pit of her stomach told her as much. Was this what a puddle of warm butter felt like?

Romy pulled her down into his arms. He touched his lips to hers and closed his eyes. Heat sizzled through Maggie in explosive starbursts. Before it burned her to a crisp, she sat up, putting her hands on his shoulders.

His face beamed, mirroring hers. "Well, if that's what happens when a tree falls on me, I'd gladly do it again tomorrow."

"Oh, no you won't. I never want to live through that scare again."

They laughed, hugging each other. Maggie sent up a prayer of thanks to God for leading her to Romy.

EPILOGUE

Four Years Later

"Maggie, where's your pepper shaker? I think the dressing needs a little more before we stuff the turkey." Emma looked around the kitchen, drying her hands on a towel.

Maggie pointed in the direction of the stove. "It's in the cupboard next to the—"

"Mama, where's Papa?" The screen door slammed after three-year-old Jerry raced into the porch.

Maggie scowled at her son. Romy wouldn't be happy with Jerry. They'd been working on his manners for a several weeks now. "I told you before, you shouldn't interrupt Mama when she's talking."

"But where is he?"

"Can you apologize to Aunt Emma first?" Maggie put a firm hand on his shoulder. When would he remember to be polite?

He looked at his aunt. "Sorry." Turning back to his mother, he inquired, "Where is he?"

"He's getting the car ready to go get Grandpa and Grandma from the train."

"Can I go?" He hopped from one foot to the other.

"Don't be so loud or you'll wake Dianne." Maggie peeked at her three-month-old sleeping in her bassinet in the dining room. Even in sleep, her daughter's nose looked so much like Romy's. She smiled down at her.

"And, no, you can't go today. Maybe when they go home again."

"Awww…" He turned and ran out the door, letting it slam behind him.

"Sorry, Emma." Maggie went back to her job of rolling out a piecrust. "Did you find the pepper?"

"Yeah, no problem." Emma stirred the dish of dressing once more.

"Thanks so much for coming over today to help me get all this food ready for tomorrow." Maggie brushed the extra flour off her fingers. "Cissy wanted to come today also, but Little Al came down with the flu yesterday. I hope she and Harry can come tomorrow with the kids."

Emma's eyes met Maggie's. "I'm just so happy we can all be together for Thanksgiving. It's so wonderful that the folks and Katie will be with us, too."

Maggie swallowed past the lump in her throat. "I know. I haven't seen them since Romy and I went to Wisconsin for our short honeymoon. At least the economy is picking up now, so they have money for the trip here."

"I'm sure Danny and Vivi helped them out so they could come."

Maggie nodded. "Probably true."

Emma looked around the kitchen as she stuffed the turkey. "You've done so much with your kitchen. Of course, I haven't been here since summer."

"Getting the electric lines finally installed along the road sure helped a lot this fall." Maggie paused to see if the crust would fit in the pie pan. "Now, at least we have water piped into the house from the pump house. It's so much easier to wash dishes. And the bathroom is a godsend with the two little ones."

Emma clucked her tongue. "I can't imagine living without either one. It must be so nice that your rooms are upstairs now, also."

Glancing in Emma's direction, Maggie brushed her hands on her apron. "Oh yeah. It's so much more private for us. The four of us live up there, even though I still do all the meals down here. Romy's sisters are now using Pa's old bedroom, which has so much more room for them. Pa fits much better in the girls' old room. Of course, it helped when Harry and Ted got married and moved out."

Emma washed her hands at the sink. "That makes things easier for you to care for the kids. You're always so busy taking care of your adopted family. I don't know how you did it for so many years."

"I really can't remember either now." They both laughed. "I guess you block out the hard times. Romy said we're hoping to get an electric stove next year. That will be a great help, that is, if we can afford it."

After the stuffing bowl was empty, Emma started closing up the bird. "Understandable. The economy is improving, but with the war going on in Europe, who knows what will happen to us. At least, President Roosevelt says we're staying out of this one."

"So far . . ." Maggie leaned over to place the three pies into the oven. "With England and Canada declaring war on Germany, I can't imagine we can stay out forever."

"We'll pray the president keeps his word. At least, most of the family are farmers and wouldn't have to get called up if war comes." Emma plunked the turkey in the roaster.

"True, but remember Katie's fiancé works in a factory. He'd most likely get drafted."

Setting the cover on the roaster, Emma paused. "I wonder when they're getting married. She's already twenty-three years old."

Maggie had had the same thought many times about their youngest sister. "She's just taking her time."

"She doesn't know what she's missing. Married life is terrific."

The porch door slammed. Romy walked in, followed by his son. "I couldn't agree with you more, Emma." He walked up behind Maggie and embraced her, planting a loud kiss on her neck. "I've never been happier." He kissed her again. "I'm not going anywhere."

"I can't argue there." Maggie leaned back against her husband. "God has led me to you, and I'm here to stay."

THE END

ABOUT THE AUTHOR

Connie Cortright has been a history buff all her life, reading biographies and history since grade school. Naturally, when she considered writing a story, her first thoughts turned toward historical fiction. Her novels are set in America's Midwest and reflect her own Wisconsin farming roots.

Her life has been the fulfillment of her girlhood dreams: becoming a Lutheran schoolteacher, marrying a pastor, and having lots of children. Her life has taken her across the country and beyond as she followed her pastor-husband in his service to various churches with their four sons.

Their sons are married to wonderful Christian women, with eleven grandchildren scattered from Wisconsin to Washington to British Columbia to Missouri. Connie accompanies her husband on his mission work in Europe. They try to see most of their family at least once a year and are very thankful for Skype!

Connie loves reading books (especially historical romance) and now writing her own stories. Her book is available on Amazon.com. She can be contacted at Facebook and at www.conniecortright.com.